Praise for B.J. Daniels

"A well-written, Western-themed romantic suspense
novel that will keep readers guessing throughout."
—*RT Book Reviews* on *Forsaken*

"Action-packed and chock-full of suspense."
—*Under the Covers* on *Redemption*

"*Unforgiven* is B.J. Daniels at her finest."
—*Under the Covers*

"Daniels, as usual, proves she's as adept with
family relationships as she is with deep intrigue
and suspenseful action."
—*RT Book Reviews* on *Cardwell Ranch Trespasser*

"The mystery and danger thickens from
the first page, weaving a spell around readers."
—*RT Book Reviews* on *Justice at Cardwell Ranch*

"An explosive tale of love, trust and the twisted ties
among an embattled family."
—*RT Book Reviews* on *Crime Scene at Cardwell Ranch*

B.J. DANIELS

ATONEMENT

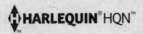

Recycling programs
for this product may
not exist in your area.

ISBN-13: 978-0-373-77846-1

ATONEMENT

Copyright © 2014 by Barbara Heinlein

Printed in U.S.A.

I happily dedicate this book to my two favorite quilt clubs: Hands All Around and Quilting by the Border. These talented ladies inspire me— and they're a whole lot of fun. And yes, I can see a book set at a quilt retreat in the future.

PROLOGUE

SO THIS IS how it ends.

It was his first thought when he opened his eyes and found himself tied to the steering wheel of a speeding car, reeking of alcohol—worse, dead drunk with it—and about to die.

Through the windshield he saw that he was barreling along a rutted desert road lined with cacti bathed in moonlight. Sobered by the realization, he slammed his foot down on the brake. Nothing. Panic washed over him like an ice shower.

He stomped on the accelerator only to find it tied down, as well. With his hands roped to the steering wheel, he couldn't turn the car off the dirt track he was now bumping along. Nor could he grab the emergency brake—let alone open the door and bail out.

Bailing was the one thing he'd excelled at in life. That, however, was no more than a fleeting thought as he hit a jarring rut in the road, the speedometer wavering just this side of eighty.

Ethan thought of all the mistakes he'd made, the people he shouldn't have double-crossed and the few he'd actually cared about. He didn't have long to mourn his misspent youth, though. Ahead the dirt road made a ninety-degree turn to the left to avoid a deep rocky ravine. It was a turn he realized he wouldn't be making.

That was when the hair rose on the back of his neck as he realized he wasn't alone. He knew the smell of death, would have noticed it sooner had it not been for the reek of his own fear the moment he'd opened his eyes and seen what was happening.

As the car hit another rut in the road, the body in the backseat rose with it. He saw the man's face and let out a shocked curse of regret and pain. Buck Morgan. The gangly wrangler hadn't known what he was getting into. Buck's body dropped with a sickening thud as the car came down hard.

Ethan felt something give. The ropes that bound his wrists suddenly felt looser. He freed one hand, but still couldn't reach the emergency brake or the gearshift. He remembered the small knife he always kept in his right front pocket. Even if they hadn't taken it, what were the chances he could get it out of his pocket before…

It was there. In an instant, it was in his hand. He thumbed the blade open and frantically sawed at the rope around the steering wheel as car roared toward the cliff.

The wheels bounced out of the road ruts and wiped out several large cacti before the dark chasm opened up before him. A scream tore up out of his throat as the knife ripped through the last of the rope. He grabbed for the door handle.

Seconds later the car left the road and soared out through the moonlit night. He watched in a kind of sick awe as the vehicle seemed to hang suspended in midair over the abyss. A bubble of laughter buoyed up, but not for long. He was a fool if he thought he could cheat death the way he had cheated everyone in his life.

CHAPTER ONE

FROM THE MIDDLE of the corral, Dillon Lawson tugged gently on the halter rope, urging the filly in a circle. She was a beauty and he couldn't help feeling a sense of pride in her. The filly was smart, too. He'd known that the moment he'd looked into her eyes after she was born.

He'd named her Bright Beauty, struck dumb by the miracle of birth and the courage he'd seen in the foal as she'd stumbled to her feet for the first time.

Now as she trotted the tight circle around him, he could feel her gaze on him. The breeze lifted her red mane and she seemed to prance as if wanting to please him.

His heart swelled. His father wouldn't have approved of the way he'd gentled her. Burt Lawson "broke" his horses, the same way he'd tried to break his sons. The thought brought with it fresh pain. For whatever reason, their father had always been meaner to Ethan. It was why Dillon had spent years trying to protect his brother—only to fail him in the end.

Not even this beautiful Montana spring day or the filly he'd nurtured since birth could keep his mind off his brother—and the upcoming one-year anniversary of Ethan's death. Dillon wasn't sure what was worse, the guilt that he'd let his brother down or the grief of having lost the last member of his family.

"Ethan!"

With his mind on his brother, Dillon thought he'd only imagined the voice. He looked over, surprised to see a woman he didn't recognize at the corral fence. He lived so far out of town he seldom had strangers come in off the highway. Nor had he heard anyone drive up. He did a quick glance to the yard. No vehicle. Where had she come from?

His gaze returned to the woman. She'd climbed up the corral fence and now clung to the top rail. A mass of curly dark hair floated around a face dominated by huge blue eyes. That was all he was able to take in before she spoke again.

"Ethan." She said the name like a curse. He'd thought he must have heard her wrong the first time she'd said his brother's name. This time he heard anger in that one painful word. Anger and disappointment.

A chill ran the length of his spine.

She thought he was his brother.

That realization came like a kick to his gut. He slowed the filly to a stop and pushed back his Western straw hat. A warm sun slipped toward the west, making the breeze that blew down from the Crazy Mountains suddenly feel cold. The snow-fed breeze was a reminder that this was Montana in the spring and, like life, it could change at a moment's notice.

Dropping the halter rope, he took off his hat and, stepping toward her, tried to clear his throat. A lump had lodged there. If this woman had mistaken him for Ethan, then she must not know about his death.

As he drew closer, the woman's eyes narrowed. Her anger confused him. But then again, who knew what his brother had been up to before he died? Ethan had always attracted trouble like a magnet to metal, and Dillon had known little about his brother's life the past few years. That was the way Ethan had wanted it.

He was within a few feet of her when he saw her eyes fill with tears, then all the color suddenly bled from her face. She teetered on the corral railing for a moment before starting to slump backward in a faint.

Dillon took two long strides, bounded over the corral fence and managed to catch her before she hit the ground. Holding her in his arms, he looked down at her and felt his eyes widen.

The woman was *pregnant. Very pregnant.*

Her thick lashes fluttered. Those big blue eyes opened and zeroed in on him.

The roundhouse slap she gave him was hard and did more than surprise him.

"You *bastard.*"

"You've made a mistake," Dillon said.

"The mistake was ever falling for you."

He shook his head sadly. "I'm not who you think I am."

"*You're telling me?* Put me down."

Dillon did as she'd ordered and watched her struggle to get her feet under herself. Seeing him had been a shock for her, that much was clear. And yet she'd come here looking for him, as if…

He frowned as he tried to make sense of this. Ethan had been dead a year tomorrow. Why would she think he was Ethan? Not to mention… He stared at her swollen belly. The woman looked as if she might deliver that baby at any moment.

"You knew my brother?" he asked suspiciously.

She had dropped her large shoulder bag. She now bent to pick it up from the dirt before turning to glare at him. "I just want my money," she said as she slung the bag over her right shoulder.

"*Your money?* Are you talking about the insurance money?" The check had come only a few days ago. Apparently his brother had taken out a half-million-dollar policy on himself and made Dillon the beneficiary. Ethan had always been full of surprises. This woman was apparently another one.

"Insurance? Is that what you call it? Just give me what's mine and I'm out of your hair for good," she said, and glanced toward the mountains as if she couldn't bear looking at him any longer.

Sweetgrass County was rimmed with snowcapped mountain peaks, making some people think it was paradise. Dillon was one of those people. The moment he'd seen the Crazy Mountains, he'd known this was where he wanted to settle—rather than the logging town in western Montana where they'd grown up. His brother, Ethan, had hightailed it the moment he turned eighteen and apparently had never looked back.

When her gaze returned to his, Dillon saw that she hadn't been admiring the breathtaking Montana scenery. She'd apparently been trying to tamp down her anger—and failing.

"Why don't we go into the house?" he suggested. "I think we can settle this easy enough. Just let me get the halter rope off my horse—"

"If you think you can sweet-talk me, you're dead wrong. And you sure as the devil aren't seducing me. Not again." Her hand went to her stomach and he felt his heart drop.

She wasn't really going to try to convince him that she was carrying Ethan's baby, was she? He'd never been the brightest kid in school, but this one was a math no-brainer. Even if the woman did look as if she could give birth any moment, his brother had been gone twelve months tomorrow.

"Look, I'm not sure what your story is, but that baby you're carrying? It isn't—"

"If you dare say it isn't yours…" Her right hand dipped into her shoulder bag. An instant later he was staring down the barrel of a .45.

CHAPTER TWO

DILLON RAISED HIS hands and took a step back. "Take it easy. Like I said, if you'll come in the house, I can take care of this. But first, put down the gun. There's no call for any gunplay."

This was not her first rodeo, Tessa Winters thought as she took in the cowboy. She'd come all this way on a hunch that Ethan might have gone to Montana, but she'd still been shocked when she'd actually tracked down the lying bastard.

"You won't be charming your way out of this."

He shook his head. "Not my intention. If you put away the gun, I'm sure we can resolve this."

She eyed him warily, torn between her anger and his apparent calm. There was a time when she would have weakened. That time had long since passed.

Her gaze narrowed as she realized that he must have come straight here after he'd run out on her. His big hands were callused and his skin was tanned, as if the man had actually been doing some honest physical labor.

Looking at him now, she couldn't help but think about the first time she'd seen him. With his tousled sandy-blond hair and big blue eyes, he'd been the most handsome cowboy she'd ever run across. Like now, he'd been wearing a Western shirt that accentuated his broad shoulders and slim hips, and jeans that— Tessa shook off those dangerous thoughts and reminded herself what was at stake here. He might look good—the physical Montana lifestyle had made him even more attractive—but under the facade was a liar, a coward and a thief.

"Please." He motioned to the gun. "You're making me nervous."

"You *should* be nervous." But she lowered the gun.

"Okay," he said, slowly putting down his hands. "Let me see to my horse and then we'll go up to the house and take care of this." He climbed the corral fence and approached the wary filly slowly.

Tessa could hear him talking softly to the horse as he removed the halter rope, then stroked the filly's neck. Her ire rose as she saw how gentle and loving he was to the horse. It hurt even more to think of how easily he had abandoned her and their child.

When he finished with the horse, he climbed back over the fence and motioned toward the house. She followed. Distrustful as to what he was up to, she kept her fingers around the grip of the .45 in her bag. He thought he knew her, but he had no idea who he was dealing with. Pregnancy had changed her in more ways than one.

Tessa felt like a loose cannon, and knew a large part of it was the hormones her doctor had warned her about. Given the way she was feeling, it surprised her that more pregnant women didn't kill the men in their lives.

Truthfully, she was so angry with Ethan that she didn't know *what* she would do. She'd spent six months telling herself to let it go. Forget about him and the way he'd conned her. Finally, she'd given up kidding herself. She had to look him in the eye one more time before she could let it go. Probably bringing the gun hadn't been her best choice, though. But she wanted him to know that she was dead serious.

The cowboy mounted the steps of the house and pushed open the door, holding it for her. *Now* he was going to act like a gentleman? She gave him a withering look as she entered. Behind her, she heard him step in and close the door.

"How about we discuss this over a cup of coffee?" he asked, but didn't wait for an answer as he moved past her.

She sighed, wondering how long he thought he could stall before she lost her temper. Since becoming pregnant, she'd found herself on a roller-coaster ride shifting between tears and anger, which had left her exhausted. But she was nonetheless determined. It was bad enough Ethan had seduced her with his lies, knocked her up and then taken off on her. Stealing her money, though? That had been the last straw.

Tessa looked around the old farmhouse, surprised to see how neat and clean it was, as she told herself that once she'd settled things with Ethan, she would get back to being calm, confident and in control of her normal self again. At least she hoped so.

"Who cleans your house?" she asked suspiciously as she stepped toward the kitchen doorway.

"I do," he said over his shoulder.

She watched him set about making a fresh pot of coffee. When had he learned to make coffee? Or maybe he'd known all along and, like everything else, had played her. Just when she thought he couldn't make her any angrier.

Looking away to keep from pulling the pistol and shooting him, she was shocked that the kitchen was as clean and uncluttered as the rest of the house. This was *not* the Ethan Lawson she knew.

Until that moment she hadn't considered that the reason he'd left her and the baby she was carrying was because he had another family back in Montana. The thought felt like one of his horses standing on her chest. She fought to take her next breath—and worse, not cry.

Was it possible the reason he was always broke was because he'd been sending the money he made home to a family? She hadn't thought he could hurt her any more than he had, but she'd been wrong.

"Who else lives here?" she asked, her voice breaking.

He turned to look at her. "Just me and a couple cattle dogs. Why don't you have a seat? Have you had breakfast? I could make—"

"I'm fine." She didn't even want coffee. And since

when had Ethan learned to cook? She just wanted her money and she'd be on her way. Well, not quite. There was that other small matter, she thought, her hand going to the shoulder bag again.

He motioned her into a seat at the table and placed a mug of coffee in front of her. "I made decaf because of the…" He waved his hand toward her pregnant belly.

"*Baby*. It's a baby, Ethan, and stalling isn't going to do you any good. Just give me my money—"

"Hang on a second." He left the room and she half expected to hear the sound of his pickup engine revving up outside as he pulled another disappearing act.

To her surprise, he returned a few minutes later with several photos and what appeared to be two newspaper clippings.

She watched him drop them on the table next to his coffee before he pulled out a chair across from her, turned it around and straddled it.

"Let's see if we can clear this up," he said, and shoved the photos and the folded newspaper clippings across the table to her.

She didn't even give the items a glance, wondering what he was up to. Whatever it was, it wasn't going to work. Had she really thought that by coming here she could settle this? With a curse, she started to get up from the table, her hand going to the gun in her bag.

"*Pl*ease. I think this will help." He said the words

almost as gently as he had spoken to the filly. Reaching over, he pushed the newspaper clippings aside to expose the top photo.

She gave him an impatient look. Then, settling back down with a sigh, she glanced at the snapshot lying on the table. Shock rippled through her. Her gaze shot up to him. He looked as if he was waiting patiently. She dropped her gaze to the photo again. Her fingers trembled as she picked it up to make sure her eyes weren't deceiving her.

The boys were about ten in the snapshot. Both were grinning at the camera, their cowboy hats pushed back. They wore Western shirts, jeans and boots, and stood next to what appeared to be an old barn.

Her gaze moved to the second photo, an older version of them. She lifted it from the table, still shocked to see the two identical faces. They appeared to be in their teens in this shot. They were dressed much the same as they had been in the other photograph, but in this one, neither was smiling at the camera.

"Identical twins," he said as if she hadn't already figured that out.

She tossed the photos back on the table and glared at him. Did he really think she was going to fall for this? The photos appeared to be authentic. But she sure as the devil didn't have him mixed up with some other cowboy—even an identical brother.

"Fine, let's pretend you aren't Ethan. Let's pretend you're his twin. But being identical and all, you know where he is, right?"

"I do." His gaze went again to her stomach. He looked worried, as if he feared she was going to faint again. "Maybe you'd better look at the newspaper clippings."

A feeling of dread washed over her as she reluctantly picked up the first clipping and unfolded it.

Her pulse roared in her ears. "What is this?" she demanded, even though it was clearly Ethan's obituary.

He pushed the other clipping closer to her and waited.

Tessa swallowed, telling herself this was some kind of trick. She picked up the second clipping and unfolded it. The first thing that caught her eye was the photograph that ran with the article. It was a shot of what was left of a car that had crashed and burned in some ravine in what looked like the desert.

"Take a look at the date on the newspaper clipping," he said.

Her heart plummeted as she saw the date—*a year ago tomorrow.* How was that possible? She was eight months pregnant! For a moment, she didn't know what to make of it.

Then she looked at the cowboy sitting across from her. "Is this some kind of joke?"

"My brother's death isn't a joke. At least not to me."

Tessa shook her head as she glanced again at the

photos of the twin boys, then at the young men. She couldn't tell the brothers apart. Nor could she be sure which of them was Ethan.

She raised her gaze and narrowed her eyes at him. "If your brother is really dead, then unless you're a triplet…" Her hand went to her belly.

"Are we back to that?" he asked, sounding sad.

Tessa stood abruptly. "If it wasn't Ethan who I met last year, then it was you masquerading as him. That means you're the one responsible for this," she said, her hands covering her stomach, "and for stealing my money."

He shook his head. "My name is Dillon. Dillon Lawson. And you and I have never met before I looked up a while ago and saw you climbing my corral fence." His eyes lowered to where the baby was growing inside her, and she saw his gaze soften. "But if I thought for a moment that you really were carrying my brother's child…"

Tessa felt such a wave of sadness. She really *had* believed that when he saw her, saw how pregnant she was, he would do the right thing. "It's my own fault. I knew the kind of man you were the moment I met you. A charming saddle bum who was as dependable as the weather. You said you were trying to change. I should have known better. As it turns out, you're more despicable than even I could have imagined."

Her eyes burned, but she angrily fought back the tears as she looked into his face. If his brother was dead, then this was the man she'd fallen desperately in love with, the man who had promised her the moon and stars, the man who'd lied to her from the word *go*. Ethan wasn't even his real name. He'd used his dead brother's first name, probably thinking that she'd never track him down, since he'd lied about his last name.

She hugged her stomach protectively. "Fine," she said, hating the emotion she heard in her voice. "You want to pretend this isn't your baby and that you don't know me? Just sign this and we're done." She pulled the form from her shoulder bag and shoved it across the table at him.

He picked it up and took a moment to look at the form that would give him no rights to their child. When he'd finished, he looked up at her again. "I can't sign this. I thought I made myself clear. I'm not the father of your baby. Believe me, I would remember if we'd ever…" His gaze locked with hers for a moment. He actually flushed. "If we had ever… met. And with Ethan dead a year ago tomorrow…" He raised a hand to keep her from interrupting him. "I should also warn you that I am undersheriff of Sweetgrass County, so if this whole charade is about extorting money from me or from my brother's insurance policy…" He pushed the form back across the table toward her. "I also would suggest you reconsider whatever it is you're planning to do with that .45 you're reaching for in your bag."

"Undersheriff?"

He nodded. "If you like, I would be happy to show you my star."

She shook her head, hating what a fool she'd been, was still. She hadn't expected much when she'd come all this way. Knowing Ethan, she'd realized there was little chance of getting back the money he'd stolen from her. But she'd expected him to be at least man enough to sign the form.

When he'd left without a word, he'd made it clear that he wanted nothing to do with his child. That hurt more than his leaving her. He knew how she felt about family, since she'd never had one.

Obviously, none of that mattered. He'd never planned to make this right, knowing he would never have to. It was her word against the county lawman's.

Snatching up the paper, she shoved it back into her shoulder bag and fought not to cry. "I thought I saw something…good in you." She met his gaze, losing herself for a minute in all that pale blue. Tears burned her eyes. She shook her head. Nope, she wouldn't give him the satisfaction of knowing how much he'd hurt her. "I don't ever want to see you again. If you ever come near my baby—" Her hand dropped into her shoulder bag.

"I would advise you not to threaten an officer of the law again by pulling that gun."

"Just so we understand each other. You can take my money and hurt me, but never my baby. *Never*. Undersheriff or not." She gave him one last look, turned and walked out. He didn't try to stop her.

CHAPTER THREE

DILLON WATCHED THE young woman walk down the road to where she'd left her newer-model compact car. Apparently she'd wanted to surprise him. Well, she'd done that, all right.

He couldn't make out the plate number from where he stood, but it looked like a California license plate. His brother had been killed in Arizona. Not that far away, possibly.

What Ethan had been doing down in Arizona, Dillon had no idea. Had this woman even ever met Ethan?

On the form she'd tried to get him to sign, he'd seen that her name was Tessa Winters. But that might have also been a lie, just like swearing that Ethan was the father of her baby. Hell, he realized with a start, the woman might not even be pregnant.

He half wished he'd arrested her for trying to scam him.

As the dust settled behind her car, Dillon felt as if he'd imagined the entire encounter, like a bad dream. And yet it nagged at him. He kept recalling her expression when she'd seen the photographs. There was no way she could have been acting. She'd been *shocked,* but not half as shocked as she'd been when she'd looked at the newspaper clippings.

She hadn't known Ethan was dead.

Dillon shook his head. It didn't make any sense. Maybe that was why it had left him so upset. When she'd gotten a good look at him earlier, she'd fainted. Or at least she'd pretended to.

He tried to brush off the whole incident. The woman had tried to run some kind of con on him. It hadn't worked. Case closed.

Going back to the table, he gathered up the photos and clippings. The newspaper clippings were worn from looking at them so many times. It had been a horrendous accident. According to the coroner Dillon had spoken with in Arizona, speed and alcohol had been involved.

He was hit again with guilt for not saving his brother. The fact that he'd tried when they were younger didn't count. He should have tried harder, he thought as he put the photos and newspaper clippings back in the drawer where he kept them. Ethan was gone. He had to accept that. Or at least try to live with it.

But the woman had left him stirred up. He couldn't work with the filly now. The horse would sense his tension. He'd thought he was handling the one-year anniversary of his brother's death fairly well—until the woman had shown up.

Gathering himself up, he decided the best thing he could do was some good, hard, physical labor.

He headed for the horse stalls. Nothing like mucking stalls to wear himself out.

It had been a mild winter. Today the sun felt warm on his back as he walked to the barn, but the breeze had a nip to it, and he'd heard on the radio earlier that there was talk of snow in the mountains in the next day or so.

Spring in Montana could be a terrible tease. One day would be beautiful and the next as much like winter as a day in January. Dillon had seen thirty-six springs come and go. His father used to say a bad Montana spring after a long winter was what separated the men from the boys.

Maybe it was true. His mother certainly hadn't fared well on those snowy spring days. She said an unpredictable spring broke not only its promise, but ultimately your heart. Dillon figured that might also be true of the man she'd married. It probably explained, too, why his mother had left on a snowy spring day.

He shook his head at the thought. His mother should have left the old man many springs before she did. Dillon had given up hope of her ever escaping, so he'd been as shocked as his father when she'd finally done it. Not by packing up and leaving, like she should have done years before. No, it had taken an aneurysm to free her of Burt Lawson. She'd died in her sleep in the bed next to him.

Burt Lawson was a heartless bastard. Anyone who'd ever met him would tell you that, including his two sons. That was why no one had expected that Erma's dying would break the old man the way it had—especially not Dillon. Apparently Burt had had a heart after all. Her passing had killed him, turning him into an even more bitter old man before death took him.

Dillon pushed away thoughts of the past and, entering the barn, picked up a shovel and went to work.

He spent the rest of the day doing backbreaking labor, but as hard as he tried, he couldn't get the incident with the woman off his mind. He told himself she probably wasn't even pregnant. There were forms a woman could buy to look that way. But his mind kept coming back to why she would come all the way to Montana when it was so easy to prove she was lying.

He hated things that made no sense. It was one reason why he'd been drawn to law enforcement. He liked to think that crimes could be solved with a cool, calm logic. He was a man who believed in justice.

Just thinking of the .45 in the woman's shoulder bag made him sorry again that he hadn't arrested her. She'd threatened an officer of the law with what he assumed was a loaded weapon, *and* she'd tried to extort money from him in the most egregious way.

Well, she'd realized her mistake once she'd seen the photos and Ethan's obit, he thought. Her attempt to blame Dillon had failed, so she'd packed it up and left before even telling him how much money he'd allegedly stolen from her.

And that form releasing the biological father of any right to the baby... That, he was sure, had been for pure show.

After she'd learned that he was undersheriff of this county, she'd backed down quickly enough. Had she done her homework, she'd have known that. Nope, she wouldn't be back to try to shake him down again.

So why was he wondering where she'd gone?

TESSA TRIED TO still the pounding of her heart as she drove into Big Timber. It had always been like this. The man evoked feelings and desires in her like no other man ever had. She'd seen something in him, a sweetness that he'd tried hard to hide. Wasn't that why she'd overlooked her misgivings and let him into her heart?

She shook her head, furious with herself. After everything the man had done to her, part of her had been drawn to this rancher version of Ethan even more strongly than to the old Ethan. It was when she'd seen him working with the filly. She remembered the way his large, tanned, callused hands had stroked the horse's neck, the soft words he'd uttered as he'd removed the halter rope.

Chastising herself under her breath, she couldn't believe she'd let him sucker her in again, and now she was leaving without her money—or the signed form that would relinquish his rights to their child. She felt like pulling the car over and just sitting and bawling.

But Tessa swore that she wouldn't shed any more tears for the man. She couldn't believe he'd used his dead brother's name. What kind of man did that?

If it was true and the real Ethan Lawson had been killed in a car wreck one year ago tomorrow, then no wonder the man she'd known hadn't mentioned that he had an identical twin. He had stolen Ethan's identity. Was it any surprise that a man like that would steal her heart *and* her money?

Sick to her stomach at the realization, she wished she'd asked for copies of the newspaper clippings. But she should be able to verify it online....

Part of her argued for putting it all behind her. How could she, though, when she was carrying the man's baby? She couldn't have him showing up one day and trying to take her child.

Ahead she slowed as she spotted a motel not far from the Yellowstone River just outside town. The small Western town of Big Timber, Montana, didn't quite live up to its name. She didn't see any big timber. The pioneers must have cut all the trees down when they'd built the town. How ironic, she thought as she pulled in front of the motel unit marked Office.

After checking in, Tessa used her phone to go online to verify Ethan's death. She felt foolish. But when the man she'd known as Ethan had disappeared, even if he had given her his real last name, she still wouldn't have thought to search for him online. A self-professed saddle tramp, he'd appeared to be a cowboy who worked on ranches where he got room and board. She had doubted he'd ever had an apartment, paid a utility bill or owned more than his old pickup and his saddle. Which meant no paper trail, so she hadn't even bothered to look.

No, when he'd taken off without a word in the middle the night with her money and hadn't returned, Tessa hadn't gone to a computer to find him. She hadn't planned on going after him at all. What would be the point? She certainly hadn't wanted a man like that back.

But then she'd found a dog-eared snapshot he'd left behind, and very pregnant and running on emotions like gas fumes, she'd changed her mind about finding him. She'd wanted to look him in the eye one last time.

And now she had.

FRANK CURRY COULDN'T believe how much time had passed since he'd turned in his star and gun and walked away from the only job he'd ever loved. He'd been ready to quit being sheriff, furious with the system that couldn't find his ex-wife, Pam Chandler, and put her behind bars.

Pam had attacked him, tried to kill the only woman he'd ever loved and done horrible things to the daughter he hadn't known existed until a year ago.

Now as he stood looking at the calendar hanging on his kitchen wall, he was thankful that his undersheriff, Dillon Lawson, had insisted he take a leave of absence instead of quitting.

His six months were up today and he was anxious to get back to his job. He'd missed being sheriff and had come to realize how much he needed it. For months now, he'd been on a quest to find Pam and put an end to the horrible things she'd done to the people he loved. He'd been crazed and was now thankful he'd finally found peace.

Glancing up, he peered out the window at his ranch yard and realized what had caught his eye. A bird had landed on the telephone line that ran from his house to the barn.

Frank blinked, his pulse jumping with both surprise and pleasure. He froze, afraid to move for fear the bird would fly away. Or worse, that it would prove to be a pesky magpie instead of a crow. He'd studied crows for years, having had a family of them on the ranch.

The crows had been the one constant in his life, other than his job. He'd named the birds, could tell them apart by their calls and thought of them as family. He'd been more than heartbroken when last year one of his crows had been killed. The family had left, warning other crows of the danger. For months he hadn't seen a crow on his property.

Until now.

He told himself it was sign that the worst was behind him.

AFTER A RESTLESS night, Dillon was surprised to get a call from Frank Curry. "Frank, it's good to hear from you." It was early, but he was up, dressed and ready to go to work.

"I wanted to see how you were doing," the sheriff said.

Frank's six-month administrative leave was coming to an end. Dillon hoped the sheriff was calling to say he was ready to come back to work. Frank had been the best sheriff he'd ever run across—that was, until Frank's ex-wife had done everything possible to break him. Dillon had feared that the woman was going to succeed.

"How *I'm* doing?" Dillon said with a laugh. "Shouldn't that be what I'm asking *you?*"

"I'm fine. I've been doing a lot of repairs around the ranch, riding my horse up in the Crazies some and, of course, visiting my daughter."

"How is Tiffany?" Dillon asked.

"Okay." In other words, the same hateful girl who'd tried to kill her father. Dillon knew that the sheriff had spent a lot of time at the state mental hospital, visiting her. Recently he'd heard that a court date might be set for Tiffany's hearing. If found competent, she would stand trial as an adult even though she'd been only seventeen when, allegedly brainwashed by her bitter mother, she'd tried to kill Frank.

"Guess what? There's a crow sitting on my phone line to the barn," Frank said.

Dillon could hear how that cheered Frank. He knew Frank needed something positive in his life.

The sheriff had always enjoyed watching the crows that had taken up residence in his yard.

"They are so much like humans," Frank had once told him. They'd been on a stakeout, and Frank had pointed out the way the crows reacted to each other. Dillon had never paid much attention to the birds before that. He'd always thought a crow was a sign of death or some dark omen or another.

But Frank saw the birds as good luck. He'd watched his family of crows grow on his ranch and had become very attached to them. Then Frank's daughter, Tiffany, had killed one out of spite. The rest of the birds had left and hadn't returned. Until now. Maybe.

"One of the crows saved my life that day," Frank had told him. "It flew at Tiffany, distracting her and allowing me to get the gun away from her, otherwise I wouldn't be here today."

Dillon wasn't sure he believed the bird had purposely helped Frank, but as long as Frank did, that was all that mattered. He'd quit asking Frank if his crows had come back.

"Dillon, I was worried about you. I know what today is," Frank was saying. "How are you holding up?"

It surprised him that Frank had remembered, with everything the man had been going through. "Ethan's on my mind, of course, but I'm okay. Thanks for thinking of me, though. How are you doing?"

"I'm thinking I will come back to work today."

"That's the best news I've heard yet," Dillon said, and couldn't help smiling. Frank sounded better. No, more than that. He sounded good. Had he finally accepted things?

While the entire country had been looking for Pam Chandler for months, she hadn't turned up. It was as if she'd dropped off the face of the earth. Dillon had feared that Frank's obsession with finding his ex-wife would be the downfall of not only his career, but also his life.

Even though Dillon had finally talked him into taking six months, he'd had little hope that Frank would return to the job if Pam wasn't found. It had been so hard to see Frank go down that long, dark road. He'd feared Frank would end up finding Pam, killing her and going to prison.

"How was New Mexico?" Dillon asked now.

Frank laughed softly. "I should have known you were keeping track of me. I chased down a lead, but no one down there has seen Pam since she cleared out a year ago. How is the drug investigation going?"

A shipment of cocaine with a street value of over five million dollars had disappeared from a plane that had crashed in the Beartooth Mountains, south of Big Timber, early last summer. The pilot had been killed in the crash, and four others ended up dead before it was over, two of them murdered by an unknown assailant.

"No more leads," Dillon said. "The DEA has the case. I assume you didn't find a connection to the drugs in New Mexico?" He'd seen the phone numbers on one of the drug runner's cell and had discovered, as he was sure Frank had, that the man had called the ranch where Frank's ex-wife had been staying. It was a thin connection and apparently it hadn't panned out.

"I couldn't find anything that would suggest they knew each other in New Mexico, even though they'd lived in the same town. Nor did I find any connection to Judge Bull Westfall where Pam had been staying."

"I'm sorry, Frank. As you know, we have an APB out on Pam. But we haven't gotten any hits." Normally an easygoing, excellent sheriff, Frank had been pushed to his limit by his ex. Pam was dangerous. She'd done terrible things to Frank since their divorce. One of the worst was not telling him she was pregnant when they'd split eighteen years ago, and raising her daughter, Tiffany, to hate the father she'd never even met—until last year. Since then, Frank had been working to keep the girl out of prison—and getting her the mental help she needed at the state hospital.

"I should let you go. You probably need to get to work. Speaking of work, I'm headed that way myself. See you at the office." Dillon had been acting sheriff in Frank's absence and realized how little he liked being the boss. "Your star and gun are in my desk drawer. It's great to have you back."

Dillon had almost mentioned the woman who'd shown up at his ranch yesterday, but figured he could talk to him about it later back at the office. Frank was a good sounding board, and he'd need it. The woman had thrown him for a loop.

He left the house and drove the twenty-five miles into Big Timber from his ranch out in the valley. He'd just crossed the Yellowstone River, the water a clear cool green, when he spotted Tessa Winters's car. It was parked in front of a motel on the edge of town.

He slowed, telling himself there was no reason to stop. He'd said his piece yesterday. But it bothered him that the woman was still in town. She'd made this already hard day even tougher with her accusations. Just seeing her car put him in a foul mood.

What was she still doing here? He couldn't bear the thought that she might go around town telling people that a man she thought was Ethan Lawson had not only impregnated her, but also abandoned her and stolen her money.

Against his better judgment, he swung into the motel parking lot, pulled alongside the woman's car and got out.

All the curtains were drawn across the motel room windows. This time of the morning any guests from last night were long gone—except for Tessa Winters. Leaning down, he peered into her car. His brother's vehicles had often been filled with fast-food containers and beer cans, growing up. Ethan had never been neat.

Wouldn't a person expect Ethan's "girlfriend" to be just as bad? The immaculate interior of her newer-model car seemed to prove she was lying about ever living with his brother. He tried the passenger-side door. Locked. He knew he should just walk away. More than likely the woman was just getting a late start this morning. She would clear out of town and he could put her accusations behind him.

But being the law enforcement officer he was, he walked around the car and took down the license plate number. He realized he was still upset that the woman had tried to shake him down. For all he knew, she might have a police record a mile long.

Stepping back to his own vehicle, he ran her plates. No priors. The woman was squeaky-clean. Even the car checked out.

There was only one red flag. The car was owned by Tessa Winters of Rancho Mirage, California—a town not that far at all from where Ethan had been killed near Parker, Arizona.

CHAPTER FOUR

SHERIFF FRANK CURRY *loved her.*

Nettie Benton felt a rush of heat as she watched Frank get out of his pickup and start up the steps to the Beartooth General Store.

She'd waited years to hear those words, and finally had six months ago. That knowledge was the only thing that had kept her going in the months since he'd confessed how he felt about her. She'd seen little of him during that time. She'd known he'd been trying to find his ex-wife, and she had lived in fear of what he would do when he did. She'd never seen him so angry, and while she didn't blame him for wanting to kill Pam, she prayed he would come to his senses before he did anything that could land him in prison.

They would all sit easier if Pam was gone for good, Nettie especially, since the crazy woman had tried to run her down out in the street in front of the store. But that had been months ago, and there'd been no sign of Pam since.

The bell over the front door jangled, and Frank walked into the store. At just the sight of him, Nettie felt like she had as a girl. Frank Curry was a large broad-shouldered man who looked like an old-time sheriff. He had a thick, drooping, blond mustache flecked with gray, and a weathered Montana look that belied the gentleness in him. He wore jeans, boots, a uniform shirt and a gold star, his gray Stetson resting on a full head of graying blond hair.

To her he would always be that young man who'd shown up at her house on a motorcycle, wanting her to run away with him. His hair had been long and blond as summer wheat back then. He'd been wild and carefree and had made her heart race at just the sight of him.

No wonder her mother had talked her out of going off with Frank. Instead Nettie had married dull, safe Bob Benton. His parents had given them the store, which was something Bob had never had one iota of interest in running.

The store, though, had saved her during all those years of marriage to Bob. But now he was gone, and the ink on the divorce papers had dried a long time ago.

All water under the bridge, Nettie thought as she smiled at the sheriff. "Glad to see you back in uniform." Like everyone else, she'd been worried he would never go back to being sheriff. Just as she had worried that he would never love her again. She'd broken his heart. Or at least that was what he'd told her all those years ago.

He gave a slight nod, his smile racing straight to

her heart. "It feels good. I'm sorry I haven't been by for so long—"

"You don't have to do that," she said as he made his way to her. "No apologies are necessary."

"Yes, they are. You asked me to fix your office door months ago. Is it still sticking?"

She nodded and smiled. "I just don't close it."

"Otherwise you would be locked in?" He shook his head.

"It's no big deal. I can always call Kate across the street to come get me out. Anyway, you've had more important things on your mind. The usual?" She was already getting him an orange soda from the cooler.

"I've missed you," he said as she opened the bottle on an old-fashioned opener on the wall and handed it to him. Their fingers brushed and she felt that familiar thrill.

She didn't want to tell him how much she'd missed him. Or how much she'd feared he would never come back. She'd survived on what he'd said before he left. He loved her.

"Is this your first day back at work?" she asked.

He nodded and took a drink.

He'd changed over the past six months. She couldn't put her finger on what it was, though, but he seemed reconciled. A man like Frank Curry believed he could "fix" most anything—or at least should be able to. He'd blamed himself for Pam being the way she was.

"I'm so glad you gave up on finding Pam," Nettie said.

Again he merely nodded.

She thought of the man who'd taken off out of the store, murder in his eye, to find Pam. So what had changed? she wondered as she studied him. Pam Chandler was still dangerous. She was still out there somewhere. Nettie lived with that knowledge every day. She didn't cross the street to the post office or the Branding Iron Café without looking around for the crazy, vindictive woman. She no longer walked down to the store at night unless someone was with her. At the house, she locked all her doors, even in the daytime, something pretty much unheard of in most of rural Montana.

"I'd better be going," Frank said. He had a deep voice. It had always sent heat racing through her blood. His gaze met hers and she felt a catch in her throat. "I was thinking you might want to go to a movie tomorrow night."

He was asking her for a *date?* It had been so long in coming that she didn't answer at first, out of shock.

"That is, if you're free." He sounded not so sure of things between them. Understandably, since it wasn't that long ago that she'd given up on him and had spent some time with another man.

She shoved that thought away. "I would love to go," she said, her voice cracking with emotion.

He smiled then and he was the Frank Curry she'd fallen so desperately in love with so many years ago.

That love had lingered and only recently begun to bloom again, like a glacier lily coming up after a long, hard Montana winter.

Stepping down the hall, he took a look at her office door.

"Frank, I don't want you to be late for work. The door can wait."

"It looks as if I'm going to have to take it down and plane off some of the wood. The store must have shifted on its old foundation. I'll fix the door this weekend. Just don't get locked in."

"I won't." His concern warmed her heart. She pushed aside her worries about him as he leaned over and kissed her softly on the mouth. He tasted of orange soda and smelled of the outdoors. She wanted to wrap her arms around him and hold him to her, but he was already drawing back, saying, "Don't want to be late my first day back on the job." And he was gone, the bell over the door jingling.

Nettie moved to the window to watch him leave, her fingers pressed to the glass, her heart pounding. She had waited so long for this.

Please don't let anything spoil it.

TESSA STARTED AT the knock on her motel room door. Her first thought was, *No one knows I'm here. No one but Ethan, or whatever the man wanted to call himself.*

At the second knock, she moved to the door and asked, *"Yes?"*

"Ms. Winters, I'd like to have a word with you." Ethan's voice, though more authoritative. Just the sound of it hurt. "It's Undersheriff Dillon Lawson."

"I believe we said all we had to yesterday," she called through the door.

"Not quite."

She gritted her teeth and opened the door. For a moment she was taken aback by the uniformed man standing in her doorway. He wore a pale gray Stetson over his longish blond hair, a tan uniform shirt with his name tag and a gold star. A gun was strapped to his slim hips, over a pair of jeans that ran down his long legs to his boots.

Ethan was as handsome as any man she'd ever known, no matter what he was wearing. But in a uniform, he looked so responsible, so nice, so safe, that he threatened to break her heart all over again.

"What do you want?" she demanded.

"Just to talk. May I come in?"

Tessa hesitated. "I don't see what talking—"

"Please."

The break in his voice made her relent. She stepped aside to let him enter the room but left the door open. She'd made the bed, a habit her mother had taught her and one she couldn't break even when it was a motel. The air smelled of pines and the Yellowstone River nearby. She breathed it in and braced herself for whatever was to happen next.

He saw the bed and looked surprised.

"I can't stand an unmade bed and I wasn't quite ready to leave yet."

He'd removed his Stetson and now held the brim in his fingers. "Where are you going?"

"Not that it concerns you, but back to California. I have a job there, you might recall. I had a life there before I met *you*."

"Do you have family there?"

She studied him. "Are you asking as undersheriff or as the father of my baby?"

He didn't answer.

"As you already know, I don't have family, but I have friends in California," she said into the silence that stretched between them. She felt awkward standing in the small motel room. There weren't a lot of places to sit in the room, other than the bed and one straight-backed chair by the desk. She wondered how long this was going to take. "I'll be just fine, not that I think you honestly care about me or the baby."

"You said you have a job. Where do you work?"

She eyed him suspiciously. "Why are you—"

"Please, just humor me, all right?"

Tessa sighed. "I work as a supervisor for a landscaping firm."

He seemed surprised, which only annoyed her. "How much money did you say my brother took from you?"

She ignored the *brother* part, wondering what he was doing here. Apparently he wanted to continue this pretense. But to what end? Yesterday he'd threat-

ened her with arrest for pulling a gun on him and trying to scam him. Surely he hadn't come here today
to do just that, had he?

"All of my savings. Just under five thousand dollars, as if you don't know that, too."

He looked down at his boots for a moment. "I
was thinking…" He slowly raised his gaze. "If you
really knew my brother, then you should have some
way to prove it."

She put her hands on her stomach. "The proof, as
they say, is in the pudding. Anyway, why would I
have come all the way to Montana looking for Ethan
if I hadn't known him? Or at least someone who'd
pretended to be him?"

"That's what I'm trying to figure out. Truthfully,
I can't see you with my brother. You seem to have
too much going for you to get involved with him."

She chuckled at that. "I should have been smarter.
Neither of us is denying that."

"I guess what I'm trying to say is that you and
Ethan must have been together for a while before—"
His gaze dropped to where her hands still rested on
her stomach. "Before you say he left you."

"Three months. I met him last April, three months
before I got pregnant. That would have been a month
after you stole his identity." She couldn't help being
angry. What was he insinuating? That this wasn't his
fault because clearly she was just plain easy? Those
were fightin' words.

"Then you must have photographs of the two of you together."

Tessa felt her pulse jump. "You know damned well I don't."

"I beg your pardon?"

"Do we really have to continue this charade? *Ethan* took everything that tied him to me and the baby when he left, including photographs of the two of us, along with my money. He even killed the ones on my cell phone, not that there were many. Ethan didn't like having his photo taken."

"Didn't you find that strange?"

She laughed. "I did until I met you. Now we both know why you didn't want me to have any proof, don't we?"

"So you have no evidence that you ever even knew my brother."

Tessa glared at him. "Isn't that the way you planned it?"

"Then I guess we're finished here." He settled his hat on his head, tipped the brim and started for the door.

That was it? He was just going to walk out again? What had he really come here for?

And that was when it hit her.

"Aren't you curious how I found you, since you lied not only about your first name but also your last? You were so careful not to leave anything that would tie me to you. You must wonder how I found you."

The lawman stopped short of the door and turned

to look back at her. She reached into her shoulder bag and saw him tense, but she didn't pull the .45. "I was wondering why you stopped by here this morning. Did you just realize that you'd dropped something when you left me in the middle of the night? Of course you would want to make sure I don't use it to embarrass you, to prove what you did."

He frowned. "I don't know what—"

"Admit it. You came for *this*." She held up the dog-eared, faded photograph and let out a bitter laugh. "I'm so stupid. Of course this was why you asked me about photographs. You realized you must have dropped it in your hurry to get away the night you left."

His frown deepened.

"I'll bet you've been racking your brain, wondering how I could have found you. You never told me enough to lead me to you in Montana. So what could it have been? Then you remembered the photograph." She looked at him, her expression filled with disgust. "Here, take it," she said, thrusting it at him. "I'm not going to bother you again. I'm going back to California and you will never see me or my baby again."

He seemed to hesitate for a moment before he stepped to her and took the photograph.

ONE GLANCE AT the photo and Dillon had to pull out the chair and sit down. He bent over the snapshot, tears blurring his eyes. "Where did you get this?"

"I just told you. You dropped it. I almost threw it away when I found it. I thought, how egotistical that he carried around a photo of himself. I remembered seeing you with it a few times when you didn't know I was watching. Clearly it meant something to you, so I thought the sentiment must be about the place."

"Why didn't you show me this yesterday?" he asked without looking up.

"As if it would have made a difference."

He glanced up then and met her blue gaze. He'd been in law enforcement long enough that he had gotten pretty good at telling if a person was lying. This woman had thrown off his instincts from the moment he'd met her because of his grief over his brother's death. Her story hadn't held water, and yet… "You said you found me through this photo?"

"I tried Hard Luck Ranch from the logo on the side of the pickup in the background, but there was more than one, so I just looked up the brand on the cattle in the pasture behind you in the photo." She shrugged. "It led me right to your ranch."

It surprised him that she'd been that clever, but clearly the woman was smart and very determined.

"Now that you have your photograph back…"

It was obvious she wanted him to leave. Her disgust tore at his insides. He hated to think that what she was saying about his brother's stealing her money and leaving her might be true. But he feared it was.

Which meant what? That Ethan hadn't died in that car crash? His heart leaped at the thought, but quickly plummeted. Ethan was dead. Unless somehow there'd been a mistake in identifying the body, since the vehicle had apparently exploded on impact—

"This photo isn't mine," he said. "That *is* me in the picture, though. Ethan took it the last time I saw him, almost two years ago."

He could see that she didn't know what to make of that. For once, she looked as confused as he'd felt from the moment she'd appeared at his corral fence. "Tell me about my brother."

She let out a small laugh. "You have to be kidding." Her gaze met his, challenging him to tell the truth.

He only wished he *knew* the truth. "You say you met him last April?" A month after he'd buried his brother. Or at least what was left of the man he'd thought was his brother. "Please, tell me about him."

Tessa stared at him, her blue eyes firing with anger and pain. Ethan had hurt her badly—and she believed he had been that man masquerading as his brother.

"Tell you about him? You mean other than his being a liar and a thief and a coward?" she asked sarcastically.

"There must have been something you loved about him."

Tessa had to swallow the lump in her throat. Since Ethan had left her, the pain in her heart had dulled.

Being this close to the man now made her recall something she'd sensed in him the first time she'd met him. A sadness born, she'd thought, of compassion.

He'd told her he'd made mistakes in his life. That he had wanted to change for her. He'd made her believe that her love could bring out the man she'd sensed was in him. She'd wanted to believe that. There'd been something about him....

Tessa sat down on the edge of the bed and looked at the man sitting in her motel room. She told herself she wasn't up to this charade. That was what it was, wasn't it? This man was trying to confuse her, right?

And yet he looked heartsick, like a man who had lost his brother and thought she could bring him back.

She took a breath and let it out slowly. "He was... charming and funny and a little vulnerable. He made me feel..." She swallowed again and said, "Do we really have to do this? If Ethan was killed a month before I met the man I thought was him—"

"Where did you meet him?"

Tessa sighed and told herself to indulge him; whatever it took to get him to sign away his rights to the baby she was carrying. Even better, get him to write her a check for the money he'd stolen from her. Showing him the photograph had touched him in a way she hadn't expected.

"At church."

He actually looked surprised. "I would have thought—"

"A bar?" She could see that he wanted to think the worst of her. "*Ethan* was on a construction crew fixing part of the church. I had stopped by to bring some cookies I made for an upcoming potluck.... He asked me what kind of cookies I'd made and said they were his favorite."

"Snicker doodles."

She met his gaze. "Yes."

"You gave him one, and that's when he asked you out."

Tessa hesitated a moment before she shook her head. "He didn't ask me until a few days later at a church garage sale."

"He must have liked you right from the start. Do you mind?" He took one of the plastic-wrapped cups and got up to fill it with water from the bathroom. He looked shaken, making her feel as if she, too, was on unfamiliar, unstable ground. Was it possible Ethan had fooled not just her, but also his brother and the rest of the world? She was no longer so sure this man was the one she'd known.

"So you fell in love with him." It wasn't a question.

She nodded. "We'd set a date to get married."

That surprised him, she saw. "What happened?"

"You know what happened," she said irritably, realizing she was buying into his act—and not for the first time. He'd played her for a fool once. She was determined he wouldn't again. "You took my money and skipped town." She stood up.

"You know it wasn't me." He said the words softly, his gaze holding hers.

She stared into his eyes for a long moment, then she lowered herself back onto the edge of the bed. She felt a small chill ripple through her. This *wasn't* the man who'd hurt her. Hadn't part of her known that the moment she'd seen the way he'd handled the horse yesterday?

"I don't understand." Her voice broke as her eyes welled with tears.

"There is only one explanation," the undersheriff said. "If you're telling the truth, then my brother is alive."

CHAPTER FIVE

FRANK HAD WANTED to tell Lynette—he'd never called her Nettie—about the crow he'd seen on the telephone line at the ranch. But he already regretted telling Dillon. He knew it was silly, but he feared he'd jinxed it, and when he went home the crow would be gone.

He couldn't explain it, but the crows gave him a feeling of well-being, as if everything was right with the world. The birds fascinated him, as well. He recalled one morning when he and Lynette had sat in his patrol pickup and watched two young crows playing on the main street of Beartooth.

It had been a game of tag, the young crows dancing around, teasing each other with a twig between them. Before that morning, Lynette hadn't understood his fascination with the birds.

"They *are* like us," she'd said after watching the young crows play.

He'd told her how they made extended families, taking in uncles and aunts, any crow that needed a place to stay. He still wasn't sure exactly how they communicated among themselves, but they did. There was one thing he did know, though, for certain. Crows were better at making and keeping their families together than humans.

Frank shoved that thought away. He was in too good a mood to think about the past now. He and Lynette were going on a date. He smiled. And he was going back to work, back to a job he loved and had almost given up because of—

Nope, he wasn't even going to think his ex-wife's name. He'd put that all behind him. Over the past six months he'd worked hard at the ranch, filling his days so full that at night he couldn't think. He would walk into the house, often too tired to eat, and would fall into his bed.

All that was in the past, he told himself, and yet he wasn't sure he would ever be able to quit locking his doors at night or stop keeping his loaded gun within reach beside his bed. So maybe not everything could be put to rest in the past.

Frank had barely reached the sheriff's department, retrieved his service gun and gold star, when he got his first call. A domestic dispute. Never his favorite. But it was nice to be back in the saddle, so to speak.

"WHAT ARE YOU saying?" Tessa demanded as she stared at Dillon. It was hard to look at him and not see Ethan. But more and more she was seeing subtle differences between the two men that had nothing to do with their looks.

"There is only one way you can be carrying my

brother's baby," he said. "And that is if Ethan didn't die in that car crash last March."

"Then who did?"

"I don't know."

She shook her head. "If the person behind the wheel wasn't him, then why didn't he come forward?"

Dillon let out a short, hard laugh. "He wanted everyone to believe he was dead." He shook his head, as if amazed that his twin could be that cruel. A thought seemed to strike him. "What name was he going by when you met him? You said he'd lied about his last name."

"Ethan *Cross.*"

He nodded. "That makes sense. It's our mother's maiden name."

"You really are his twin brother." She suddenly felt awful for calling him a liar. "I'm sorry I doubted you."

His smile was benevolent as he held out his hand. "Maybe we should start over. My name is Dillon Lawson."

"Tessa Winters," she said, her hand disappearing into his large, warm, callused one. She couldn't tell which of them was trembling. Maybe both of them were, given what was becoming apparent. "Is it really possible?"

"With Ethan, anything is possible. Even probable."

"Why would he let everyone think he was dead?"

"My guess is that he was in trouble and needed to disappear. How better than letting everyone believe he had died in the car wreck?"

"Everyone, including his *twin* brother?"

"We haven't been close in years. Also, he's apparently good at disappearing." He reached into the back pocket of his jeans and pulled out his checkbook. "You said he took five thousand dollars from you?"

"Not quite. But I don't want your money."

He raised a brow. "You wouldn't have come all this way unless you needed it."

"I'll manage. More than anything I wanted to look into Ethan's eyes one last time." She hated to admit that she'd actually thought about giving him another chance. Not for herself, but for their daughter. She couldn't bear the thought of her little girl growing up without a father.

How foolish she had been. The man had let everyone believe he was dead. He'd lied about more than she could have imagined. Now all she wanted was for Ethan to sign the form giving away his rights. The last thing she wanted was him coming in and out of their lives and bringing his troubles with him.

"I'm sorry."

She met Dillon's blue gaze and wondered why she hadn't seen it before. They might be identical twins, but where Ethan had tried to be gentle and caring, Dillon just was.

"What I really want is for him to sign the form. He didn't want this baby. I don't want him showing up years from now and trying to lay claim to my daughter."

"You're having a girl?" His voice broke. He cleared his throat. "I'm going to have a niece?" He smiled as she nodded, and she felt her heart lift at the joy she saw in his expression. She'd so wanted her daughter to have family, especially since she herself had grown up without any.

"I'll see what I can find out about Ethan," Dillon said, suddenly looking uneasy. "In the meantime, I would imagine you'll be going back to California. I'll let you know when I find him."

Tessa shook her head. "I didn't come all this way to give up that easily. If Ethan is alive, I'm finding him—with or without your help."

"I DON'T THINK that's a good idea, Tessa. Not only are you pregnant—when are you due?"

"Three weeks."

"*Very* pregnant, and not trained for this sort of thing, and we have no idea what kind of trouble my brother is running from." Even as Dillon said the words, he saw the stubborn lift of her chin. Determination burned in her blue gaze.

"You said you hadn't seen him in two years," she argued. "I, on the other hand, have firsthand knowledge of your brother during the past year. Between the two of us, we stand a better chance of finding him if we work together than alone."

He studied her for a moment, remembering the .45

in her shoulder bag. He didn't doubt that she could take care of herself under normal circumstances. But these weren't normal. Whatever his brother was running from, it must be something big if it had forced him to fake his own death.

"You have to think about yourself and your baby," he said. "If I'm right, my brother was involved in something bad. This could get dangerous."

She crossed her arms on top of her stomach and stared him down. "Then I have already put myself and my baby in danger by finding you, haven't I?"

Dillon worried she might be right about that. "Still—"

"You don't owe me anything. You can wash your hands of me right now. But I *will* find Ethan. As hard as he tried, he left me somewhat of a trail. You are only one of my leads."

"Leads you aren't going to share unless we do this together."

She smiled.

He considered the woman. From the moment he'd laid eyes on her, there had been something in her demeanor that had gotten to him. Her story had been preposterous, and yet… And yet he hadn't been able to let it go.

He'd thought she was trying to con him when they'd first met. The lawman in him reminded him that he might be falling for the worst con of all, because he desperately wanted Tessa to be carrying Ethan's baby—and she would know that.

He recalled how Sheriff Frank Curry had never opened the DNA test that had been run on the girl claiming to be his daughter, Tiffany Chandler. Frank had said he didn't need to. Tiffany was his daughter.

Dillon knew Frank wanted to believe Tiffany was his daughter. Just as Dillon wanted to believe this woman had known his brother and was now carrying his child.

"You still aren't sure about me," she said as if reading his thoughts.

Did he believe she was carrying Ethan's baby or did he only want to believe it? He thought of the photograph that Ethan had left behind and how he'd used their mother's maiden name.

"I believe you knew my brother, and if you're telling the truth…" His gaze went to her stomach. He saw something move across the surface. Before he could react, Tessa took his hand and placed it on her swollen belly.

His eyes widened as the baby kicked his hand. He felt its little foot just below the surface. The movement awakened some primitive emotion deep inside him, because he felt an instant connection to this child she was carrying. Ethan's baby.

Tessa smiled. "That's your niece."

He nodded, praying she was telling the truth, because it would mean Ethan was alive—or at least had been only months ago—and part of his brother lived in this woman. Being his brother's identical twin, Dillon felt as if he was part of this child, as well.

If what she said was true, Tessa had been close to his brother, something he himself hadn't been for years. If true, she, too, had loved Ethan. No doubt still did. Because of that, he couldn't let her go after Ethan alone. The only way he could protect her and this baby was to keep her close. If it was true, she might know more about his brother than he did. Between them, they might stand a chance of finding Ethan—if he really was alive.

He couldn't help being skeptical. It came with the job. He met Tessa's gaze. His brother was alive. But where was he now? And how was Dillon going to find him? Ethan hadn't used his real name when he'd met Tessa. That must mean someone had been looking for him.

"I'll see what I can find out through regular channels," Dillon said. "In the meantime, I don't want you staying in a motel." Before she could argue, he quickly added, "Come stay out at the ranch. I have plenty of room. You'll be more comfortable there."

"And you can keep an eye on me."

"And vice versa."

She pretended surprise. "Did you think I might suspect you'd go after Ethan without me?"

He smiled. "In the meantime, I want you to have this." He began to fill out a check for five thousand dollars.

"I already told you—"

"It's just a loan until we find Ethan and he can pay you back what he owes." He held out the check.

She glanced at him and the check for a moment before taking it. "A loan. Only until we find Ethan."

Part of him called himself a damned fool. He could be five thousand dollars poorer tomorrow—if she didn't steal him blind at the house before disappearing as quickly as she'd appeared in his life.

But once he'd felt that tiny foot against his palm, Tessa Winters had had him.

THE FIRST THING Dillon did was check to see if anyone had disappeared around the time of Ethan's alleged death in the desert. He found what he was looking for in a short police report about a wrangler who'd been reported missing from a dude ranch near Palm Springs. The man had left behind his truck and some of his belongings.

There was just the one mention of the missing man. No follow-up. The man's name was Buck Morgan. His former address, though, was Wisdom, Montana.

Dillon had a bad feeling the man was now buried in the local cemetery under Ethan's headstone. He remembered the day he'd laid his brother to rest. There hadn't been a funeral. No one in the area knew Ethan, and Dillon wouldn't have taken his brother's remains back to western Montana. Too many bad memories there for both brothers.

Had Ethan been watching the day Dillon had placed the ashes in the container at the grave site? That thought made him both angry and incredibly sad—and even more determined to find his brother, if indeed he was still alive.

The last Dillon had heard, his brother was working on a ranch over on the Powder River near Eka-laka, Montana. But that had been two years ago, and Ethan had never stayed in any one place long.

Dillon put in a call to the ranch just in case the owner might have known where Ethan was headed next. Possibly Wisdom, Montana?

When the ranch owner answered, he introduced himself as Undersheriff Dillon Lawson of Big Timber.

"Ethan Lawson, oh, you bet I remember him," the female ranch owner said, giving Dillon a bad feeling he knew what was coming next. "He left here owing me money. Any chance you're a relative?"

"Brother. How much does he owe you?"

"Two hundred."

"I'll put a check in the mail today," Dillon said, wondering how much it was going to cost him by the time he was through looking for his twin. "Do you happen to know where he went after he left your ranch?"

"Not likely, since he left in the middle of the night. The two of them absconding in the night like the thieves they were. The other one got me for five hundred. I don't suppose you want to pick up his tab, as well?"

"The other one?"

"Luke Blackwell. Running with him, your brother

was headed for trouble. I hired Luke against my better judgment, since when I checked the ranch he'd worked for I was warned that he'd gotten involved with the rancher's granddaughter. Luke gave me some song and dance about the girl chasing him. I weakened. Big mistake. Last I heard, Luke did some hard time in Deer Lodge. Not surprised."

"Do you know what he went to prison for?" Dillon asked.

"Felony theft. He was caught stealing a backhoe. The bum actually tried to get me to give him a recommendation before the parole board hearing, promising to offer him a job when he got out. Like I would ever let him back on my ranch. If you're looking for your brother, he'll be wherever Luke went after he got out. The two were thicker than thieves." She chuckled bitterly.

Dillon asked for her address, thanked her for the information and hung up. He quickly checked to see how Luke Blackwell had fared with the judicial system.

Luke had done only eighteen months in prison before his release. He had gotten a rancher by the name of Halbrook Truman of the Double T-Bar-Diamond to promise him a job when he got out.

The Double T-Bar-Diamond was in Big Hole country over by Wisdom, Montana. Dillon felt his heart beat a little faster. He'd never trusted coincidences. As he started to place a call to the ranch, he changed his mind. He hadn't been to that part of southwestern Montana in years. It was only a half day's drive, one he wouldn't mind taking.

Also, he was curious why Halbrook Truman had hired Luke Blackwell. Felons had a hard time getting jobs. If the rancher had checked into Luke's past at all, he would have found out just how unreliable the man was—not to mention that he'd gone to prison for theft. But maybe Luke had proved he could change and now still worked at the ranch.

With Sheriff Frank Curry back at work, there was no reason Dillon couldn't follow up on this. He called the cell phone number Tessa Winters had given him before he'd left her at the ranch. She answered on the second ring, sounding breathless.

"Are you all right?" he asked alarmed.

"Fine, I left my cell phone on the porch. I was down at the corral admiring your horses."

With relief, he asked, "Did Ethan ever mention working on a ranch called the Double T-Bar-Diamond?" He heard her start to say no just before he quickly added, "For a man named Halbrook Truman?"

"Halbrook," she said. "I *have* heard that name. Who is he?"

"A rancher over in western Montana. I think Ethan might have worked for him before he left for Arizona. I'm going over there to talk to him."

"Not without me."

He smiled and shook his head, telling himself he should have known she wouldn't sit tight for long.

The woman was resolute. Look how she'd found *him*. He wondered if he would have ever known there was even a chance Ethan was alive if she hadn't shown up at his door.

"In that case, how do you feel about a road trip? It will also give us a chance to talk." There was so much he wanted to know. About Ethan—and whatever trouble his twin had gotten himself into.

But he was also very curious about Tessa Winters.

CHAPTER SIX

DILLON GLANCED AT the young pregnant woman in his passenger seat. Not for the first time, he saw her turn to look behind them.

"Is everything all right?" he asked.

She seemed startled by the question and reticent to answer. "You'll think I'm silly, but I've had the strangest feeling I was being followed."

"All the way from California?"

"Crazy, huh?"

Maybe. Maybe not. Who knew what kind of people his brother had gotten involved with? It scared him, though, to think that the trouble might have followed her.

"You said on the phone earlier that you recognized the name Halbrook," he said.

She nodded. "A man stopped by a day or two before Ethan left. Ethan went outside to talk to him, but I overheard them arguing. Ethan mentioned the name Halbrook. It's unusual enough, I remembered it."

"Did you ask Ethan what the argument was about?"

"He told me he owed the man money. I asked how much and suggested he use the money I had

in savings to pay the man. I hadn't liked the look of
the man and didn't want him coming back around."

"Ethan didn't jump at that?"

"He said he didn't want my money, that it was for
our house." She scoffed at that now. "He knew I'd put
the money in both our names. Talk about trusting."

"Tell me about you," Dillon said, and glanced over
at her. "If you don't mind."

"What do you want to know?"

"Whatever you'd like to share with me."

TESSA THOUGHT ABOUT that for a moment. More to the
point, what did she really know about Dillon? He
wasn't his brother—that much was clear. He was a
man who worked both as an undersheriff and at his
own ranch. He was kind and generous and compassionate, and he'd taken an entirely different route in
life than his brother had.

What scared her was that in Dillon she glimpsed
what she had wanted to see in his twin. She knew
it was crazy, but Ethan had been just enough like
his brother that she felt she already knew Dillon.
She *trusted* him, and trust didn't come easily to her.
Ethan's betrayal had only made her less trusting.

"I was born and raised in California. My parents
were killed in a car wreck when I was two. I was
in the car, but I miraculously survived. A neighbor
lady took me in and raised me until her death, when
I was sixteen. After that, I was on my own." She'd
purposely left out the part about the foster homes the

county had put her in. She'd barely survived those with her life. That had been the real miracle.

Dillon studied her for a moment before turning back to his driving. He seemed to sense the parts she'd left out and was kind enough not to ask.

"You want more for your daughter," he said after a moment.

"Of course I do," she said. "I suppose that is the real reason I came all this way looking for Ethan. I wanted to give him another chance to be a father to our daughter."

"What about another chance with you?"

She shook her head. "He used up his last chance when he left the way he did."

DILLON COULD SEE what his brother had seen in Tessa. Ethan would have liked her independence, the fire in her, not to mention her beauty both inside and out. Ethan had chosen well. So why had he burned his bridges when he'd left?

Because he'd known he wouldn't be back?

"I'm sorry my brother hurt you," Dillon said as the Montana countryside blurred past, a tableau of shades of green from the new bright grasses to the deeper, richer shades of the cool pines. The mountains rose around them, most still snowcapped.

"It was my own fault." She turned as if to gaze out at the passing landscape.

"You must have seen something good in him. Isn't

it possible he really did want to change? Really did want everything he said he did?"

She let out a sound that made him hurt inside. "Better to think that than I'm a fool who was taken in by a handsome cowboy, right?"

He could see that Tessa had thought herself smarter. She'd let herself be fooled by a man. She hadn't yet learned that love was a heart thing, often with no brain involved.

He glanced in the rearview mirror. He hadn't thought to check for a tail. Then again, he hadn't thought he needed to. There were cars and pickups and a couple semis behind them. If they were being followed, he couldn't tell.

"There was no warning?" he asked, hoping to get her talking about Ethan.

"The signs were there. I just chose not to see them."

"Signs?"

"He'd been more moody in the days right before he left. Antsy and uncharacteristically impatient. More secretive, too. If I asked him where he'd been or what he was looking at on the computer—"

"He had a computer?" This surprised Dillon. Ethan had ranted about the new technologies on his visit two years ago. He'd said that was why he worked on ranches. He didn't have to learn how to use a computer, let alone a smartphone.

Tessa's chuckle had a bitter edge to it. "No, *he*

didn't own a computer. Other than his old pickup and his saddle, had he ever owned anything?"

"So he used yours. Do you still have it?" He could see that she understood at once.

"I checked it after he left. I thought…" She looked away.

He knew exactly what she'd thought. An online romance with another woman.

"He had said he was looking for a new saddle. I showed him how to use a search engine. He wasn't dumb. He didn't ask for my help after that."

Dillon knew his brother wasn't shopping on the internet for a saddle. So what had he been looking for? "Did he find a saddle?"

Another short laugh. "He *wasn't* looking for a saddle. He was looking for a gun."

"A *gun?*" Dillon asked.

"He had guns—a .357 he kept rolled up in its holster beside the bed, and a hunting rifle, a .30 Winchester, that hung on the rack in his pickup. Both were old. I suspect they meant something to him?"

"Our uncle Jack gave him the .357 before Jack died. The Winchester was our grandfather's." Dillon was a little surprised, given his brother's lifestyle, that he'd somehow managed to hang on to them.

He'd never thought of Ethan as being sentimental. Nor had he seemed like someone who cared about possessions. More and more Dillon was realizing how little he knew his twin.

He cracked his window, needing air. The more

he learned about his brother, the more sick at heart he became. The lush spring Montana landscape was a tapestry of contrasts, from the new bright green grass to the dark pines of the mountains, from the blinding white snow capping the peaks to the cloudless blue of the sky. The sweet scents reminded him of springs when they were boys.

The one thing he knew now without a doubt was that Tessa had known his brother. When and for how long? Well, that was still the question, wasn't it? But he wouldn't be looking for his brother unless part of him believed her, believed Ethan was alive.

"So what kind of gun was he looking for online?" He couldn't fathom that, even if Ethan had wanted another gun, why he would look for it on the internet. Not when he could pick one up at a local gun show. Again, it didn't sound like his brother.

"He'd deleted the sites he went to. But I hadn't told him about how the computer kept a history of the sites visited." She shrugged, giving away more than she probably meant to. Even back when they'd been talking marriage, she hadn't completely trusted the man she'd fallen in love with.

"Why would he feel the need to lie about what he was looking for?" Dillon asked after a moment.

Tessa seemed to pull herself out of the past. She came out of it angry again, but he suspected it was more with herself than Ethan. "Why would he lie about *everything?* I have no idea. I just know that he was looking at antique rifles. I saw on one site that a similar rifle to the one he was viewing went for a hundred and fifty *thousand* dollars."

"So he was just looking."

"I guess so. He'd been saving his money. I thought for a house for us, but he could have been saving it to buy a rifle, for all I know."

Odd. Again not like his brother. Dillon couldn't see him wanting an antique rifle even if he could afford it. So what was that about?

"Did you ever ask him?"

She nodded. "He got defensive, said it didn't have anything to do with me and that I should stay out of his business. It was the same day the man had stopped by whom he said he owed money to."

"The day you heard Ethan mention the name Halbrook?"

She nodded. "Ethan stormed out, but came back later and apologized. He was gone the next morning with my money."

"But he left the photo," Dillon said.

"Only because he dropped it, he was in such a hurry to clear out."

"Maybe. The thing is, if he was in trouble, which I think we can assume, then maybe he dropped it on purpose, knowing you would find me."

TESSA SCOFFED AT that. "Why didn't he just contact you himself if he wanted your help?"

"Because he's too stubborn. Ethan likes to believe he can take care of himself. He wouldn't ask for my help ever." He looked over at her, something soft and tender in his gaze. "But he would want you to find me because he'd know I'd take care of you and the baby if anything hap—"

"You think he *sent* me to you?" She couldn't help but laugh. "Ethan didn't exactly seem worried about what was going to happen to me and our baby when he took my money and left."

"I think you're wrong about that."

"Wouldn't it have been a whole lot easier if he'd just left me your name and address?"

He turned his attention back to the road. She saw his jaw work. "Would you have come all the way to Montana to see his brother?"

She studied him for a moment. "No."

"I didn't think so. You strike me as an independent woman with a lot of pride. Ethan obviously knew you. He knew you'd track down the ranch from the photograph." He glanced over at her. "He knew you were smart and resourceful. He knew you'd find me."

Tessa let that sink in as she watched the countryside blur past.

She had never seen such beautiful, remote country. They had traveled along Interstate 90 through pine-studded mountains past Paradise Valley and over the Bozeman Pass. From there they drove along clear rivers, winding through more mountains to reach Butte, home of the huge open-pit mine, before leaving behind civilization again.

She hated reliving those last few weeks with Ethan. Worse, she hated to admit even to herself how badly he'd hurt her. How badly she'd let him.

Could Dillon be right? Had Ethan cared about her and the baby? He had an odd way of showing it. But if he was in trouble... She reminded herself that Ethan had apparently faked his own death and changed his name—pretty drastic behavior even for him. Which, according to his brother, indicated that he'd been in serious trouble.

And then he'd met her.

So why hadn't he kept running? Surely a wife and baby hadn't been in his plans.

As much as Tessa hated doing it, she stewed over the days before Ethan left. He'd been angry about her questioning his time on the computer. He hadn't wanted her to know that he was looking for a rifle. That made no sense.

"Had Ethan gotten angry with you before?" Dillon asked, as if he'd noticed her chewing at her lower lip and glowering out the window.

"He was just looking for an excuse to cut and run," she said.

"My brother has always been...complicated."

She chuckled at that as she glanced over at Dillon. She couldn't help remembering what he'd said about her being strong and smart, what he'd figured out about her after meeting her *twice*. She suspected he was a good undersheriff, good at dealing with most people. But not his brother, apparently. He'd said he hadn't seen Ethan in two years, hadn't even known where he was.

She couldn't help being curious. The brothers were identical twins and yet one had become a lawman and the other an outlaw. "I take it you and Ethan weren't close?"

He shook his head. "It's a long story." And clearly one he didn't want to get into.

Ahead, a town appeared on the horizon. Tessa was relieved for a change in scenery as well as subject. At the edge of town, the sign read Welcome to Wisdom And the Big Hole Valley, Land of Ten Thousand Haystacks.

"Those are the Bitterroots," Dillon said, pointing to the snowcapped mountains.

The whole scene was breathtaking. The Big Hole River wound through the valley, with the Bitterroot Mountains as a backdrop. There was a lushness to the country, a new-spring green that was almost blinding.

They followed the Big Hole River out of town, rolling along a gravel road, a jackleg fence on each side. In a field next to them a half dozen horses took off running through the tall grass, the wind blowing back their manes. Overhead, cumulus clouds floated on a sea of blue.

Not far down the road, she noticed the Posted signs. They were orange and stamped with the Double T-Bar-Diamond Ranch name.

"Is this ranch as large as it seems?" she asked,

after they'd gone for miles with the Posted signs on both sides of the road.

"Montana has some huge ones," Dillon said, and slowed as a massive log arch appeared on the right-hand side of the road ahead. The arch was made of log and metal. An ornate design of a huge elk had been cut into the metal.

Suddenly Tessa sat up straighter. "I think Ethan told me about this place."

Dillon glanced over at her. "The Double T-Bar-Diamond Ranch?"

"Not by name. But if I'm right, there's a large rock fireplace in the living room of the lodge with a huge elk mount over it. Ethan said the owner of the ranch was so proud of the elk because it was the first one he'd ever killed. Apparently he liked to brag about it and his other possessions. I could tell Ethan didn't like the man. But when I showed an interest by asking about the ranch and when he worked there, Ethan said he didn't want to talk about it. He said it wasn't a place he wanted to remember and then he changed the subject."

DILLON COULD HAVE told her that Ethan probably hadn't wanted to talk about most ranches he'd worked, because more than likely he'd left under unpleasant— if not downright criminal—circumstances. Dillon thought of the one over on the Powder River and the two hundred bucks it had cost him. He wondered what it would cost him at this ranch.

He checked his mirror. Dust boiled up behind the pickup, obscuring anyone who might be following them. "What makes you think this is the ranch?"

"Its size," she said. "I got the impression the man was very wealthy. But also that arch we just drove under? Did you see the elk artwork in the metal part?"

He already suspected Ethan had worked here. Now he was afraid of what they would find out about his brother as they came over a rise and a sprawling house came into view. Dillon hoped it hadn't been a mistake bringing Tessa with him.

The house was a single story made of stone and log with a green metal roof. The roof and the house seemed to run forever along the river's edge.

Dillon parked in front, bracing himself for more bad news as they got out and approached the gigantic carved wooden door.

A woman answered a few minutes after he'd pushed the doorbell. A military march song echoed through the house as she asked, "Yes?" She was dressed in a maid's uniform.

"We're here to see Mr. Truman."

She nodded and led them into a massive living room. Dillon spotted the fireplace, a towering stone masterpiece, and the elk mount dwarfing the room. It looked like something out of Boone and Crockett. He and Tessa shared a look. It appeared he'd been right about his brother following Luke Blackwell here.

At the sound of boot heels on the stone floor, they

both turned. One look at the man and Dillon knew this had to be Halbrook Truman, the ranch owner. He carried himself like a man in a hurry to get whatever he wanted with no doubt in his mind that he would succeed.

The fiftysomething rancher appeared distracted, so it took a moment before he looked up and actually saw them. His gaze went from Tessa to Dillon before he stumbled to a stop. *"Ethan?"* He started to laugh, shaking his head as if nothing surprised him anymore. "You're the last person I expected to see—especially wearing a damned sheriff's department uniform. Did you make Luke one of your deputies?" The man guffawed at his own joke.

For the second time in two days, someone had thought Dillon was Ethan. He'd lived so long separately from his brother that he'd forgotten what that was like.

"I'm Undersheriff Dillon Lawson. Ethan was my brother." He couldn't help using *was*. Part of him still wouldn't let himself believe that Ethan really was alive. He couldn't bear the thought of losing his brother all over again if not.

Halbrook let out a grunt. "Yeah, right. Call yourself whatever you please, since we both know that the rumors of your demise were greatly exaggerated. But you'd better be here to return my property." The rancher glanced at Tessa. "All of it, including the ring I gave my fiancée. I hope to hell you didn't knock up Ashley, too."

So Halbrook had heard about Ethan's death, but unlike Dillon, he hadn't been fooled by it. "What property might that be?"

The rancher narrowed his gaze. "What the hell is this?" He laughed again but there was no humor in it. "You foolin' with me, son? You should know better than that."

"As I told you, I'm not Ethan. I'm his twin brother. I take it he never mentioned he had an identical twin." Dillon tried not to let that hurt him. He remembered Ethan saying once that he felt like a carbon copy, not the real thing.

"You have some credentials on you?" Halbrook Truman asked.

Dillon produced his driver's license, along with his badge and one of the photographs he'd shown Tessa, of him and his brother. For years he hadn't had to explain about his twin because Ethan hadn't been part of his life. It felt strange now.

The rancher's eyes widened as he took in the photo. His gaze swept up to meet Dillon's and narrowed. "He never said anything about having a twin." Suspicion laced his tone. "If you're not Ethan, then what are you doing here?"

"I wasn't sure Ethan had worked for you. Now that I know he did, I'm hoping you might know where he is."

Halbrook fidgeted with the coins in his jeans pocket for a moment before moving to a cabinet along the wall. A door swung open, exposing a built-in bar.

Before, the man apparently hadn't thought he was really dealing with law enforcement. Now he seemed worried. Why was that, if Ethan had taken his property from him? Wouldn't he be glad to have the law involved?

"You didn't say what my brother took that you were hoping I was bringing back, along with your fiancée's ring," Dillon said to the man's back as Halbrook poured himself a drink and took a gulp from the crystal glass. The alcohol seemed to fortify him.

"And you didn't say why you're really here, if you weren't even sure your brother worked here or not," the rancher said without turning around.

"Luke Blackwell."

Halbrook turned slowly and raised a brow. "I didn't know we were talking about Luke."

"You offered Luke a job when he got out of prison," Dillon said. "You were instrumental in getting him out."

"I like to help a man who wants to change." The rancher shrugged and poured himself another drink. "He also apparently lied when he vouched for your brother." Dillon noticed that the man's hands were shaking, but not from fear or nervousness. Halbrook Truman was furious.

"Luke doesn't still work for you?"

Halbrook laughed in answer.

"When did my brother and Luke leave your employ?"

The rancher pretended to give that some thought. "Let's see. I'd say it was in the middle of the night the first part of February a year ago, as I recall. I found my safe open and empty the next morning and my fiancée, Ashley, gone, along with some of my hired hands."

"You called the sheriff?"

The man's expression darkened. "It was a personal matter."

Dillon didn't like the sound of that, given that Ethan had allegedly died in a car accident a month after leaving this ranch. The wreck had been ruled an accident, since alcohol was involved. Dillon had had no reason to suspect anything. Until Tessa showed up. So who had been in that car? Who had really died that night?

He pulled out his notebook and pen. "If you could give me the name of the ranch hands who left with my brother…"

"I don't see the point."

"I need to find Ethan. One of the others might know where he is. Or I could talk to your current employees—"

"Luke Blackwell, Tom Grady and Buck Morgan. You want the name of my fiancée, too?" The alcohol seemed to have loosened his tongue. Or maybe he didn't want Dillon talking to his employees. "Ashley Rene Clarkson."

Dillon wrote down the names and asked, "Do you know where they went after they left here?"

The rancher cocked his head. "If I knew, I wouldn't still be looking for them, now, would I?"

"You're looking for them?"

Halbrook seemed to regret his words. He waved off the question with a dismissive sweep of his hand. "It's no big deal. They took some money. I'd forgotten all about it until I saw you."

He was lying. Dillon had seen the man's fury. Halbrook Truman wasn't a forgiving man. He thought of what Tessa had told him about the conversation she'd overheard with Ethan and some stranger. Had Halbrook hired a man to get back whatever the bunch of them had stolen?

"It would help if I knew what they'd taken," he said. "If my brother owes you money—"

"I don't need your money." The rancher downed his second drink. He seemed calmer as he put down the glass. "I'm sorry, I would have offered you a drink but I'm assuming you're on duty," he said to Dillon. "And—" he turned to look at Tessa "—you're—"

"I'm fine," she said, her tone crisp. "But would you mind if I used your bathroom?"

"There's one down the hall on the right. Help yourself," Halbrook said, and watched Tessa until she disappeared around the corner. "That your doing?" His eyes narrowed. "Let me guess, *she's* the one interested in finding your brother." He laughed. "Ethan *has* been busy. Looks like you'd better hurry and find him."

Dillon changed the subject, asking some general questions about the ranch while they waited. Halbrook was happy to talk about his "spread." Apparently he hadn't bragged about what he had to only Ethan. He was ready to brag to anyone who would listen.

"My great-grandfather made his fortune in the gold fields and started this ranch," Halbrook boasted. "It has grown with each generation."

"That's a nice elk," Dillon said, nodding to the mount over the fireplace.

"I killed him when I was twelve. One shot to the heart. Gutted him myself. Had to quarter him to get him back to the ranch. Scored four hundred on Boone and Crockett." The man swelled with pride as he looked at the elk.

Dillon saw Tessa coming down the hallway. She looked pale. He feared coming here had been a mistake. Bringing *her* definitely had been. She didn't need to hear more bad things about the father of her baby. He hated to even think how many ranchers his brother had ripped off or how many of them had a score to settle with Ethan.

At least now he had an inkling of why his brother might be on the run. Even on a good day, he suspected Halbrook Truman was a force to be reckoned with. What had Ethan stolen? Clearly something the rancher wanted back. Could it be the reason Ethan had faked his own death, if indeed that was what had happened?

Dillon had a bad feeling that he'd better find his brother before the rancher did.

CHAPTER SEVEN

Ethan Lawson woke in a cheap motel, hungover and depressed. He glanced toward the window. The curtains were closed, but through a thin space between them, he could see that it was too light outside. It was too quiet, too. Earlier he had been vaguely aware of vehicle engines starting, followed by a scraping sound.

He swore as he sat up. The motel room was hot, the window partially steamed over as he stood and walked to it to part the curtains. "Snow." He cursed again. A good four inches had fallen overnight. What was he doing in this godforsaken country this time of year anyway?

As his head cleared, he remembered why he wasn't down south in the desert. He let the curtain fall and turned, tempted to go back to bed. But he couldn't remember the last time he'd eaten, and it would be dangerous to stay here any longer.

He moved into the bathroom, turned on the shower and while he waited for the water to warm, he relieved himself in the toilet. It was after he'd showered that he'd accidentally seen himself in the mirror over the sink. He'd known he probably looked the way he felt—terrible. But still, the image had been shocking.

A couple weeks' growth of sandy-blond beard gave him a homeless appearance. He couldn't remember the last time he'd gotten a haircut, as he ran his fingers through the curls at his neck. How long had it been since he'd even looked at himself in a mirror?

He let out a bitter laugh at the thought. He couldn't even face himself, and with good reason. Forcing himself, he locked eyes with his image. They really were windows into the soul. What he saw broke his heart.

The irony didn't escape him. Here he was trying so hard to stay alive, and part of him had already died. Those eyes looking out at him were those of a corpse.

"There is a faster way to kill yourself if you're interested," the barmaid had told him last night when he'd asked her to just leave the whiskey bottle. "I would think a cowboy like you would own a gun. Can't afford a bullet?"

He'd chuckled. What did she know? Maybe he had a good reason to drink himself to death. That thought had made him take a drink straight from the bottle last night. But after that, he'd lost his taste for it and had left, angry and sick at heart.

Now he dressed and opened the motel room door, telling himself that he needed to pick up a razor and some shaving cream before the next motel. Maybe a pair of scissors to trim his hair.

His old pickup was capped with snow and now the only rig left in the motel lot. He glanced out, checking the street. He thought of that barmaid again. If only he *could* drink himself to death. He doubted he could stay alive long enough, though, for the booze to kill him.

Every morning he woke with the same thought. *Things could be worse. A lot worse.* Then he would remember what was at stake. The only way things could be worse was if he failed.

That thought usually brought back the vivid memory of being in a car, racing toward an abyss and a fiery death at over eighty miles an hour in the desert. Unconsciously he checked to make sure the knife was still in his pocket. His lucky knife, he called it since escaping that car. Bailing out of it would probably have killed him if he hadn't been drunk and landed in sand. He'd rolled, ending up against a cactus. He was still pulling spines out of his backside almost a year later.

But that had been a whole lot better than what had happened to Buck Morgan, he reminded himself.

He went out to the pickup, made a swipe at the deep snow on the windshield, all the time watching the street. He probably wouldn't even recognize the men who'd been paid to find him and kill him. He likely wouldn't see them coming. Some days he wondered why he even bothered. He'd surely mess this up, too. Wouldn't it be easier just to end this once and for all?

But then he thought of Tessa and was reminded of why he was doing this.

The street was still quiet in this part of Colorado. All the small mountain towns looked alike. The moment you drove out past the city-limits sign, there was nothing but miles of sagebrush and antelope until the next little burg.

It will be over soon, he thought as he went back inside the motel, picked up his duffel bag, then, making sure he hadn't left anything behind, went out and started his truck.

His pistol was loaded, stuck in his waistband under his shirt and jacket, reminding him he wasn't just the hunted, but was also the hunter. As he pulled away from the motel, he looked around for a store and an internet café.

Survival had now come down to only a matter of which of them found their prey first.

DILLON SEEMED LOST in thought as they left the ranch. Tessa could see that he was taking the news about Ethan maybe even harder than she was. She felt like such a fool. She'd actually thought that Ethan had panicked about marriage and fatherhood and that he'd only taken her money because…

Because he never had any of his own. What had he done with the money he'd made from his construction job? He'd often had a few beers at the local bar after work, but other than that he didn't spend much. He'd given her a little to help with the rent after he'd moved in, and had promised her more when he could afford it.

What had happened to whatever money the three men had stolen from Halbrook Truman's safe? For that matter, what had happened to the man's fiancée?

"What do you think Ethan took from back there?" Tessa asked as they drove back toward Wisdom.

Dillon shook his head.

"Seems that if it was money, Halbrook would have jumped at the offer you made to repay it."

"Does seem that way. I suspect this is less about what they took and more about the man's pride."

She couldn't argue that.

"Tell me more about this rifle Ethan was looking at online," he said.

"It was popular during the Civil War, a Henry .44-caliber rimfire, lever-action, breech-loading rifle."

He glanced over at her. "You know a lot about rifles, do you?"

She laughed and shook her head. "Only because Ethan seemed so interested in this particular one. Are you thinking one of them was what Ethan helped steal from Halbrook Truman? But why, if Ethan was in on taking the rifle, would he be looking for it online?"

"I was just thinking about that. If an antique rifle was what they took, my guess is that someone else has it. Maybe Luke double-crossed him and he's thinking Luke will try to sell it online. But we don't even know if there is any connection between Halbrook and this rifle. That model definitely isn't rare."

"No, it isn't," she agreed. "I checked. Nine hundred of them were manufactured between the summer and October of 1862. By 1864, production had peaked to 290 a month. By the time production ended in 1866, approximately fourteen thousand had been manufactured."

He laughed. "You do your homework."

"The thing is, though, one in excellent condition can bring in a hundred and fifty thousand dollars. Not peanuts, and yet not enough to kill someone over—especially if you were already rich."

Dillon nodded. "Except that Halbrook Truman is angry and wants his property back. We don't know that this rifle Ethan was looking for has anything to do with him or what was taken from him. Or that Halbrook had anything to do with why Ethan has pretended to be dead for a year. But it does make me wonder."

The town of Wisdom appeared again on the horizon.

"I was thinking we'd stop at that café we saw in town and have something to eat." He looked over at her. "You need to take care of yourself and my niece."

She smiled, touched by his concern. "I'm not upset about what he said about Ethan."

"Still, I'm sorry my brother—"

"You aren't your brother's keeper."

He laughed and pushed back his hat to rub his forehead with his free hand as he drove. "Oh, I don't know about that. I always tried to protect him." He shook his head.

"*Protect* him?" She saw Dillon swallow.

"Our dad. He had this idea that you had to break the spirit of a wild horse—or a wild boy. I stepped between them enough times to take the brunt of it, but—"

"You were a *boy* yourself."

Dillon looked away. "Ethan was always…too… tender. I think that's why the old man went after him instead of me. Ethan felt things too strongly. It made him seem—well, at least in our father's eyes— weak. The old man thought he could toughen him up. Instead…"

"Ethan's a man now, capable of making his own choices in life," she said firmly. "Just because he might have gotten a raw deal as a kid, he doesn't get to spend his life blaming his behavior on that."

Dillon glanced over at her, no doubt surprised by the fierceness of her words. "Was your childhood—"

"Fine. It was just fine." His sudden compassion made her want to bite back her heated response. She looked away and was grateful he didn't push the subject.

The café was small and rustic, like a lot of cafés she'd seen off the beaten path in Montana. Over lunch they talked about the magnificent country outside the café window. It was spectacular, especially in contrast to the desert of Southern California. As Tessa listened to Dillon talk, she could hear his love for this state. That love warmed her. She'd always longed for a place with deep roots but had never had it. Ethan had told her once that he'd left home at eighteen and professed he preferred to be rootless. So unlike his twin, who had planted obvious roots here.

After lunch, Dillon talked for a few moments with the elderly woman who had waited on them. Tessa stepped outside, needing to feel the sunshine on her face. The air smelled of pine and water. She breathed it in.

She'd lied to Dillon—and to herself. Hearing even more bad news about Ethan *had* upset her. She wondered which of the cowboys had "stolen" Halbrook Truman's no-doubt-young fiancée.

"What did you find out?" she asked as they walked to the patrol pickup.

"Halbrook was engaged to, and I quote, 'a woman young enough to be his granddaughter.' The waitress estimated Ashley Rene Clarkson's age as mid-twenties. 'A pretty little gold digger' was how she described her. Not that she had much good to say about Halbrook. Seems he isn't the most popular man around the county, so when Ashley took off with some of the hired hands… Well, no one was very sympathetic."

A pretty young woman in her mid-twenties. Tessa, who was now over thirty, didn't want to think about it. But she had to ask, "So you're thinking that if we find Ashley, we might find Ethan?"

He glanced at her as they climbed into his patrol pickup. "It's a lead." She nodded and he busied himself by starting the pickup.

"So how do we find her?" Tessa asked.

"I'll run all their names when I get back to the office and we'll see what comes up."

"You don't sound as if you hold much hope in finding them."

He sighed. "The best place to hide when you're like my brother and his cohorts is on a ranch outside town, where you get room and board and wages that are often off the books."

"No paper trail," she said. "But isn't that the first place Halbrook Truman would look for him?"

AFTER MEETING THE rancher, Dillon could tell Tessa was as worried as he was about his brother. They drove toward Big Timber, the beautiful spring day now lost on them. He could see her stewing over on her side of the pickup—the same thing he'd been doing for miles.

"We need to find out where they went after they left Halbrook's that night," Tessa said after a long while. "According to him, they left the first part of February. Ethan wasn't allegedly killed until a month later. Did they split up or did they stay together during that month? Wouldn't it make sense that they would go through the money quickly and have to get jobs?"

"Probably." Tessa continued to surprise him. What surprised him more than anything was that Ethan had picked a woman with a head on her shoulders. This wasn't the type of woman his brother normally hooked up with, or at least that had been the case growing up. Was it possible Ethan had really loved her? Maybe had even wanted this baby?

"Ethan had obviously blown through his share of the money by the time I met him," she said. "He was working as a carpenter. He told me he was saving his money, but now I wonder if even that was a lie."

"Let me see what I can find out about the others," Dillon told her. "Maybe one of them left a trail."

"I don't like Halbrook Truman."

He chuckled at that. "Me, neither."

"If he's looking for Ethan…"

"Yeah, that was my thought, as well. We need to find Ethan as quickly as possible."

When they reached the ranch, Dillon asked, "Will you be all right out here alone?"

She smiled at that. "I live in a gated community in California and was robbed three times. This is the safest place I've ever been. I'll be fine. I also have my .45."

"I was thinking more of the baby."

"I still have three weeks, and I'm told first babies

are usually late." She smiled. "Don't worry. I'm taking care of myself. You can go catch bad guys."

He nodded, but she could tell he was reluctant to leave her even to go into work for a short while. If they were right and Halbrook Truman was as dangerous as they both feared, then she'd just put herself and her baby into his line of fire.

ETHAN LAWSON LIKED to think he'd had an epiphany the night he almost died. He'd watched his car fly out over the edge of that cliff—and then drop to explode in the rocks below.

After the cactus incident, he'd lain in the warm sand, staring out at the stars, too shaken to move. The smells of the desert had risen around him in those moments before he'd caught the stringent odor of the burning car and its contents.

Cheating death should have felt more invigorating. But while he was a lot of things, stupid wasn't one of them. The men who had tried to kill him— the same ones who'd killed Buck Morgan—weren't through with him. He'd known that when he surfaced, they would be waiting. One thing had been clear. He could never be Ethan Lawson again. Even with a new identity, they would probably find him.

The epiphany, though, was realizing he had to change. He wanted desperately to change, given that for some reason he'd been awarded a second chance.

He'd sat up and looked around. Miles from town, he hadn't been sure which way to go. They would be coming soon to make sure no one had walked away. He'd become aware of the cactus he'd collided with, but he hadn't had time to worry about that just then.

Staggering to his feet, he'd headed west, away from the smoke billowing up from the ravine, away from that life.

Even then he'd been skeptical. How could a man in his thirties change, let alone outlive his sordid past? He figured he didn't stand a chance, but he had to try.

He'd always been a saddle tramp, going from one ranch to the next. He'd picked up a few skills, could throw a hammer with the best of them.

Even *he* thought it was ironic that his first job as this new, improved person was as a carpenter on a church. When Tessa Winters had walked into his life... Well, he'd believed there actually might be salvation for him.

That moment was stamped on him like a brand. He'd been up on the roof, tacking down a few shingles that had come up in the last windstorm, when he'd looked down. She'd been coming up the walk toward the church. Her hair, dark as obsidian, shone in the sunlight and fell in lustrous waves over her shoulders.

A breeze had flapped one of the shingles he hadn't gotten tacked down yet, and she'd looked up. It was at that moment that he'd regretted his past the most. If he could have changed it—or himself...

Now he stared at the long road ahead, remembering how filled with hope he'd been at that moment and even more later when Tessa had told him she was carrying his baby.

But his old man had been right about one thing, at least. There were consequences to a life ill spent.

He sped up, the old pickup rattling and snow blowing and drifting across the blacktop as he continued north. There was no saving himself, but there might still be hope for Tessa and his baby.

CHAPTER EIGHT

AFTER THE UNDERSHERIFF left her at the ranch, Tessa started dinner, then felt at loose ends. She wandered around the farmhouse. She knew she should have been worried about Halbrook Truman and what Ethan had taken from him that had probably put them all in danger.

But her thoughts kept coming back to Dillon. Everything she'd ever heard about identical twins said that even when raised apart they wore the same kind of clothing, married the same type of spouse, even shared the same values.

How did she explain the differences between Ethan and Dillon?

She found herself at the door to Dillon's bedroom. He'd left it slightly ajar. One little push with a finger and the door opened all the way. She had to admit she was curious about him. For a moment, she merely stood in the doorway to his bedroom, assuring herself she wasn't going in.

But then she spotted something on his bedside table that made her change her mind. The bedroom was as neat as the rest of the house. There wasn't the clutter that took over most people's homes.

Dillon lived simply. She liked that about him, since she was much the same. His bed was made, she noticed, and there was no clothing strewn around. Had this been Ethan's house... She broke off that thought, not wanting to go there. Ethan had never owned a home. No doubt never would. He'd talked about buying a house when they set the date for their wedding....

Another train of thought she didn't want to take.

While she couldn't help comparing the brothers, they had little in common other than their physical appearance, from what she could tell.

At the bedside table, she looked down at the photo album that had caught her eye. Gingerly she picked it up. She didn't think Dillon would mind. Either way, her curiosity had overridden any guilt she had for coming in here and snooping.

Taking the photo album, she headed for the door. As she did, she couldn't help but stop at the closet, open it to glance inside—everything was neatly hung or stacked. She closed it and left the room.

Curling up on the couch, she opened the album. The photos at the beginning were old, some of them faded. She assumed they were of older relatives. She slowed as she saw a man and woman. The man looked enough like his sons that he had to be their father. Someone had written in ink on the tiny white strip at the bottom of the snapshot: *Burt and me*. The two appeared to be in their thirties.

The woman in the shot was tall and pretty. She

had a sweet, patient-looking face, but there were lines, as if raising two twin boys had taken its toll on her.

Tessa noticed that the woman was standing a good foot away from her husband, neither touching. Or maybe it wasn't raising the twins that had taken its toll on her.

The photos had been put in the rest of the album at random. There were some of the boys when they were babies on the same page with ones of an older-looking Burt Lawson beside a horse. He was scowling at the camera.

There were only a few snapshots of the boys as young men.

She made a point of listening for Dillon's pickup engine coming up the road so she could return the album before he came into the house. The house remained quiet, though, as she studied each page, trying to get a feel for the two young men.

Tessa knew she was looking for clues as to their differences. She had just turned the page when she saw an older photo of one of the boys lying in bed, a large bandage on his head. He looked to be about four or five. She couldn't tell which brother it was, nor was there any indication of what had happened, since this one had nothing written beneath it. She wondered if their mother had written something on the back of the photo.

The photographs were adhered to the pages by a plastic cover. In most places, since the album was old, the plastic had stuck to the pictures. Tessa hurried into the kitchen for a knife. She'd always been short on patience, but she carefully worked the plastic up enough to peek at the back of the snapshot.

Ethan, five, after the accident.

The handwriting was shaky as if even when this was written the writer was still traumatized.

How close a call had it been? Tessa wondered as she studied the boy's pale face. Ethan had never mentioned it, of course. He hadn't really opened up to her about anything, let alone his childhood in Montana.

Still, she couldn't help wondering if the head injury was what had made the boys different. She'd read somewhere that during a prison study, they'd found that many of the inmates had experienced trauma to their heads when they were young.

The theory was that something inside the brain had gotten messed up, like wires getting crossed or receptors no longer touching. She couldn't remember the specifics, just that it was a theory on why a normal kid had turned into a criminal.

Worried Dillon would catch her snooping, she quickly returned the album, partially closed the bedroom door and hurried into the kitchen to check the chicken dish she had cooking in the oven.

DILLON HAD NEVER walked into his house to the smell of food cooking. He stopped just inside the front door and breathed in the wonderful smell as if it might be his last breath.

It surprised him, the well of emotions the wonderful scents evoked as he hung up his hat. This house had been his home for years, and yet this was the first time it had felt truly like a home.

He moved toward the sound of music, stopping in the doorway. The radio was on and Tessa had just finished setting the table. She began to move with the music as a slow dance came on the radio. Her eyes closed as she danced with an invisible partner.

Dillon watched her, entranced by the look on her face as she danced around the large old kitchen. Before he could stop himself, he moved to her and took her outstretched hand. Her eyes flew open as he stepped closer and began to dance with her. After a moment, her other hand dropped to his shoulder and she gave him an embarrassed smile.

They moved like that to the country song about lost love and broken hearts. She moved well for a woman so pregnant.

"You like to dance," he said, smiling at her.

She nodded. "I do."

He didn't ask if she'd danced with Ethan. His brother was there between them as it was. As the song ended, their gazes locked for a moment. He reluctantly let her go.

"Dinner is ready," she said, quickly stepping away to gather up the hot pads.

"You didn't have to cook," he said, the sight of her leaning over to open the oven reminding him how pregnant she was. "Shouldn't you be sitting with your feet up or something?"

She laughed. It, too, seemed to make the house come alive. "I'm more comfortable when I'm moving."

"I just don't like you cooking for me," he said, and quickly added, "I mean I do. I'm grateful, but—"

"I know what you mean."

"Seriously, what is that amazing smell?"

"It's just a chicken casserole. I found the chicken frozen in your freezer. I didn't think you would mind."

"Mind? I could kiss you." The words were out of his mouth too quickly to rope them back.

"You'd better taste it first," she said, turning her back to him. "I also made apple crisp. I hope you like it."

"I *love* it," he said as she started to reach into the oven. "Here, let me do that." He took the hot pads from her. "It's the very least I can do." He placed the bubbling casserole on the trivet she'd set at the center of the small kitchen table.

Tessa had already pulled up a chair and was reaching for her napkin.

His big farmhouse kitchen suddenly felt too small as he closed the oven door, put away the hot pads and took his seat at the table.

An awkward silence fell between them, making him fear that his comment about kissing her had caused it.

He cleared his throat. "You're doing all right?"

"Fine." She didn't look at him as she scooped some casserole onto his plate and some for herself. He'd always loved a woman with a healthy appetite. He'd found, though, that those kind of women were few and far between. He hated taking a woman out to dinner when she was on some special diet. It took all the fun out of it.

With Tessa, that didn't seem to be a concern. But then again, she was eating for two now. Other than the baby bump, she was slim, strong looking, as if she did physical labor as part of her job managing a landscaping business.

"The baby?"

"Is fine." She finally looked at him. She smiled across the table. "We're both fine." She seemed pleased by his concern, though. She met his gaze for a moment, then looked away.

He wondered if, when she looked at him, she still saw Ethan. He pushed that thought away and took a bite of his casserole. The taste rushed through his senses. Without realizing it, he closed his eyes and let out a groan of satisfaction. "Mmm."

At the sound of her chuckle, he opened them.

"So you like it?" she asked, clearly amused.

"I have never tasted anything better."

"I doubt that's true, but thank you."

"I'm serious. I have to have this recipe."

That made her laugh again. "You actually cook?"

"Of course." He frowned. "How else do you think I get fed?"

She shook her head, smiling, all the awkwardness between them gone.

"My mother was a pretty good cook. But after she died, Ethan and I had to take over that job. Ethan…" He laughed.

"He could burn water."

"I always thought he was just pretending to be helpless in the kitchen so he could get me to do the cooking," Dillon said.

"I wouldn't put it past him," she agreed. "How old were you?"

"Fourteen." He looked away, embarrassed by her look of sadness for him.

"What do you think made the two of you so different, other than your father's feelings for Ethan?"

Dillon shrugged.

"I was reading about inmates in prison who had suffered head injuries." She didn't look at him when she asked it.

He wondered who had told her. Ethan? Or had she met someone in town? If so, how did a conversation like that even come up?

"Ethan got bucked off a horse when he was five. He hit his head on the corral fence. Doc said it was one of the worse concussions he'd ever seen. For a while we didn't think he would come out of the coma. I was the one who'd put him on the horse." He didn't mention that it was his father who'd let out a high-pitched whistle, knowing the horse would take off, to see, as he'd put it, "if the kid could at least ride a horse." Either way, Dillon hadn't been able to save his brother that time, either.

"You can't blame yourself," Tessa said, seeing that this had been a weight on his shoulders for years. "You were five. It was an accident."

"But Ethan was…different after that."

She could have kicked herself for saying what she had earlier. "The head-injury thing is just a theory. He could have been born the way he is."

He smiled and reached across the table to cover her hand with his. "We've all wondered what made Ethan the way he is." She looked down at his hand. It was so large and sun browned. There were several scars. Without thinking, she began to trace one with the finger of her free hand.

"That one was from the day I fell out of the hayloft and tried to catch myself by grabbing the chain with the hook on it," he said, actually smiling at the memory as he watched her trace the scar.

"Ouch."

"And that one…" She hadn't realized she'd moved her finger to trace the second one. "That one was from a knife game Ethan I had come up with when we were six." He drew his hand back to look down at the scar. "My mother blamed me for coming up with the game in the first place. We were typical boys, always finding ways to hurt ourselves."

She thought of Ethan's hands and his lack of scars and how their mother had blamed Dillon. How, at even such a young age, had he become responsible for his brother?

They ate to the sound of birds singing outside the open kitchen window. The breeze stirred the curtains, sending in small gusts of spring air. The casserole was Tessa's favorite. She hadn't realized how hungry she was until she'd taken that first bite. After they'd finished, she'd served the apple crisp and was pleased to see how much Dillon had enjoyed it.

He insisted on doing the dishes. He'd wanted Tessa to go into the living room, where she would be more comfortable. Instead, she'd stayed in the kitchen, pulling up a second chair to put her legs on. The baby had been kicking all day. They were both having trouble getting comfortable.

As he put away the last dish, he turned, his gaze going to her baby bump. He frowned, immediately looking concerned. "Have you been to a doctor?"

"Of course. They have them in California, you know."

"I mean, everything is okay, right?"

"Everything is fine and proceeding as to be expected."

That seemed to relieve him a little. "Maybe I was wrong about you staying out here so far from the nearest hospital."

"It's only twenty-five miles into town."

"But what if you go into labor?"

"I will have plenty of time to drive into town."

His eyes widened in alarm. "You call me the moment anything happens. I'll send an ambulance."

She began to laugh as she slipped her feet off the opposite chair and got up. "I won't need an ambulance. Women have babies every day and in places far from the nearest hospital. I'll be fine." But his concern still touched her. She brushed a hand over his arm as she moved past him. "I think I will call it a day, though."

"Let me know if you need anything," he said after her.

"I will."

Tears suddenly rushed her eyes. Being pregnant had swamped her with emotions for months now. But these tears made her chest ache. Since Ethan had walked out on her, she'd accepted that she would be having this baby alone. She had no family. And while she had friends, it wasn't the same as family.

She'd never given a thought to Ethan's family. He'd told her that both his parents were dead. Since he'd never mentioned siblings, she'd assumed he was an only child. Dillon had been such a surprise in so many ways. And now her baby had family, and that filled her with such emotion that it brimmed over and spilled down her cheeks.

Tessa hurried to her bedroom, not wanting him to see her tears. She quickly closed the door and leaned against it as the sobs broke free.

CHAPTER NINE

ETHAN CHECKED HIS rearview mirror for the hundredth time. He reminded himself that Wyoming was a huge state, almost a hundred thousand acres. What were the chances that he'd run into anyone he didn't want to see?

At a gas station, he'd shaved and cut his hair. For a long time he'd stared in the mirror, seeing his brother instead of himself in his reflection, something he'd tried to avoid for a lifetime. He'd wanted to be different from Dillon. Had done a bang-up job of being different, he'd thought with a curse.

Now as he drove, he worried about this lame plan of his. What he should have been doing was hightailing it in the other direction, he thought as he drove up Highway 85, keeping to the two lanes rather than the interstates. He should be getting on a slow boat to Argentina. The dumbest thing he could do was keep heading north. Hell, look how dangerous even Arizona had turned out to be.

He knew he was taking a terrible chance, but he had to find Luke. The last time he'd seen him, Luke, Ashley, Buck and Tom were headed for South Dakota's Black Hills. Luke had wanted him to come along and had gotten angry when Ethan had insisted on going his own way.

"I think it would be better if we all stayed together," Luke had said. His dark eyes had glittered the way they did when he was excited. Or angry.

"Just give me enough of my share of the cash to get me to New Mexico. I know a place down there I can get work," Ethan had said, lying through his teeth. Even back then, he'd had a bad feeling about what they'd done. Maybe worse, what he thought Halbrook Truman would do.

Luke had been sweet-talking Ashley for weeks before the actual seduction. "She knows the combination to the safe," Luke had told him a few days before. "She says Hal doesn't trust banks and keeps bundles in there." Luke loved calling their boss Hal because it pissed the man off.

Ethan hadn't liked any of it and had said as much. He didn't draw lines in any moral ground often, but this was felony territory.

"Ashley says this is money Hal's hiding from the government, so don't you see? He can't call the sheriff on us. There is only one little snag. Ashley is going to have to go with us. Tom and Buck want to go with us, too."

Ethan had sworn. "Why don't you invite the whole ranch?"

Luke had talked him into going along with the robbery even though he'd been against it. He remembered something one of his teachers in elementary school had written on his report card. *Ethan seems to be a follower and often doesn't use good judgment in whom he follows.*

Luke was only a little this side of crazy. He loved to push the boundaries, tempt death. It was what got him high. Unfortunately he was as close to a friend as Ethan had managed over the past ten years.

His elementary teacher had been right—he always gravitated toward the Lukes of the world. He liked them, liked to be in their orbit. He was indeed a follower.

It wasn't until high school that one of his teachers had mentioned his lack of a moral compass. Or maybe it was one of the sheriff's deputies who used to pick him up and drag him home. Ethan's old man hadn't tried to analyze what his son's problem was. He'd just beaten the crap out of him.

"What the hell is wrong with you?" Burt Lawson used to bellow at the top of his lungs.

Ethan wondered himself. He had no qualms about ripping people off, and yet his identical twin had a moral compass that kept him as straight as one of the highways through Wyoming.

He hadn't heard from Luke after they'd gone their separate ways. He'd gotten a job as a wrangler on a dude ranch in Arizona and had been pretty content until Tom Grady had tracked him down.

"Just wanted to give you a heads-up," Tom had said over the phone. "Some detective is apparently looking for us."

"I thought Luke said Hal wouldn't go to the law?"

"*Private* detective. I'm not sure this is about the Double T-Bar-Diamond. He seems most interested in you."

That had given Ethan pause. "So what did you tell the detective?"

"Nothing, I haven't talked to him. I just heard that some guy had been asking around about you. Have you heard from Ashley?"

There'd been something in Tom's voice. Did Tom have a thing for the woman, too? "So Luke and Ashley aren't together?" He'd thought from the beginning that Luke was only playing her. It would have been just like Luke to dump Ashley and Tom Grady, and leave them to pick up the pieces.

"They were still together after Deadwood. I left them in South Dakota."

He'd recalled that they were all going gambling. "Did Luke lose his share of the money?"

"I don't know. He still had most of it when I left. Ashley's is probably gone, though."

Ethan knew that if Luke Blackwell was broke, he'd be looking for money—anywhere he could find it.

"The thing is, Ethan, if I can find you, then I'm pretty sure this detective can. I just thought you might want to cut out of there before that happens."

Ethan had looked out the window to see a man walking slowly around his car. "Too late," he'd said into the phone.

LUKE BLACKWELL WOKE to an empty bed. Again. He lay back with a sigh, telling himself he should be glad the woman was gone. Again. But it still pissed him off.

"Well, I'm not taking you back this time, Ashley," he said as he swung his legs over the side of the bed and looked out the curtainless window at the falling snow. The pines were already snowcapped, the boughs bent under the weight of the spring storm this high in the mountains.

He realized the roads out of town might close again, which could explain why Ashley hadn't returned. This place was accessible only part of the year as it was. It was one reason he'd chosen it. A little too isolated and small, though, for big-city girl Ashley Rene Clarkson.

As he pulled on his jeans, Luke told himself that he should be thankful she wasn't here. The jeans were ice-cold, just like everything else in the tiny cabin. He checked his cell phone for messages. She had been whining and carrying on about the weather, the isolation, him and everything else in general before she'd left.

No messages. No calls, but then again, that shouldn't have surprised him. Ashley was the only one who had this number.

Still, he thought as he pulled on his boots and clomped into the kitchen without bothering to lace them, he should have heard from her by now—even if it was one of those calls to bitch at him. Usually by now she'd have run out of money or was feeling sorry and was ready to come home. He and his father, boy, could they pick 'em. He remembered his old man saying he'd been left more times than a Greyhound bus terminal.

"Must be hereditary," he said under his breath as he put on a pot of coffee. He still liked coffee perked in a real coffeepot. It made the whole cabin smell good.

He hadn't worried the first couple days Ashley had been gone. She'd gotten ticked off before, gone on a runner, but always ended up back on his doorstep. It wasn't as if she had anywhere else to go.

Or at least that was what he'd thought. She wasn't stupid enough to try to go back to Truman, was she?

He hadn't thought about Hal and the Double T-Bar-Diamond for months, but Ashley was out of her share, and his was running low. At the thought, he felt his heart drop.

"She wouldn't," he said with a curse, and grabbed his coat before storming out into the snow. He had hidden what he thought of as his ace in the hole in a place he thought Ashley hadn't known about. But as he hurried through the snow toward the barn, he recalled the way she'd gotten the combination to Hal Truman's safe. The woman was nothing if not sneaky and underhanded. She reminded him of himself, which was probably why they'd stayed together this long.

He had figured they would part ways pretty

quickly after they'd left the Double T-Bar-Diamond Ranch over a year ago. The charm usually wore off fast. He'd planned to leave her at some filling station while she was in the restroom. Or maybe sneak off at a café and leave her with the check. Either would have given her the message.

But there had been something about Ashley. He couldn't even put his finger on it. Maybe he was impressed that she had given up marrying Halbrook Truman to run off with him. Hal had offered her a life of leisure. True, he'd wanted her to sign a prenup. That was what had set her off and made her decide to rip him off instead of taking the trip to the altar.

"I'd sleep with one eye open if I were you," Buck Morgan had said when Luke and Ashley had hooked up.

"Don't talk about my woman."

"*Your* woman? She's the kind of woman who changes horses in the middle of the stream. Worse, if she'd double-cross Halbrook, she wouldn't hesitate to stab *you* in the back. Probably literally."

That was when he and Ashley had parted company with Tom and Buck. Luke told himself the wrangler had just been jealous. But part of him knew exactly why Buck had tried to warn him. Ashley was headstrong, a spoiled rich girl from back East who had come West looking for a cowboy and some Old West excitement.

"Just don't hurt her," Tom Grady had said in parting that day.

"Or make her mad," Buck had added with a laugh.

Luke wondered how any man could keep Ashley from getting mad. He'd apparently made her mad enough this time not just to leave and not come back for several days—but possibly to take his ace in the hole.

Inside the barn, he shook off the snow from his hair and coat as he walked toward the small old tack room. He'd spent many hours in that room as a young boy, he recalled with a smile. It was where he'd nailed his first girl, so it had sentimental value.

He took out his key and unlocked the padlock he kept on the door. The inside smelled musty. A few pieces of old horse tack hung on the walls. It took him a moment for his eyes to adjust to the dim light. He should have brought a flashlight, he thought, his heart pounding.

Too anxious to wait for his eyes to adjust, he knelt down and reached under the bottom shelf. A curse erupted from his lips.

The rifle was gone, and so was Ashley.

DILLON COULDN'T HELP worrying about Tessa. The next morning after rising to find her cooking breakfast, he'd given up telling her to take it easy. Clearly the woman would do whatever she wanted. The best thing he could do for her and her baby was find his brother.

At work, he spent some time digging up everything he could find on Halbrook Truman. The Double T-Bar-Diamond was one of the earliest ranches established in Montana. It had been started by Halbrook's great-grandfather, the man he'd been named for. The original Halbrook was a rough and tough miner who, just as Dillon had been told, had made his fortune in Montana gold.

His great-grandson had been a brawler in his youth, in and out of trouble, which could explain why he'd helped Luke Blackwell. But Dillon suspected there was more to it and wondered if Luke had worked for the ranch before.

What he found on the man hadn't sent up any red flags. He was about to give up when he stumbled across two mentions of the Double T-Bar-Diamond Ranch. There'd been a shooting when the now fifty-two-year-old Truman had been in his twenties. Halbrook Truman's first wife, Mary Louise, had been shot on the ranch. It had been ruled a hunting accident, although the hunter was never caught, as far as Dillon could tell.

To his surprise, he found there'd been a second shooting on the ranch, one of the wranglers. Dillon jotted down the victim's name, Jimmy "Slim" Ryerson. He couldn't see what this had to do with finding his brother. But on a hunch, he checked for an obituary on Ryerson. Sure enough, Slim Ryerson had been from Cutbank, Montana. He was survived by a sister.

Dillon got a phone number for the woman and called before he could change his mind. The shooting, now more than twenty years ago, couldn't have anything to do with Ethan, and yet it might have a whole lot to do with Halbrook Truman—the man looking for his brother.

Emily Curtis answered on the third ring, identifying herself as Em.

"This is Undersheriff Dillon Lawson of Big Timber, Montana," he said. "I'm calling about your brother Jimmy."

Silence.

"At the time of his death, he went by Slim and he worked at—"

"The Double T-Bar-Diamond Ranch." Her voice was ice. "I know where he worked and where he got himself murdered." She let out an irritated sound. "Just goes to show you what you can do if you have enough money. You can get away with murder. Why are you calling me about this anyway? It's been years."

"I'm looking for my brother. He worked for the Double T-Bar-Diamond Ranch. Ethan Lawson?"

"Never heard of him, but if he crossed Halbrook Truman, he's probably dead."

Dillon felt his pulse jump. "Is that what happened to your brother?"

"Who did you say you were?"

"Undersheriff Dillon Lawson with the sheriff's department in Big Timber, Montana. I'd appreciate anything you can tell me."

Silence, then, "Jimmy said there were things going on at the ranch that he didn't like. He never said what, just that he was leaving at the end of the season. The next thing I knew, he was dead."

"He never said what things?"

"No, but apparently Halbrook Truman has always thought he was above the law."

This was too vague to be helpful. "What makes you think Halbrook had anything to do with your brother's death?"

"Jimmy was raised just fine. If he saw something going on he didn't like, he wouldn't have gone along with it." Unlike Ethan.

"Well, I appreciate your time."

"Are you going to do something about Jimmy's murder?"

Dillon sighed silently, wondering how many times he would say these words in his lifetime. "Without evidence—"

"That's exactly what the sheriff in the Big Hole fed me," she said with obvious disgust. "Have a nice day." She slammed down the phone. *That's something that can only be done nowadays with a landline telephone,* he thought.

TESSA WAS OUT by the corral with the filly when she heard the sound of a vehicle coming up the road. She glanced at her watch. It was too soon for Dillon to be coming back. Unless he'd gotten worried about her and had come home to check on her.

In the distance, though, she saw that the truck was shiny black. Goose bumps suddenly rippled over her skin when she recalled that the man who'd confronted Ethan in her yard months ago had been driving a black pickup. She didn't fight the strange feeling, but instinctively moved toward the shadow of the barn as the engine noise grew louder.

The black pickup stopped in front of the house. Tessa held her breath as she pressed herself into the dark shade along the side of the barn as a man wearing a cowboy hat climbed out. She couldn't tell from this distance if it was the same man.

He glanced toward the corral and the horse. With a sickening realization, she saw that she'd left her sweater hanging there. She'd discarded it earlier as the sun had finally warmed up the spring day.

The man's gaze went to her car, then the house, before he moved in that direction. He was tall, broad across the chest, dressed in jeans and a black T-shirt. His baseball cap shaded his face, making only a deep shadow under the brim. But she had seen a black pickup enough times on her way to Montana that she'd suspected it had been following her.

She moved quickly along the side of the barn to the door and slipped in just far enough so that she could still see if the man came in her direction.

Tessa waited, the smell of hay permeating the air of the barn. It was cool in the shade and she shivered, wishing she had her sweater, but she didn't dare try to retrieve it for fear the man would see her.

She told herself that the man might be a neighbor

here to see Dillon. Wouldn't she feel foolish when that turned out to be the case?

The man came off the house porch and walked to his pickup, but he didn't get in. He stood, his back to her for a long moment, before he turned, his gaze going again to her sweater on the corral fence.

Without warning, his eyes shifted toward the barn and the open doorway. She ducked back even though she knew he couldn't have seen her from where she stood.

All her instincts told her he would check the barn. She turned and looked around, trying not to panic. She spotted the ladder up into the hayloft. The man wouldn't climb up there to look for her, would he? Not unless she was right and he was the man she'd heard talking to Ethan the day Ethan had mentioned the name Halbrook, and now that man was here looking for her.

She hurried to the ladder and quickly climbed. It was cumbersome being this pregnant. But she'd always been a tomboy who'd climbed trees with the best of the boys, and she'd kept active throughout her pregnancy.

At the top of the ladder, she moved behind some hay bales. She had just settled in when she heard the barn door creak all the way open. He had come out here looking for her, just as she'd feared.

She heard him step inside the barn. Something on him jingled. Something on a gun holster? Or keys? She held her breath, afraid to move a hair.

He stopped moving. It sounded as if he was directly under her.

She had no choice. She had to take a breath. She steadied herself with a hand on the stack of hay bales.

Through a crack in the floorboards of the loft, she could see him directly below her. If she dislodged even a little of the hay and it sifted down… Her heart leaped to her throat as he moved to the ladder and began to climb.

The sound of an engine filled the air. The man heard it about the same time she did. He stopped climbing the ladder. Like her, he must be listening.

Definitely an engine of some kind, and whatever vehicle it was, it was headed this way.

The ladder creaked with his weight and then he was climbing down, the jingling sound receding as he moved to the door of the barn.

She waited. She didn't hear him, but that didn't mean he wasn't still standing down there.

The engine she'd heard now rumbled into the yard. Not a vehicle. A tractor, she thought. It must be a neighbor.

Then she heard voices, two men talking over the low rumble of the tractor engine. One of the voices was the same as the one she'd heard down in California when the man in the black truck had come by to see Ethan.

She moved quickly from behind the hay bales. The barn doorway was empty. Tessa carefully climbed down the ladder and hurried to the barn door. The man was talking to the farmer on the tractor. It appeared the farmer was giving him directions, pointing to the east.

She heard the man thank him and start for his truck. Tessa had to grab the wall for support, her heart was pounding so hard. The man hadn't wanted directions. That had been a ruse. He hadn't wanted to get caught in this yard.

While she hadn't gotten a good look at the man's face, she remembered that voice. Her blood turned to ice. The day she'd seen Ethan talking to the man in California, she'd sensed the man was dangerous. That was why she'd offered Ethan her money to pay the man off.

Now as she watched him drive out of the ranch, she knew with certainty that the man hadn't given up. Only, this time, he'd come looking for *her*. She reminded herself that it hadn't been the man who'd mentioned Halbrook by name. Ethan had. He'd apparently thought Halbrook had hired the man to find him. But had he? Or was some other trouble hunting Ethan?

CHAPTER TEN

THE ANONYMOUS CALL came in just moments after Dillon had hung up from talking to Emily Curtis. His mind had been on Halbrook and his brother. Which meant it was also on Tessa and the baby.

The moment he answered the call, he froze. "I'm sorry, what did you say?"

"We found a body." The person on the other end of the line spoke in a low whisper as if trying to disguise the voice, but it was clearly a kid. He couldn't tell if it was a girl or a boy, although he would bet a boy. Whoever it was, he suspected it was a prank.

"Who is this?"

"It's in that old mine near the creek on the sheriff's place. It's a...lady." The line went dead.

Dillon stared at the phone. It *had* been a prank call, hadn't it? He thought of all the old small mines around from back when gold brought people to Montana. Frank had mentioned one time that there were several on his property, though none so deep that he'd been concerned about them being dangerous.

A dead woman's body found on the sheriff's property? Dillon hoped the call had been a prank. He stood up. Frank's office was just down the hall. He thought of the how the sheriff had changed. He was so different from the crazed man who'd turned in his star and gun to go find—and kill—his ex-wife.

He'd assumed the change in Frank was due to the six months he'd been away from a job he loved. The man had come back seeming…almost at peace, as if finally resigned that Pam might never be caught—let alone brought to justice. Was there another reason Frank had finally put Pam Chandler out of his mind?

Dillon had been about to go down the hall and tell the sheriff about the call. Instead, he picked up his keys and headed for the door. If there was a body on the sheriff's property, then he'd better take a look.

"Frank," he called down the hall. "I have to run an errand. I'll be back."

Frank waved to him and Dillon saw that he was on the phone. On his way out of the building, Dillon noticed Deputy Bentley Jamison pulling in.

"I just got a call on a possible body that was found," Dillon told him. "I'd like you to come with me." As the two were driving away, Dillon saw Frank come out of the building. He glanced in their direction, but appeared distracted as he got into his patrol pickup and took off in the other direction.

Dillon realized that he'd gotten the call about the body because the sheriff's line had been busy.

TESSA CALLED THE sheriff's department as soon as she was sure the man was gone and she could get to the house. She'd left her cell phone on the kitchen table this morning. She was told by the dispatcher that the undersheriff was out on a call and couldn't be reached unless it was an emergency.

"No." The man had left. She didn't doubt he would be back. But probably not today—not with that farmer working in a field so close to the house. The man had come out when he'd figured Dillon was at the sheriff's department. She didn't think that had been a coincidence.

"No, it's not an emergency," she said into the phone. "If you could just tell him that Tessa called."

She hung up, still shaken. She recalled how upset Ethan had been after the man had paid them a visit. He'd been afraid of the man, she realized. Ethan had seen him drive up and had gone outside to talk to him, telling her to stay inside. She had watched the two of them arguing, overheard just enough to assume he owed the man money.

Why hadn't she demanded to know what was going on? How could she have even considered marrying a man with such a past? Worse, she knew now why she hadn't forced the issue. She'd been afraid to learn the truth.

It made her angry with herself. She'd just kept telling herself that Ethan was trying to change, that he had changed, that the past didn't matter. He had wanted to put his past behind him. Hadn't he said that dozens of times to her? She'd believed him, believed her love and their baby were all he'd need for a fresh start.

What a fool she'd been. Ethan's past was still threatening her and her baby. She hated to think what it had done to him—or maybe was still doing. Was he caught up in it, too, so that their paths would eventually cross again? Or had he just run because running was easier than dealing with the past, let alone changing? She might never know. Ethan could be dead. She and Dillon could be chasing a ghost.

Tessa started dinner to keep busy, but she couldn't still her thoughts. She had told Dillon that she knew Ethan better than he did. That he needed her if he hoped to find his brother. Big talk, especially since she doubted either of them really knew Ethan.

Now, though, she was even more determined to find him—dead or alive. She couldn't have his past hurting her and her baby. Dillon would help her find his brother, help her escape the people from Ethan's past.

That thought warmed her. Dillon hadn't asked for any of this, and yet he'd insisted she stay here. They were family, he had said.

Could he be right about Ethan leaving the photograph for her to find? If Ethan knew his brother at all, he would have known Dillon would help her. Not just help her, she thought as she remembered his concern and the way his face had lit up at the idea of a niece. Dillon would be there for her.

At first being around him had felt strange. She would find herself staring at him. He looked identical to Ethan, and yet she saw the differences between them. Dillon was the man Ethan had said he wanted to be.

She shook off those thoughts as she finished preparing their meal, then sat down at the dining room table and opened her laptop. She recalled how surprised Dillon had been when she'd told him about Ethan wanting to buy a rifle.

Ethan had talked about buying a new truck after they got married. He'd also talked about getting a better job, about saving to buy them a house. He'd said all the right things—but he hadn't even been honest about his real name, she reminded herself. She'd thought her last name and her baby's would be Cross.

"You were *such* a fool," she said to herself as she touched the mouse pad and brought the computer to life.

But did any woman really know the man she was in love with? Or did she just see what she wanted to?

Tessa checked her emails first. There were some from friends asking if she was all right because they hadn't heard from her. She'd told only a couple friends that she was going to Montana. She hadn't told anyone why.

There was also an email from her boss saying they missed her and would be glad when she got back.

She couldn't worry about that now. Going to History, she began to go through the sites where Ethan had been searching. It had surprised her that he'd been looking for a Henry .44-caliber rimfire, but why he'd been so obsessed with that particular firearm, she'd had no idea.

Now, though, she was pretty sure it was what had been taken from Halbrook. Dillon's theory made sense. She checked a few of the listed sites that specialized in antique Civil War weapons before she noticed several other sites Ethan had visited that she hadn't seen before.

When she clicked on one, she saw that Ethan had also been searching for Luke Blackwell—his cowboy cohort.

SHERIFF FRANK CURRY'S ranch was small compared to many Montana ranches. The ranch had some nice bottomland, where Frank raised hay and alfalfa. From there, the land rose, climbing up into the rocky foothills.

As they drove, Dillon saw some of the cattle Frank ran. He continued on up the road until he came to a small bridge over the creek. Pulling over a few dozen yards from the bridge, he signaled to Deputy Jamison.

"I see them," Jamison said. Four kids, all about twelve or so, were jumping off the bridge into the deep water of the creek. "You think these are the kids who allegedly found the body?"

Dillon chuckled. The kids had seen them drive up in the patrol SUV. Just from their expressions, he was betting one of them was his caller.

"Get ready," Dillon said under his breath as he

and the deputy started to climb out. "The guilty ones are going to run."

Two of the taller of the boys suddenly turned tail and took off through the bushes downstream.

"Stop! Sheriff's Department." They didn't. Dillon sprinted after them with Jamison at his heels. They split up when the boys took different forks in the trail. Dillon heard Jamison catch his.

Ahead, his boy ran down a narrow game trail that wound through the brush along the edge of the creek. Dillon had to tackle him to bring him down, since the kid was wearing only cutoff jeans and was wet from swimming.

They hit the dirt, crashing into the brush. Dillon hauled the kid up.

"I didn't do anything, so why are you chasing me?" the boy demanded defensively.

"Why did you run?" Dillon eyed the boy. "You're one of the Thorton boys. Once I recognized you, I would have tracked you down anyway."

The kid inspected a scrape on his arm from the brush. "Police brutality," he muttered under his breath.

"When an officer of the law tells you to stop, you stop," Dillon said. "Also, when you find a body, you report it."

"I did report it." He clamped his mouth shut as he realized what Dillon had just done.

"Come on, we're going to call your fathers."

"Don't do that," the kid said. "I'll show you where we found her."

Jamison appeared, his boy in tow. Dillon took in the two boys. They were skinny and already brown as nuts. He recalled sunny, warm days, playing in the creek or hiking up in the mountains this time of year.

Jamison's kid looked scared. He was blond with a buzz cut. A lot of ranch boys got their hair cut by their mothers in the kitchen, with a towel around their shoulders and their ears twisted if they moved. Dillon remembered it well.

He saw the two boys exchange a look. Jamison's kid said, "Just tell them, Charlie."

"We didn't do anything wrong," Charlie said defiantly. He looked like a Charlie, Dillon thought. Devilment danced in his blue eyes. He was obviously the ringleader of this bunch. Put any kids together and a leader would emerge—often the kid they *shouldn't* follow. Which, in his brother Ethan's case, would have been the kid he made his best friend.

"Charlie—"

"I already told them I would take them to her, Hank."

Dillon glanced at the scared kid, Hank. One of the Hanover boys from down the road, he was betting. "What's your name?"

"Hank Hanover."

"Take us to where you found the body," he said. He knew both families and also knew that both fathers would be tougher on the boys than Dillon once they heard what the boys had been up to. Parents in these parts still disciplined their children, teaching them to respect not only their elders, but the law.

The boys exchanged another look between them. "Let us get our clothes," Charlie said.

THEY FOLLOWED A winding path along the creek. The boys obviously knew the area well. As they climbed out of the creek bottom, they left behind the thick chokecherry bushes and young newly green willows. The boys led them into the rocky foothills dotted with scrub pine. The land turned drier, the rocks larger.

It was early in the season and yet Dillon still found himself watching out for rattlesnakes. He'd never liked snakes, unlike most boys. He still didn't. He saw Jamison looking around as well, both of them no doubt reminded of the highway patrolman who had pulled over a vehicle. Wanting to get a photo of the rig for his investigation, he'd walked off the road and up a small hill, only to step into a den of rattlers. Dillon still had to smile when he thought about the motorist's reaction when the highway patrolman began shooting.

He let Jamison and Charlie get ahead of them. "So, Hank, tell me about the day you and Charlie found the body."

The boy glanced toward Charlie's retreating back.

The undersheriff took a guess. "What did you find on the body?"

The kid swallowed what appeared to be a huge lump in this throat. His eyes widened. "How did you—"

"What was it? Money? Jewelry?"

Hank swallowed again and Dillon swore silently. Just as he'd feared. The scene would be contaminated. Kids. "I assume the money is gone." One look at the kid told him that was a given. "But I am going to need the jewelry and anything else that you kids took off the body."

Hank nodded more quickly. "I don't have the gun."

Dillon felt his heart drop. They'd more than contaminated the scene. "Did either of you consider that you might be interfering with sheriff's department business?" He sighed. "Who has the gun?" Hank shifted his gaze to Charlie.

The old mine went in only a few feet into the side of the hill. At one time, it had been boarded over, but the boards had long ago rotted away, leaving a gaping hole in the earth that was hidden from the road below by a large rock and some bushes. Only someone exploring this hillside would have been able to find the old mine. Or someone who knew it was there to begin with.

They'd come the most difficult way. He noticed an old road, the ruts almost invisible for the tall grass— but still, a road that could have been used to drive up, either in a pickup or on a four-wheeler, to dump a body.

"Wait here," Dillon ordered. Jamison stayed with the boys as he approached the opening. The first thing he saw was a woman's athletic shoe. It lay on its side a few feet inside the four-foot opening. Past it, he spotted the remains.

He could tell it had been a woman because of the hair and the clothing, along with the purse that had been upended, the contents dumped out on the mine floor beside her. The boys' doing, he suspected. But he didn't need to check her identification. Dillon knew.

He turned from the opening, feeling sick to his stomach. Growing up on a ranch and later as a law officer, he'd seen more than his share of dead things. What made him sick was finding Pam Chandler's remains on her ex-husband's property. Add that to the sheriff's complete change of attitude, and Dillon feared he already had his killer, even without the gun.

FRANK FELT NUMB. He'd heard Dillon reading him his Miranda rights earlier, but the sound seemed far, far away. A beam of sunlight from the sunset had broken free of the clouds over the Crazies and painted the side of his old barn in a shimmering gold as Dillon had recited the words.

From the telephone line, a lone crow had watched. Its beady black eyes caught the light occasionally to shine like a wink.

"So you just came back to see me get what I deserved?" he'd asked the crow.

"Frank. *Frank?*"

He'd shifted his gaze back to the undersheriff. He'd always liked Dillon. It was one reason he'd made him undersheriff. The main reason, though, was because he was a good law enforcement officer. He was kind and caring, levelheaded, and believed in justice. Frank trusted him with his life.

"Frank, I need to know that you understand your rights."

He'd nodded and actually smiled.

The shock had begun to wear off on the ride to the sheriff's department. It had gotten dark by then, lights popping on across the wide valley.

Pam was dead.

Her body found in an old mine on his property.

She'd been murdered.

No doubt killed with his gun that she'd taken the night she'd attacked him in his house.

Had this been her plan all along?

Frank had waited for some emotion to hit him. He didn't even feel a sliver of regret or sympathy. All he felt was relief.

"Are you all right?" Dillon asked.

"Lynette and Tiffany are finally safe." That was when he remembered his date with Lynette. He had been getting ready to leave for it when the sheriff's patrol SUV had pulled up in his yard.

He'd known when he'd seen Dillon's somber expression that he wouldn't be making his date tonight with Lynette. He'd also known that the evidence against him had to be overwhelming.

Frank let out a bitter laugh as he realized what his ex had done to him. Pam had gotten revenge even in death.

CHAPTER ELEVEN

DILLON CALLED TESSA to let her know he would be late before sitting down across from Frank in the interrogation room. The digital recorder turned slowly, along with the ceiling fan over their heads.

"I didn't kill her," the sheriff said.

"How can you explain the change in your attitude?" Dillon asked wearily. "Frank, you were obsessed. You wanted to throw away your career. When you left here, we both knew you were going after her with one thing in mind."

"I'll admit I wanted her dead."

Dillon sighed and shook his head. "So what happened?"

"I told you—"

"Right, that you didn't kill her. But if that's true, then what's with this change of attitude?"

"It's hard to explain. I woke up one morning and I realized I was tired of putting my life on hold, living in fear of Pam and what she would do next. I couldn't keep waiting for her to be caught—I figured it could be years before she struck again—but if I did wait I was going to lose Lynette again. I couldn't let that happen."

Dillon heard the emotion in Frank's voice. "So you finally asked her out."

Frank's laugh was painful. "But even then, I waited too long."

"I need you to tell me the truth."

"I swear I don't know anything. How long has she been dead?"

"Frank—"

"You have to know I didn't kill her. Even if I had found her... I had a gun on her that night she attacked me out at the ranch. I couldn't pull the trigger. That's how I ended up with a concussion and Pam ended up with my gun." Frank let out a bark of a laugh. "That's the gun that was used, right? Of course it is. She must have planned this from the start."

"Frank—"

"Dillon, you know Pam took my gun the night she attacked me out at the ranch."

"I know you *said* she took your gun."

Frank stared at him. "You don't really think—"

"This isn't about what I think. It's about evidence, Frank. You know that. There is no evidence that Pam attacked you or that she took your gun. It's just your word against—"

"A dead woman who was trying to destroy me."

Dillon had seen Frank after a woman, allegedly his ex, had tried to run down Nettie Benton. That was really when the sheriff had snapped. That was when Dillon had feared Frank would kill Pam if he found her.

"Pam always had to have the last word," Frank was saying. "Or in this case, the last laugh." His face suddenly clouded. "What about Tiffany? Has she been told?"

"Pam's name is being withheld from the press until next of kin is notified."

"Next of kin, Dillon? You can't tell Tiffany without me there."

"Frank, you have to know that once she hears her mother was murdered and you are a suspect, you will be the last person your daughter is going to want to see."

Frank nodded and Dillon asked, "When was the last time you saw Pam Chandler?"

"The night she ransacked my house and put me in the hospital. But Kate at the Branding Iron saw her try to run down Lynette in front of the store."

"Kate saw what she thought was a woman," Dillon said. "She couldn't testify that the woman behind the wheel was Pam Chandler."

"You know damned well it was."

"Frank—"

"I know. No evidence." The sheriff frowned. "Wait a minute. Was that the last time anyone saw her alive? That was six months ago! Are you telling me she never left here? What about the pickup she took from the Westfall Ranch? Wasn't it abandoned in Minnesota?"

"North Dakota. A stolen car was found a few days later in Minnesota."

Frank shook his head. "All the time I was looking for her, she was already *dead*?"

"Bentley is getting a warrant to search your house, Frank. If there is something you want to say…"

Frank rubbed a hand over his face. "I think I will call a lawyer now, Dillon."

NETTIE PACED THE living room. Through the window, the sky had darkened. Had Frank forgotten about their date? It wasn't possible. He'd seemed as excited about it as she had when he'd stopped by the store.

She smoothed her hands over her hips. The fabric of the dress felt silky. She'd already changed three times. She wanted to look nice, but not desperate. The clock on the wall chimed. Too late now for the first show. Maybe he was thinking they'd go to the second one. Still… She was wondering if she had time to change into something more casual when she saw the lights coming up the road.

Relief flooded when she saw it was a patrol pickup. She hurriedly stepped away from the window. No time to change now. She checked herself in the hall mirror. On a downhill slide toward sixty, she was no longer that young girl that Frank said he'd lost his heart to. But she'd kept her figure, though it was fuller.

She met her gaze in the mirror. Even her cheeks were flushed with excitement. She felt young and happy. Her heart seemed to fill with it as she heard Frank's knock at the door.

Nettie ran her damp palms down her thighs, over the silky dress, and stepped to the door.

As it swung open, the smile on her face faltered, then died as she recognized Deputy Bentley Jamison standing in her doorway, his hat in his hand, his expression solemn.

She shook her head and took a step back. "Don't tell me Frank was in an accident. Don't—"

"Nettie, Frank's been detained for questioning."

She stopped her retreat, freezing in place. When she'd seen the deputy's face, she'd been terrified that Frank had been in a vehicle accident and that he was dead. If he'd been hurt and taken to the hospital, she would have heard from a friend who worked there.

"Detained for questioning?" she finally managed to say.

"He asked if I would come by and let you know."

Not call. Come by. Her chest ached. "I don't understand."

"I'm sorry."

She could hear how sorry he was in his voice. He started to turn to leave. In two hurried strides, she reached him, grabbing his arm. "Detained for questioning? What is it you think he's done?"

"Nettie—"

"Tell me! Don't make me hear it as gossip," she pleaded. As the biggest gossip in the county, she couldn't bear the thought.

Bentley turned the brim of his Stetson in his fingers for a moment. Even though he was new, he'd lived here long enough that he had to know how fast news like this traveled.

"Please," she whispered, her fingers still gripping his arm.

"Pam Chandler's remains were found on Frank's property."

She felt her eyes widen in alarm. "Her *remains?* How long has she been dead?"

"I can't say."

"You can't say? Or you don't know?"

He sighed. "It's now a murder investigation, Nettie. Maybe the undersheriff will be able to tell you more when he comes by to question you."

"Question *me?* You think I helped Frank?"

IT WAS LATE by the time Tessa saw Dillon pull into the ranch. He'd called earlier to tell her not to wait up, but she had. When he'd called, he'd sounded exhausted.

So she'd waited, also to tell him about the man who'd come by the ranch, waited until he was sitting at the kitchen table. He'd finished a large glass of milk and a bowl of her homemade soup. She could tell he'd had a rough day, but this was something she couldn't keep from him.

"You should have called me," he said when she'd finished telling him. "This is the same man you heard threatening Ethan?"

"I didn't get a good look at him, but I recognized his voice. I think he followed me from California,"

Tessa said. "I saw a black pickup a couple times. It never came close enough that I could make out the plates. I figured there were probably a lot of black pickups around and I was overreacting."

"The man probably thinks you will lead him to Ethan. Even if he didn't follow you from California and he's working for Halbrook, then he now knows where to find you."

"He wasn't the one who mentioned the name Halbrook, though. It was Ethan."

Dillon seemed to take that in for a moment. "You're saying Ethan thought he was hired by Halbrook."

"That was my impression at the time."

He nodded, his expression sad and angry at the same time. "Then Halbrook might not be the only one after Ethan. We'll have to make other arrangements. I'm not leaving you alone out here."

"I'll be fine. I've got the .45, and I actually know how to use it." She smiled and was glad when he did, too.

Dillon was much more serious than Ethan, so when he smiled, it seemed to light him up from within. She liked making him smile. That thought, though, also made her look away.

Maybe she had confused the two men before she'd known they were identical twins. But she was no longer confused. She had loved Ethan and he'd broken her heart. She didn't want to put any of those emotions onto his brother.

"Are you all right?" Dillon asked as she got to her feet and began to do the dishes. "Let me do those. You shouldn't overdo it."

"I'm fine."

"So you keep saying." He got up and took out a new dish towel and began to dry as she washed. His hand brushed hers. She jerked back, her breathing suddenly quick and labored.

Dillon was looking at her in alarm. "Tessa?"

"I'm okay." And yet tears filled her eyes. If only she had fallen in love with this twin, the loving, compassionate, good one. She tried to still the tears, but it was as if a dam had broken. He pulled her to him, wrapping her in his arms, the hug awkward around her huge belly.

"Don't worry," he said. "I won't let anyone harm you or the baby."

She closed her eyes and leaned into him, needing his strength and his warmth. He thought she was crying because she was afraid of the man who'd come looking for her. He had no idea.

FROM YEARS OF working ranches, Ethan knew what small community ranching was across the West. Word traveled fast from one ranch to the next, from wrangler to wrangler. Cowboys moved around a lot. At least the ones Ethan had known all his life.

That was how he knew that Luke wasn't working on any of them. In fact, no one had seen Luke for almost a year.

He could be dead.

That thought had occurred to him. But if Luke was dead, then whoever was chasing them hadn't gotten what they were looking for. Buck was dead, his ashes in a grave in Montana with Ethan's name on it. But Ethan hadn't heard anything about Luke or Ashley.

Finding Tom Grady had turned out to be much easier. It bothered him how easy it had been, actually. Apparently Tom didn't have a target on *his* back. Halbrook Truman had to know that Tom had been in on everything, and yet as far as Ethan knew, Tom Grady hadn't met with the same fate as Buck Morgan—or Ethan Lawson. Now, why was that?

Those were definitely questions Ethan planned to ask when he caught up to Tom, which, as it turned out, would be soon if the roads north weren't too bad. He'd managed to follow a storm north. The snow was coming down horizontally, sweeping across the highway and obliterating the pavement.

But he kept going, driven by a need that had been eating him up inside for months. He would make this right. For the first time in his life, he would try to fix the mess he'd made.

TESSA FELT THE baby kick. She put her hand over the spot. Felt another kick. "Be patient, sweetie. The last thing I need is for you to come into the world right now."

A week ago she'd left California, determined to

track Ethan down, get her money back and make him sign the papers in her purse. At least that was what she'd thought she was doing.

But once she got here and saw the man she thought was Ethan, she'd known she was hoping to change his mind about the baby, maybe even about her. Since she'd arrived at the ranch, she'd only learned more disturbing news about the man whose child she was carrying.

Earlier, Dillon hadn't wanted to leave her to go to work, but he'd finally left, saying he wouldn't be gone long. She looked out the ranch window. The mountains Dillon called the Crazies gleamed in the sunlight even though she'd heard there was a late-winter storm to the south of them in Wyoming.

Dillon had left the window cracked open. A breeze stirred the curtains, bringing in the scent of fresh-cut hay.

Maybe the best thing she could do was go back to California, back to her job, before her daughter was born. Dillon was determined to find Ethan for her, but was that what she wanted now? What would be the point? Ethan couldn't change even if he wanted to. He'd left a trail of crime in his wake, probably for years. This latest was possibly the worst.

Even if found, what could Ethan do about the man after him?

Tessa thought of Halbrook Truman. Had he hired the man, as Ethan had suspected that day? She had to know.

When she'd pretended she needed to use Halbrook's bathroom, she had gone deeper into the house. In what appeared to be his den, she'd gone straight to his desk and rummaged through it, not sure what she had hoped to find.

All she'd known was that she didn't like him. Worse, she feared he was the reason Ethan had faked his death before she'd met him—was probably still the reason Ethan was on the run. And she worried that Halbrook was the employer of the man who'd come looking for her yesterday.

She'd found Halbrook's ranch checkbook and leafed through it. There were checks over the past few months made out to Mountain Investigations. The rest of the checks seemed to be to hired hands and the usual living expenses.

When she'd opened another drawer, she'd seen the gun. Next to it was a Tiffany ring box. She'd opened it. Empty. Had it held the engagement ring he'd given his fiancée? The same fiancée who'd taken off in the middle of the night with a few of his hired hands?

As she'd closed the drawer, she had known that Halbrook Truman wouldn't take this lying down. Just the fact that he'd held on to the box for more than a year attested to that, she thought.

In the next drawer, she found an envelope from Mountain Investigations to Halbrook Truman. It was marked Confidential.

Realizing she'd been gone too long, she'd slipped

the envelope into her shoulder bag and hurried down the hall.

Now, as Tessa looked out at the Crazies, she debated with herself why she hadn't told Dillon about it. It wasn't just that she knew, being the law and all, he wouldn't have approved. Also she hadn't wanted him to think she was anything like Ethan. Maybe, too, she hadn't been sure she could trust him entirely.

Whatever her reasoning, she'd kept it from him. Inside the envelope she'd found a report. While no names had been used, it appeared that the investigator was looking for three individuals. At the time of the report, the investigator had said he'd made contact with one individual who was still willing to make retribution and be of help in locating the others. From the postmark on the envelope, the report had been mailed last week.

How would you like me to proceed?

That had been the last line of the report, followed by the name A. B. MacMillan. Tessa realized it was time to find out if A. B. MacMillan was the man in the black pickup.

CHAPTER TWELVE

AFTER HIS TALK with Frank, Dillon called in the Montana Division of Criminal Investigation and asked Deputy Bentley Jamison to be the point man for the Pamela Chandler murder case.

"Do you want to tell me what's going on with you?" Frank asked after Dillon had finished questioning him a second time.

"Don't worry about me, Frank. You need to—"

"There's talk of a pregnant woman at your house."

Dillon laughed. He loved living in a small community where everyone knew each other. They also knew each other's business. "It's a long story."

"I happen to have some free time, if you're interested." Frank had been given another administrative leave, this one indefinite or until the case went to trial. Right now Frank was the number-one suspect. Nettie Benton was a close second, but she would have had to have help getting the body into the old mine, so the MDCI was looking at both of them.

"Frank, the last thing you need to hear about are my problems." Dillon didn't want to bother Frank, but he found himself sitting down, because the sheriff had one of the most analytical minds of anyone he'd ever known. "I don't think my brother's dead."

This took Frank by surprise. "The baby?"

Dillon nodded. "Ethan's. I believe the woman." He said it simply. Frank didn't try to tell him what a fool he was for believing her without proof.

"And the person who died in the wreck in Arizona?"

He shook his head. "I don't know for sure. I considered having the ashes exhumed, but I don't see any reason to call more attention to it and make matters worse."

"You think Ethan faked his own death?"

"It looks that way," Dillon said.

"He must have had a good reason."

"You don't think a fiancée and a baby were enough reason for my brother?"

Frank shook his head. "No, I don't."

"Me, either. I think he's gotten involved in something he shouldn't have."

"So he's on the run and sent his fiancée and baby to you."

Dillon nodded, surprised how quickly Frank had come to the same conclusion he had. "I'm afraid he's in way over his head this time."

Frank said, "Don't you have some vacation time coming?"

"That was the other thing I wanted to tell you."

"You're turning my case over to the MDCI." Frank nodded. "That's exactly what I would have done if it had been the other way around, especially given the amount of evidence you must have."

"I don't believe you killed Pam."

"You don't *want* to believe it," Frank said with a laugh. "It's all right. Given the same information you had, I would have suspected you, as well. Jamison working the case with MDCI?"

He nodded.

"Good. He worked homicide in New York. He'll get to the truth."

Dillon couldn't help the relief he felt. He didn't want to let Frank down. They'd become friends. He admired him as a sheriff. But he was also the undersheriff, and he had to do his job no matter what.

"Go find your brother," Frank said. "I hear that baby is going to be due very soon."

Dillon smiled as he got up and shook his friend's hand. "I'll be back in a day or two. I suppose I don't have to tell you not to leave town."

Frank laughed.

"So if I come back and find you and Nettie have taken off for some island without extradition—"

"That won't happen. Nettie and I aren't going anywhere. We could never leave Montana."

Dillon felt no relief to hear that. Part of him had wanted Frank and Nettie to find happiness, and if Frank had killed Pam... Well, disappearing might be the best thing for everyone.

TESSA OPENED HER laptop and typed in Mountain Investigations. She found one out of Billings, Montana, and quickly looked for the names of the investigators. There it was. A. B. MacMillan.

Part of her job for the landscaping company was doing searches for job applicants. It took her only a few minutes to find out that A.B. stood for Avery Barrows. No wonder he'd gone with A.B. He lived at an address in Rimrock Estates, was forty-nine and divorced. There were no photos of him that she could find. But she hadn't gotten a good look at the man who'd paid her a visit anyway.

She would, however, recognize his voice.

She dialed the number at his P.I. agency.

A woman answered in a crisp, professional, busy tone.

"I need to talk to Avery," Tessa said just as crisply. She was hoping that she wasn't the first apparently scorned woman who'd called for him. She had a feeling she wasn't.

"Mr. MacMillan—"

"*Mr. MacMillan* will want to talk to me, trust me. I just peed on this stick, and I've got news for him."

Silence, then, "He is out of the office."

"Right. I can come down there. I'll bring the stick and I will make the biggest fuss—"

"He's not here."

"I'll wait in his office until—"

"He's out of state on a case."

"Sure he is."

The woman's tone became even crisper. "I spoke with Mr. MacMillan just this morning when he called from Greybull, so I can assure you he *is* in Wyoming."

"When will he be back?"

"I don't know for certain. Don't you have his cell phone number?"

"He's not picking up."

"Well, I suppose that tells you something," the receptionist said. "If you'd like to leave your name, I can tell him you called."

Tessa disconnected as Dillon drove up. For a moment, she debated telling him what she'd learned. She could handle this on her own, because like it or not, she was on her own, wasn't she? Dillon had a murder case involving the local sheriff. She couldn't expect him to drop everything to help her.

"What happened?" Dillon asked when she met him on the porch.

Was she that transparent? True, she was worried about going to Wyoming and crossing paths with the man in the black pickup. But she would be armed the next time that happened, and she could feel time running out. The baby had been kicking much more, and she feared it wouldn't be that long before her precious daughter was born.

If she had any hope of finding Ethan and ending this, it had to be soon. She had the five grand that Dillon had given her. If the man in the black pickup just wanted money—

"Tessa?"

"You've done enough. You have this murder investigation. I can handle—"

"Tessa, you and the baby are my first priority right now. Talk to me."

She sighed and told him what she'd found in Halbrook Truman's desk drawer the day they'd gone to the Double T-Bar-Diamond Ranch and about her call to Mountain Investigations.

"Tessa—"

"I don't normally do things like that, but I didn't trust that man was telling us the truth."

"I know. I felt the same way about Halbrook. If anything, I admire your gumption. But I'm worried about you. The deeper we get into this, the more dangerous it feels." He met her gaze. "Tell me you weren't thinking about going to Wyoming by yourself."

It surprised her that he knew her so well after such a short time. "You have a job and this murder—"

"I've turned the murder investigation over to the state DCI and I have a deputy working with them who used to be a homicide detective."

"I can't ask you—"

"Tessa, we're *family*. I'm not about to let you do this alone, especially in your condition."

She shook her head. "I'm not your responsibility. I shouldn't have dragged you into this."

"You didn't. This was my brother's doing. He *wanted* me to make sure you and the baby were safe."

His words were a reminder that he was only doing this because he believed it was what Ethan wanted. "You've been bailing him out your whole life. I'm not your problem, and neither is my baby. Dillon, I appreciate everything you've done, but it isn't fair to you."

He glanced at her stomach. "That's my niece you're carrying. Tessa, I don't like you being involved in this as it is. It's too dangerous." He held up his hand to keep her from interrupting him. "But if you think I'm going to let you go to Greybull without me, you're crazy. We're in this together. No more keeping anything from me."

"Dillon—"

"No more arguments. You could have the baby at any time. We need to find Ethan before it's too late and find out exactly what he's running from and how to get it off his back and yours. I've taken a few days off. We'll leave right away. We can be there in a matter of hours."

ETHAN HAD CALLED the ranch where Tom worked to tell him that he needed to see him. He'd heard the panic in the hired hand's voice.

"Not here. Don't come out to the ranch. I'll meet you in town." He named a bar in Greybull. "Give me thirty minutes."

The Roundup Bar smelled of stale beer and floor cleaner. It was dark but warm, and the beer was cold. Ethan had downed two and was beginning to think

Tom was going to stand him up, when the cowboy walked in the door.

It had been months since he'd seen Tom. He looked thinner, his frown lines deeper, as if the past year had been hard on him. Ethan wondered if anyone had tied him into a speeding car with a dead man in the backseat.

"Whatcha doin' in Wyoming?" Tom said, keeping his voice down as he slid into the dark booth.

"Catching up with some old friends."

Tom looked around the bar and, apparently not seeing anyone he knew, seemed to relax him a little. He had a head of bright red hair he kept cut short and the pale skin and freckles that went with it. Because of that, it didn't take much for his face to turn scarlet—just like it was doing now.

"Bring us two cold ones," Ethan told the barmaid when she appeared. "You do still have a beer once in a while, don't you, Tom?"

Tom looked wary. He took off his hat and re-creased the crown before he finally put it down on the booth seat next to him. His face wasn't quite as flushed.

"You seem nervous," Ethan commented, watching him.

"It ain't a good idea, us being seen together."

"Why is that?"

Tom narrowed his gaze at him. "Ya hafta ask?"

The barmaid brought their beers. Ethan took a long draw on his, watching Tom over the rim of his glass. After a moment, he put down his glass and wiped his mouth. Tom still hadn't touched his.

"If you're here 'bout money, I ain't got none," Tom said.

Ethan lifted a brow. "You already spent your share?" He thought that didn't bode well, given that Luke was much more of a spendthrift.

"Maybe I invested it."

He couldn't help but laugh.

"Maybe I don't always wanna work on ranches. Maybe I'd like to get married one day, settle down, raise myself a family…."

Ethan stared at him. "Ashley."

Tom reddened again. "I didn't say—"

"You don't have to. So where is she?" He glanced around the bar before bringing his gaze back to Tom. "Is she in town?"

"I didn't say…nothing…about…Ashley." Tom had been a stutterer in his youth. Now he only stuttered when he was upset. He'd been really upset the night they'd opened Halbrook Truman's safe.

"She's not still with Luke?"

Tom picked up his beer and took a long drink.

"So she *is* still with Luke. But you've seen her, right?" He could tell he was hitting on some of the truth anyway. "Look, I appreciate you warning me about the men who were after me. Unfortunately, your warning came too late." He didn't mention that he suspected it had been planned that way. Maybe Tom had been in on it. He suspected he'd merely been used. Tom was a nice guy, just not too bright. That was what Luke used to say about him and laugh.

"They tried to kill me," he said now to Tom. "They tried to send me over a cliff in a speeding car. What I want to know is why they haven't come after you."

Tom looked stricken. "Why would they?"

Ethan opened his mouth, closed it and opened it again. "Because you were in on the heist."

Tom was already shaking his head. "You know Luke roped me into it. I wanted nothin' to do—"

"Is that what you told Halbrook?"

"Mr. Truman wouldn't kill nobody."

He shook his head at the cowboy. "Mr. Truman? The two men who almost killed me didn't have a lot to say, but you call to warn me about Halbrook and the next thing you know two men are dragging me out to my car."

"He wouldn't do nothin' like that."

Ethan stared at Tom, then laughed. "You didn't invest your share, did you? You gave the money back. What else did you give up? Your friends, as well?"

"You ain't my friends."

Ethan sat back. Tom was glaring at him, angry and upset, his face flaming. "You're right," Ethan said. He picked up his beer and downed the rest of it. It didn't taste as good as the first two. He reached into his pocket, pulled out a ten and tossed it on the table. "I need to find Luke and Ashley. I'm happy for you that you made a deal with Halbrook, but he's still looking for the rest of us."

Tom looked relieved. Ethan realized the cowboy had been expecting a fight—not for him to be so accepting.

"I don't know where they is, and even if I did know where Ashley—"

"Right," Ethan said. "You wouldn't tell me." He thought about trying to warn Tom about Ashley, but what would be the point? "Fair enough. But you'd better tell her that Halbrook hasn't given up. He wants everything we took from him—including his fiancée and that big diamond he put on her finger. If he was willing to kill me, what do you think he has planned for the woman who cuckolded him?"

"He done promised he wouldn't hurt her."

Ethan laughed. "And you believe him? Tom, he isn't going to rest until he gets us all. He's using you, and when he's done with you, you might find yourself headed for a cliff, as well." He got to his feet. "Tell me something. Did you warn Luke the way you did me?"

"I told you, I don't know where he is."

"*You* didn't find me. Halbrook did, then he told you my location so you could warn me." Ethan saw from Tom's surprised expression that was exactly what had happened. "What kind of game is he playing?"

"You know what he wants," Tom said. "If you have it—"

"I don't and I'm pretty sure Halbrook knows it, has known it for over a year, which means he's also hunting Luke and Ashley."

Tom didn't react, which told him something important. Not only did Tom know where Ashley was, but she'd also let Tom think he had a chance with her. Ethan was betting that Ashley still had Luke on the string, as well.

"I hope you're right and you can keep her safe," Ethan said as he picked up his hat, tipped the brim and walked out. "Watch your back, Tom."

CHAPTER THIRTEEN

FRANK CURRY HAD called a lawyer by the name of Marsha Zane. A woman rancher turned attorney, Marsha was the toughest around. He'd seen her in action on a couple court cases where he'd had to testify. She was a badger who dug in and came out fighting. He knew that she'd gotten guilty men off. Part of him despised a system that let that happen. Another part of him feared the system that also sent innocent men to prison.

He didn't want to be one of them.

"Tell me everything," she said after meeting him at his ranch. They now sat at his kitchen table. He'd offered her coffee but she'd waved it off. "I need the truth."

He told her what he knew. She said nothing as she scribbled on a yellow-lined notepad, but she frowned a few times, especially when he told her about ignoring a restraining order to go out to the Westfall Ranch, where his ex had been staying. She'd frowned when he'd told her that Pam had befriended Judge Bull Westfall's sister, Charlotte, and that Bull had originally given Pam not only a place to stay, but an alibi for the night Frank was attacked at his house.

"So there is no tangible proof that she broke into your house, attacked you or that she tried to run down your...friend. Unfortunately there is no law against a bitter woman turning her children against her ex-husband. Or vice versa."

"There was an eyewitness to the hit-and-run. Someone who says she thinks it was a woman behind the wheel. The truck was also from the Westfall Ranch, where Pam had been staying."

"Circumstantial at best. Judge Bull Westfall claims the truck was stolen and will say in court that he didn't think your ex stole it, right?"

"According to the judge's wife, Cora, Pam was like a daughter to him and his sister. A daughter who has gone astray, is probably sick, but still one he will protect."

"So basically you're screwed, you know that, right?"

Frank nodded. "Pam's set me up from the very beginning. Now she's found some way to frame me for her murder."

"As horrible as you say this woman is, she didn't empty a gun into herself then dump her body on your property." She saw his reaction. "Oh, you hadn't heard that, huh? Look, whoever killed her either is an accomplice in the frame-up, or killed her for whatever reason and is willing to let you take the fall. Who could this person be?"

He thought of Billy Westfall, Judge Westfall's grandson. Billy had been a deputy and a loose cannon in the department when Frank got the sheriff job. As much as Frank had wanted to get rid of the arrogant little bastard, he'd been stuck with him because of the judge's influence in the county. It was just his luck that when his not yet ex-wife had moved to the area, she'd befriended the judge's sister.

The night she'd attacked him, Pam hadn't been alone. Frank was sure Billy had been the person who'd coldcocked him. Billy would be his first guess because the bad blood between them went both ways. After Billy quit the department, Frank had refused to take him back even when the judge had asked as a personal favor.

"I can't think of anyone," he said.

Marsha sighed. She was a lean woman with pale green eyes, her skin lightly freckled. Her long graying hair was always pulled up. The few times he'd seen her when she wasn't wearing a suit and heels, she'd been in jeans, boots, a Western shirt, and her long hair had been in a ponytail, making her seem much younger than her fiftysomething years.

"There is one thing I will not put up with," she said now as her gaze locked with his. "You lie to me again and I will walk."

"Billy Westfall."

Marsha gave him an oh-I-see look. "Judge Westfall's worthless grandson. That makes sense." Her gaze narrowed at him. "Now, the second thing I won't put up with is you getting anywhere near this investigation. You stay out here on your ranch, you ride your horse, muck out your barns, build something, I don't care. Just don't play sheriff. Are we clear on that?"

"Yes." He'd been suspended with pay awaiting the outcome of the investigation. That outcome Frank was pretty sure would be his arrest and a murder trial.

"Frank, I like you. You're a good sheriff. But you've let your emotions put you where you are now. After what you told me about Pam Chandler, hell, I would have wanted to kill her myself. But now you have to be clear thinking. Pam's dead. Gone. Unless you want to go to prison, get your head on straight."

He nodded, knowing what she was saying was true. If he went after Billy, which moments ago he'd been thinking of doing, he would only make matters worse. But just the thought of beating the truth out of that little SOB had definitely been appealing.

"Don't worry. I'll get our boy Billy in front of a jury when the time comes. He'll shoot himself in the foot whether he's guilty or not."

She got to her feet and started to stuff her things into her large cowhide briefcase. "Are you planning to go see your daughter?"

He thought about what Dillon had said. Once Tiffany heard about this, he wasn't sure she *would* see him. "I'm going."

"Good. *Keep* going. Do whatever you have been doing. I want to show a jury that you're the stable one." Clearly she, too, thought his arrest and a trial was imminent. "Don't let me down, Frank."

With that, she left. He watched her drive away a moment before he noticed that there was a second crow on his telephone line.

LUKE HAD CALMED down a little by the time he got the call. He saw that it was Ashley and let it ring four times before he picked up. He knew he couldn't let her know how furious he was. He told himself to say whatever it was she wanted to hear—at least until he found out what she'd done with the rifle. She must have used his key when he was sleeping. The sneaky little—

"Hello," he said, hoping his voice sounded normal. His blood pressure was through the roof. When he got his hands around her scrawny neck—

"Luke." She sounded frantic. "Luke, are you there?"

"I'm here." His senses went on red alert. Ashley had called before after taking off. Usually she was too broke to get back and he would have to go get her. This time sounded different. "What's up, sweetheart?"

"I'm in trouble."

He almost laughed. *You ain't whistling, Dixie!* "How's that, Ashley?"

"Something's happened."

That had his attention. He could think of only two reasons the woman was stupid enough to take anything of his. One, she planned to give it back to the original owner, which would have been pure stupidity, but so like Ashley. Or two, she planned to sell it, take the money and run.

He hadn't conceived of a third option until she said, "It's Tom."

She was crying now, sobbing into the phone, making it hard to understand her. If she'd been in the room, he would have shaken her until her teeth rattled.

"What about Tom?" He had suspected she kept in contact with Tom Grady. The cowboy was drunk dumb in love with her and Ashley knew it. Luke had seen her flirting with him, enjoying the attention. "Ashley, damn it, talk to me."

"He says that if we don't give Halbrook the rifle you took, they will kill us all. Last night someone tried to run me off the road. I barely got away."

Luke knew he was callous; he'd never pretended to be otherwise. "Where is it? What the hell did you do with the rifle, Ashley? And you'd better not tell me all this is leading up to why you gave it to Tom."

She turned off the waterworks. "I just told you that someone tried to *kill* me, Luke, and all you want to know is what I did with the rifle?"

"Answer me, Ashley, or you are going to have more than Halbrook's men to worry about."

Silence. For a moment he thought he'd pushed her too far and she'd hung up. "Ashley?"

"I didn't give it to him. I don't have it."

"What do you mean *you don't have it?*"

"I know where it is, but, Luke, if we don't give it back, they're going to kill us."

He tried not to laugh. They'd found Ashley, tried to run her off the road, if she was telling the truth. At the very least, they'd scared her. Tom had told her it was Halbrook and that he was going to kill them all. Tom would know she would call him and give him the message. For all Luke knew, she'd already told Tom where Halbrook could find him.

When the cards were down, Luke had always been realistic. Sometimes a man had to cut his losses and say to hell with it. If he'd had the rifle, there wouldn't be any need for more discussion. But without that damned rifle, his options were limited.

"Luke, you *have* to help me."

As soon as his attorney left, Frank looked at his watch. He thought about calling Lynette at the store, but she might have already closed up for the day. He hadn't talked to her since he'd had to break their date. He wasn't even sure how she would feel about him now that he was under suspicion for Pam's murder.

He picked up the phone to try her house, but changed his mind. He had to do this in person. He had to look into her eyes. The thought scared him. What if she didn't believe him? Or worse, what if she wanted nothing more to do with him? Who could blame her, if that was the case? If she believed he'd killed his first wife, even an ex-wife, then how could she trust him?

Picking up his Stetson, he left the house. As he was crossing the yard to his old pickup, one of the crows called down from the telephone line.

Frank looked up. The crow called again. All crows looked alike and yet he swore he had been able to tell his apart. Just as now, he swore he recognized that crow's caw.

"Hey, there," he said, hearing the tremble in his voice. "Is that you, Uncle?"

The crow cawed again and jumped around on the line.

Frank knew if anyone had been watching, they would have thought he was crazy. "I never thanked you for saving my life. Thank you." He looked to the bird next to the one who'd cawed at him. "This your lady?" When the bird said nothing, Frank laughed at his own foolishness. "Right, you never were the type to kiss and tell. Well, it's nice to have you back. I hope you're staying for a while."

As he walked to his pickup, he couldn't help the lump that had formed in his throat. Common sense told him that these two were probably just a couple crows passing through, little chance they'd ever seen him before. Little chance they would stick around.

The light was still on at the store even though it was after closing time. Frank climbed the steps to the porch that ran across the front of the Beartooth General Store. His boots thumped across the worn boards as they had so many times before, and he found himself filled with regrets. As he reached the door, he took off his hat and hesitated.

He'd waited so long to finally ask Lynette out. Now he wondered if the odds were against the two of them ever being together. He wanted to curse the sky if that was the case. He loved this woman, had from the first time he'd laid eyes on her. He'd let hurt and stubbornness keep him from telling her how he felt, and now it might be too late. He felt like an old fool.

Gripping the door handle, he said a prayer, swung the door open and stepped inside. He would move heaven and earth if that was what it took, but he was going to spend the rest of his life with Lynette—or die trying.

NETTIE GLANCED UP in surprise as the door banged open. She hadn't heard Frank drive up. She'd been busy adding up the day's receipts and getting ready to close for the day. She stared at him, shocked at how bad he looked. Pam had done her worst to him before. Or at least they'd thought so. What had she done to him now?

He'd stopped just inside the door, hat in hand as if waiting for her to throw him out.

"Frank." Everything she was feeling seemed to come out in that one word. She moved to him quickly, feeling her eyes blur with tears, and then her arms were around him.

She buried her face in his broad chest. The man

was nearly sixty and yet he was as strong and solid as he'd been in his youth. There had always been something substantial about Frank. Something dependable.

"Lynette." He said her name on an expelled breath that rustled her hair as he bent over her. Wrapping his arms around her, he lifted her off her feet.

She closed her eyes, soaking in his warmth, relishing in his love. When he finally set her down, she looked up at him, meeting his eyes. He was such a handsome man, always had been. He was one of those men who only got more handsome as he aged.

His gaze locked with hers. "I didn't—"

She reached up to press a finger to his lips, his wonderfully thick mustache tickling her lips as she leaned up on tiptoes to replace her finger with her mouth. It was a soft kiss, a mere touching of lips, and then he was scooping her up, drawing her even closer as he deepened the kiss.

Desire, stronger than when they were young, coursed through her veins. She was that girl who used to race across the pasture to the thunder of horses' hooves, Frank at her side. He'd always been a man who loved a challenge, and he'd ridden horses as well as she had or better.

As the kiss ended, he released her and put her down. "What now, Frank?"

He raised a brow, almost making her blush.

She shook her head. "Don't tempt me." There was nothing she would have loved more than to put out the closed sign on the store's front door and go upstairs to the apartment with its queen-size bed. But she knew this man. Knew this wasn't the time. They'd waited this long. They would wait until Frank was free.

"What do we do to find Pam's killer?" she asked.

FRANK THOUGHT HE could never love this woman more than he did at that moment. "*We* aren't finding the killer. Dillon has turned the case over to Deputy Bentley Jamison, a former homicide detective in New York and the MDCI."

She shook her head as she went to the cooler and pulled out an orange soda, his usual. "They don't know Pam the way we do."

He didn't like the sound of that. "Lynette, what are you suggesting?" he asked as he watched her open the bottle and hand it to him. "Lynette?"

"I already heard where they found Pam's body and that she was killed with your gun."

The Beartooth grapevine, he thought with a curse. She'd heard more than even he had known.

She read his expression. "Well, it's true, isn't it?"

"You probably heard then that she was shot numerous times, making it appear it was a crime of passion."

She nodded. "This is all her doing."

"Probably, but still, I can't imagine she would have someone kill her just to get back at me, and I doubt a jury will, either."

Lynette narrowed her gaze. "We're talking about *Pam,* but I know what you mean. That's why we have to find out who pulled the trigger. She was evil and vindictive but definitely not a martyr."

Lynette had a sharp mind—it was another reason he loved her. He smiled and took a drink. "What are you getting at?"

"I was thinking about the last time I saw Pam. It was only in passing in Big Timber one day. I didn't even recognize her. She looked thinner and older than I had remembered. I didn't think too much about it at the time—"

"You think she might have been sick?"

"It would be easier to sacrifice yourself to screw over your ex-husband if you already had one foot in the grave and were facing a painful death, don't you agree?"

"I do."

"Good, then that is where I'll start."

"Lynette, I've already been warned by Dillon and my lawyer. I can't get involved in the investigation. I could make matters even worse."

"I didn't say anything about *you* being involved," she said. "But I'm going to help you."

"That's really sweet of you to offer, but—"

"Save your breath, Frank. I know you didn't pull that trigger. So who did? If I'm right and she had someone kill her—"

"Then the killer is still out there, Lynette."

"Exactly, and I'm going to find him."

He shook his head. "It's too dangerous. I won't hear it."

She ignored him. "Usually either love or money is involved. What if whoever killed her made it look like a crime of passion because it was? Did Pam have a lover?"

Her question took him by surprise. "Good question." And one he *hadn't* considered. "I just assumed Billy Westfall had helped her when she was in town, given the way Billy feels about me. But even though there was a rumor about the two of them being romantically involved…"

"Pam was using him, and Billy was too stupid to see it," Lynette said. "I suspect there is someone else in the picture, someone you haven't thought about. By the way, they suspect the killer had an accomplice. I heard on the Beartooth grapevine that Pam's body was dumped on your property, but she was killed somewhere else."

He nodded. "They are searching my ranch."

"If she had a lover who helped her, maybe he was the one who dumped the stolen Westfall Ranch pickup in North Dakota and stole another car that ended up in Minnesota to make us think she'd left."

With Pam dead, they might never know.

"Don't worry," Lynette said. "I will find out the truth or die trying."

"That's what I'm worried about. If you start asking a lot of questions—"

"Leave it to me."

"Lynette," he said, taking her shoulders in his hands. "I'm begging you to stay out of this. I couldn't bear it if anything happened to you. Let the MDCI and Jamison handle this." But even as he pleaded with her, he could see that nothing short of locking her up could keep her from doing this.

CHAPTER FOURTEEN

"WHERE ARE YOU?" Luke asked into the phone.

Ashley started crying again. He could hear fear in her voice. She had reason to be scared, even if Halbrook's men hadn't really found her. "I'm in Greybull."

Greybull, Wyoming. So she had gone down to see Tom Grady. Luke had heard he was working on a ranch outside of Ten Sleep.

He hated the stab of jealousy that cut through him. It was all he could do not to tell her she was on her own. Let Halbrook's men find her and kill her. What did he care?

"Where is the rifle?" he asked through gritted teeth.

In the silence from the other end of the line, he could almost hear the wheels turning in that pretty little head of hers. "I...hid it."

Hid it? Did he believe that? He stared up at the cabin ceiling for a moment as he tried to rein in his fury. "If you're lying to me—"

"I'm not lying. I wouldn't do that. Luke, I need your help. They will kill me if they find me." She started blubbering again.

"But I will kill you if you're lying. I *need* that rifle." *Just not as badly as Hal does, though, apparently.* Halbrook Truman had never seemed sentimental. Sure, it was his great-grandfather's, but to threaten to kill people over it? Or to even still be determined to get it back a whole year later? Luke cursed the man's enormous ego. Halbrook thought he was above the law, so who knew how far he would go? Or how far he'd already gone.

"*We* need that rifle," he amended. "It's our ticket out, remember? South America!" He would finally sell his ace in the hole, take the money and skip the country. Ashley had said she'd always wanted to go to South America. Unfortunately, he didn't think he would be taking her with him, but he wasn't about to tell her that. Not until he had the old Henry in his hands.

"I was worried you wouldn't want to take me now."

"Don't be silly. Where are you exactly?" he asked.

She told him the name of the motel. Sleepy Hollow.

"I'll come get you," he said. "But you need to tell me where you hid the rifle. Is it near where you are?"

"No. I hid it near our cabin." *Our* cabin? It was up here on the mountain?

"So it is somewhere inside our cabin?" he asked, thinking he would tear the place apart if he had to.

"No. I'll show you when I get back."

She hid it somewhere *outside* the cabin? A rifle

worth that much money better not be out in the weather. He could kill her himself right now. "Why would you do that?"

"I was afraid—" he heard her swallow "—you might take off without me."

"Ironic, since it seems you're the one who left *me*."

"I needed a little time away."

"With Tom."

"We're *just* friends. He's…he's easy to talk to. If anything happens to him, I'll never be able to forgive myself, though. Luke, maybe we should give back the rifle…." She began to cry again.

"Stay where you are. Don't even stick your head out the door. I'm on my way. We'll figure this out together."

NETTIE HAD NEVER thought that her nosy nature might pay off someday. She'd simply liked speculating on what was going on with people she saw from the store window. Human nature fascinated her.

Now she had a chance to turn that interest into helping clear Frank. She figured that if Pam Chandler had been sick, even possibly dying, there was one person who would know.

After stewing for a while, she did something that was inconceivable from eight to five every day of the week except for church Sunday mornings. She put the closed sign in the Beartooth General Store window and headed for Big Timber.

Judge Bull Westfall had always been more than a little protective of his sister, Charlotte. An old maid, Charlotte lived in Big Timber in a modest house. Nettie knew that Bull visited his sister almost every day.

That was why she had waited over by the large open area at the edge of town. She'd parked where she had a good view of Charlotte Westfall's house. Bull's visit didn't last long today. He'd left looking angry, but then, he looked angry most of the time.

Nettie waited for a while after he left. Maybe he'd just gone to get her a loaf of bread or some milk. When he didn't come back after twenty minutes, though, she had to assume he was gone for the day.

She was probably just being paranoid, she told herself as she climbed out of her SUV and walked up the street. Maybe Bull wouldn't mind her visiting his sister. Then again, given the kind of questions she was planning to ask, she'd bet not.

Charlotte Westfall was the heroine of her own fantasy life. She opened the door to Nettie's knock wearing a silver caftan, high heels with white fur and enough jewelry that if she fell into the Yellowstone she wouldn't surface until the Gulf of Mexico.

"Hello, dear," Charlotte said in her movie-star voice. She'd left Montana to become a movie maven back in the early 1960s. Bull had gone after her four years later. The woman he'd brought home was still beautiful, but broken.

The story was that she'd married some rich older

man who'd gotten her a few parts in some small movies before he'd died and left her a fortune.

There'd been some question about the husband's death, the word *poisoned* floating around and rumors of a torrid love affair with a movie director. True or not, Charlotte had never married again after her return. Like a character in a film, she'd spent her life pining away for a career that had never happened and a man who'd gotten away.

"Hello, dear," she repeated, and gave her once-brilliant smile.

"Hello, Charlotte." Nettie saw at once that the old dear didn't have a clue who she was. All the better, Nettie thought. "It is so good to see you. I hope I didn't catch you at an inopportune time?"

"Not at all. I was just about to have a martini. Would you like to join me?"

A martini was the last thing she wanted at this time of the day. "I would love to join you," Nettie said, and stepped inside.

FRANK STOOD IN the waiting room at the state mental hospital. Through the large windows at one end he could see the mountains.

He was afraid his daughter had already heard the news about her mother's death—and that her father was the number-one suspect. If so, he doubted Tiffany would even agree to see him.

But just then he heard a sound behind him and turned to see her standing next to a nurse's aide.

Frank swallowed as he tried to judge his daughter's mood. He hated to admit this even to himself, but sometimes Tiffany scared him. There was so much hate in her, he didn't know if she would ever be healed. Or if she *could* be healed.

Her hair had grown back in some from where she had shorn it with a pair of scissors she'd somehow gotten her hands on a few months ago. She'd refused to let anyone try to fix it, so it had grown out into what he thought was called a shag.

At least when she had to go before a judge, she wouldn't look so…disturbed. He wondered, too, if Tiffany had heard she would be standing trial as an adult, since she'd been just short of eighteen when she had tried to kill him.

He had nothing but bad news to bring her, and it must have shown in his expression, because she seemed to hesitate before she moved closer.

"What?" she demanded.

Surprisingly, this greeting was better than any he'd had in the past.

"Can we sit down?"

She shook her head. "Just tell me. Are you leaving me here in this loony bin for the rest of my life?"

"They are going to try you as an adult," he said. "You could get off with the time you've already been locked up."

"Or I might go to prison."

"There is a good chance that won't happen if you cooperate."

Her eyes narrowed. "Cooperate?"

"You have to be sorry you tried to kill me and you have to try to get better."

She scoffed at that. "Then you might as well leave me here or send me straight to prison."

"Tiffany, you're *young*. You have the rest of your life. If only you could see—"

"That my mother programmed me to kill you?"

He met her gaze. Her eyes were an incredible blue so much like his own. Every time he saw her, he found more of himself in her. Or maybe he just wanted to.

"I don't want to speak ill of your mother, but yes. She used you to seek revenge against me. She was sick." He was being as kind as he could, considering he hoped Pam Chandler burned in hell for what she'd done to this poor child.

"Are you saying she isn't sick anymore?" She'd keyed in on the *was*. So like Tiffany, he thought. The girl was intelligent. She had so much potential. If only she would get a chance to use it.

"I'm sorry to bring more bad news," he said, and sat down, hoping she would do the same. But Tiffany wasn't about to give him an inch. "Do you know if she'd been feeling bad?"

"You forget, she washed her hands of me when she thought I was beginning to believe your lies. I haven't seen her in almost a year. So did she die?" The question was asked with no emotion.

He stared at his daughter for a moment. "I'd heard

she was rail thin and that she hadn't looked well. I thought you might have known something about it."

Tiffany shook her head. "So she *is* dead." Still not an ounce of emotion. Nothing in those blue eyes.

He felt even more sick inside. "She was…murdered."

She didn't move. Her facial expression didn't change. It was if she'd heard it might rain.

"Tiffany, do you really not know how much your mother hated me?"

"With good reason."

"Even if that was true, did she have the right to poison you against me? To let you pay with your life?"

"What does it matter? She's dead, right?" Tiffany started to turn away.

"Your mother had one more plot to hurt us both."

She stopped but she didn't turn around.

"She had someone shoot her and leave my gun next to her body on my property six months ago."

Tiffany turned slowly.

"She framed me for her murder," he said.

His daughter stared at him. For the first time in a long time, he didn't see the icy cold look. There was true pain in that gaze. "Did you—"

"No. I didn't kill her. Nor would I be fool enough to kill her and leave her on my property with my gun next to her body."

"You hated her, though."

"Yes, but for what she did to you. She could have done anything she wanted to me, but I wanted her to stop hurting you."

"She told me she was done with me." This, too, was the first emotion he'd heard in her voice.

"I hated her for doing that to you. I'm so sorry."

Tiffany nodded slowly. "She's really gone?"

"She can't hurt you anymore. Only you can hurt yourself if you don't let go of this hatred she filled you with."

The girl looked so young, so fragile. A lone tear trailed over her cheek and hit the floor. Slowly, she turned and started to walk away, the nurse's aide trailing after her.

Frank felt buoyed by that glimpse of real emotion he'd seen in his daughter. He got up and watched Tiffany continue down the hall. Maybe there was hope for her yet.

At the locked doors, the nurse's aide buzzed them in. Just as Tiffany was about to go through the gate, she turned to look back at him.

He felt his heart leap to his throat. He waved, a small, unsure gesture. She met his gaze for a moment, then smiled.

It was a smile he'd seen six months ago on her mother's face right before she'd hit him with a baseball bat. It was a smile that said he wasn't as smart as he thought he was.

His own tentative smile fell. Then Tiffany was gone.

THE DRIVE TO Greybull, Wyoming, was a matter of taking Interstate 90 east as far as Laurel, then heading south into Wyoming. Dillon and Tessa left behind the mountains to travel through rolling country dotted with farmland, and finally wild country with antelope or speed goats, as Dillon called them. The afternoon sun caught on the sleek animals' coats, making they seem to glow.

Dillon had called the ranch outside of Ten Sleep and was told that Tom Grady had taken a couple days off. When questioned further, one of the hired hands had told him that he might find Tom in Greybull. Best place to try to catch him would be the Roundup Bar on the main drag.

Tessa had dropped off to sleep outside of Bridger. Dillon was glad to see her getting some rest. She looked so peaceful when she slept. He wished he could put that look on her face all the time. What worried him was what would happen when they finally did find Ethan.

No matter what Tessa said, he suspected she would take his brother back. Which meant whatever trouble Ethan was in, Dillon would have to get him out. Nothing had changed since they were boys, he thought. Except his brother no longer trusted him to ask for his help.

He put a country station on the radio, content in the quiet music and the sound of the tires on the highway.

It surprised him how comfortable he was with Tessa. He stole a glance at her. She was even more pretty in the evening light, if that was possible. But he suspected her pregnancy made her all the more beautiful.

He'd never envied Ethan. Even when their mother would do special things for him to balance out how the old man treated him, Dillon had never begrudged his twin anything. But that was before Ethan got Tessa.

Dillon turned his attention back to the road, mentally kicking himself for his thoughts. But damn it, his brother didn't deserve this woman, let alone the baby she was carrying.

Not that it changed anything. Tessa was determined to find Ethan, and Dillon was doing his best to make that happen. Part of it was personal, he had to admit. He, too, wanted to look his brother in the eyes. Ethan had let him believe he was dead. He'd let him mourn his loss for a year. What kind of brother did that, let alone a twin?

Dillon was angry, and not just for himself. No matter what kind of trouble Ethan was in, he shouldn't have left Tessa to fend for herself. Not to mention taking all her money. For the life of him, he couldn't imagine how his brother had been able to leave this woman.

While he'd known his share of women, he'd never met one he wanted to spend the rest of his life with. The past year or so, he'd been thinking he might end up one of those old ranch bachelors, too set in his ways and stubborn for any woman to put up with him. The thought hadn't bothered him.

Until Tessa. Having her at the house had made him realize how much he wanted what his brother could have had. Tessa was a keeper. Ethan was just a damned fool.

Dillon thought about the woman he'd fallen in love with in high school. Ethan had never liked her. Or at least had pretended that was the case. Had he been jealous? He shoved the thought away. He hadn't let himself think about that for years.

But he feared it was the reason neither of them had met anyone they'd wanted to settle down with. Unless Ethan really had been serious about Tessa. If so, what had happened to change that?

Halbrook Truman, Dillon thought.

"What was her name?" Tessa asked, surprising him, since he'd thought she was asleep.

Dillon shot a surprised look at her. *"Pardon?"*

"The woman who came between you and Ethan."

CHAPTER FIFTEEN

DILLON ALMOST DROVE off the road. When he swerved, the right tires lost traction in the gravel at the edge of the road before he regained control of the SUV again. Tessa could see he was upset. The knuckles on his hands, gripping the wheel, were white. All the color had washed from his face. He swallowed and shook his head as if telling himself he didn't want to do this.

But then he looked over at her and something broke in his expression. "Elizabeth." The word came out with so much pain, Tessa felt her own heart break for him, and at the same time, she felt the bitter taste of jealousy in her mouth.

Elizabeth. Her mind conjured a perfectly pale-skinned young blond woman in a spaghetti-strap sundress, smiling from under a broad-brimmed hat. Elizabeth. Not Lizzie. Not Beth. Not E. No, this young woman would never have gone by any of those nicknames, nor would any young man have dared to call her by one.

Tessa swallowed the lump in her throat and felt her eyes burn as she thought of the Elizabeths she had known. With her skinned knees, sun-browned summer limbs and mass of unruly dark curls, she'd known she would never be one of those fair beauties.

But part of her had always thought that when she outgrew being a tomboy, she would awake one morning like the ugly duckling to find she'd turned into a swam.

Now over thirty, she'd accepted who she was. The hard knocks from the Elizabeths she'd known had left her strong, determined, resilient and surprisingly content with the woman she'd become. No swan, but no longer that ugly duckling, either.

But even so, she had to brace herself. "Was she your girlfriend or Ethan's?"

"She was my high school girlfriend," Dillon said, staring straight ahead, his hands still gripping the steering wheel. "She and Ethan had never gotten along. He always said he couldn't understand why she didn't like him."

Tessa swallowed. She'd brought this up; now she had to know. "What happened?"

He frowned. "How did you…" He shook his head.

"I'm not psychic. It was something in your expression and a fairly easy guess."

He drove without speaking for a few moments. "Elizabeth and I had decided to take our relationship to the next level. I was finishing up chores, getting ready to clean up and go meet her, since we had decided that night was the night we would be together.

Ethan locked me in the barn, dressed in my clothes and went as if he was me."

Tessa closed her eyes. "Did your brother know the two of you were planning to make love that night?"

"I don't know how he would have known."

She wasn't so sure about that. "He was that jealous?"

"He said he thought it would be funny."

Tessa opened her eyes and looked over at him. The afternoon light coming in the through the windshield cast shadows across his handsome face. Pain was etched at the corner of his eyes.

"You don't believe he did it as a joke," she said.

Dillon stared out at the highway for a long moment before he shook his head. "We had planned to go to a movie. I hadn't told Elizabeth but I was going to get us a motel room. I didn't want her first time to be in my pickup."

Tessa didn't speak, couldn't have.

"Ethan knew about the movie. I guess he didn't know about the motel room. He took her up one of the logging roads in the area where we lived in western Montana."

"She had to have figured out it wasn't you."

He shrugged.

That, she saw, hurt him even more deeply than anything else. Was it possible Elizabeth really couldn't tell them apart?

"Ethan said nothing happened."

She couldn't bear what she heard in his voice.

What had Ethan done that night? It turned her stomach to think.

Dillon continued, speaking quietly, lost in the retelling. "It had started raining by the time he headed back to town." He fixed his gaze on a spot in the distance or maybe on the past.

Either way, Tessa wished she could have stopped him right there. But she had to know. She was another woman balanced precariously between these two seemingly identical men, her story racing toward its own heartbreaking end. The difference was that she wasn't in this alone. She hugged the baby growing inside her and held her breath.

"They never made it," Dillon said, his voice flat. "Ethan lost control of the pickup. It rolled. Elizabeth didn't have her seat belt on. She was thrown out." He stopped and took a breath as if his lungs had collapsed with the last of his words.

Tessa didn't breathe, either. Nor did she speak. Her throat ached with unshed tears. She wanted to touch Dillon's arm, drag him into her own arms and comfort him.

"Is your .45 loaded?" he asked, and cleared his throat.

"I reloaded it first thing this morning." It surprised her that her voice sounded normal, given the emotion she was feeling.

"Good. Keep it handy. If anyone threatens you and your baby..." He glanced over at her.

"Don't worry. I'll use it if I have to."

He nodded, holding her gaze for a moment before he slowed on the outskirts of Greybull and it began to snow.

NETTIE WONDERED IF Bull had told his sister about Pam's murder. When Pam had first come to town she'd had a hard time finding a place to live. At least that had been her story.

She'd ended up renting a room from Charlotte. Nettie suspected even then that Pam had been scheming. Judge Bull Westfall was well-known as a powerful man in the county, if not the state. Pam had worked her way into not only Charlotte's heart but also Bull's, apparently.

Nettie stepped into a living room straight from a Doris Day movie in the sixties. As Charlotte swept over to the bar to make their martinis, Nettie looked around in awe. It was as if time had stopped in 1962, when Charlotte had left the ranch to become someone else. The house her brother had bought her was done in white and gold with lots of gilded mirrors.

The centerpiece and the only real color in the room was a huge painting of Charlotte, probably commissioned by her rich former husband. The young woman in the painting was clearly beautiful, with a serene elegance that Nettie envied.

"Here we go," Charlotte said cheerfully, and handed Nettie her drink. "Isn't she beautiful?" she said, motioning to the painting Nettie had been admiring.

"Yes, beautiful," Nettie said, a little thrown by Charlotte referring to herself in the third person.

"Why don't we sit down so we can visit?" Charlotte touched her gray hair, now piled in an elaborate do on her head as she continued to admire the woman in the painting.

"Good idea," Nettie said, and lowered herself to the edge of the white couch.

"Do you like what I've done with the house?" Charlotte asked, and for a moment looked her age. Her bright red lipstick had bled into the lines around her mouth. Her face, which had once been smooth as marble, was now wrinkled with age. The hand holding her drink had age spots that even all the rings on her fingers couldn't distract from.

Nettie doubted Charlotte saw that, though, when she glanced in the many mirrors on the walls. No, Charlotte saw the woman depicted in the portrait over the white fireplace, a lithe beauty with flowing dark hair and wide-set green eyes.

"I was hoping we could talk about Pam," Nettie said, thinking this visit might be short.

"Pam?"

"Pam Chandler. She roomed with you almost twenty years ago, but I'm sure you saw her more recently than that."

"Did I?" She ran a freshly manicured fingertip around the rim of her glass. Nettie noticed that her nail polish was the same color as her lipstick.

"Oh, yes, a fine young woman," Charlotte said with a clueless air.

"Did your brother tell you the awful news?"

The elderly woman looked stricken. "Awful news?"

Nettie got the feeling that Charlotte lived in a bubble, one she was about to break, with questionable results. She braced herself. "Pam is dead." No reaction. "She was murdered."

"Oh, how awful for you," Charlotte said. "Were you terribly close?"

Nettie saw that this was getting her nowhere fast. She took another sip of her drink. It didn't taste like anything she'd ever had before. She put the almost full glass down on the coffee table and rose.

"I should be going."

"Oh, you only just got here," Charlotte cried. "You should stay." At the knock at the door, she turned in surprise. "I wonder who that is?"

So did Nettie. Before either of them could move, there was the sound of a key in the lock and the front door swept open.

"Hello, dear," Charlotte said, and raised her glass as her brother, Bull, filled the doorway.

"I was just leaving," Nettie said.

"Oh, please, don't hurry off on my accord," Bull said.

"Don't let him scare you," Charlotte said with a wink. "He's really very sweet—" she leaned forward conspiratorially "—and he's half in love with me." She winked again and took a sip of her martini.

Nettie felt a chill run through her as she hurried for the door. Bull was still blocking it, an angry scowl on his face.

"What are you doing here?" he demanded under his breath as she neared him.

"Come join us for a drink, darling," Charlotte said. "My friend and I were just having a martini."

Bull looked toward his sister, and Nettie saw his expression soften to a kind of sadness she wished she hadn't witnessed.

He stepped away from the door and let her leave without another word. But Nettie had a bad feeling this wouldn't be the last of it.

ON A HUNCH, Ethan followed Tom after they left the Greybull bar. Tom had said he needed to get back to the ranch. He'd been checking his watch like a man who definitely had someplace to be. Ethan just didn't think it was the ranch.

As it turned out, he was right.

Tom left in the direction of Ten Sleep as if he was going to the ranch, then circled back to a small, older motel called Sleepy Hollow on the edge of town.

A light snow drifted in and out of the glow of the streetlamps. The streets were dark and wet as Ethan parked a block away and watched Tom get out of the pickup in front of room eleven on the end.

As the wrangler knocked on the motel room

door, Ethan couldn't help noticing how nervous Tom seemed. He kept looking around. Was he afraid Ethan had followed him? Or someone else?

When the door opened, Ethan let out a chuckle. Even from this distance he recognized Ashley Rene Clarkson. The blonde had a strip-joint body but a baby face that seemed to make some men protective—and vulnerable.

Halbrook Truman had bought into it. Tom, too, apparently.

As Tom disappeared into the motel room, Ethan debated what to do. Tom had sworn he didn't know where Luke was. He'd also given him the impression that Ashley was still with Luke.

Ethan figured he had two choices. He could bust in and demand answers and probably get a runaround. Or he could wait and see what happened. He settled in, thinking he might be looking at a long, cold night.

The snowflakes were getting larger, floating in from the growing darkness of the storm. He hit his wipers to clean his windshield and started his engine again to let the heater run. The temperature was dropping and again he was telling himself he should be hiding out on some tropical island instead of sitting in his decrepit pickup in the middle of a spring snowstorm in Wyoming.

But then he thought of Tessa. He tried hard to keep her out of his thoughts. He'd known his share of women in his life. He'd never had any trouble leaving even one of them. Tessa was different. Tessa was also carrying his baby.

That thought cut deep, making his heart ache. She'd always been too good for him. Had he ever really planned to stay? Sometimes he bought into his own bull. But ultimately, he knew himself too well. He would never have been happy living in some suburb in California. Not even with Tessa. So why did it hurt so bad?

Not even twenty minutes later, Tom reappeared. He was carrying a suitcase. He headed for a red sports car. Moments later, Ashley hurried out. She'd put on a coat with a hood, hiding her hair and most of her face as she rushed through the falling snow to the car. To his surprise, she slid behind the wheel as Tom loaded her suitcase behind the seat and began to clean the snow off the car's windows.

What a gentleman, Ethan thought. He watched Tom go around to the driver's side. They talked for a moment. The kiss was quick and friendly, leading him to believe Ashley really was still with Luke. The one thing she wasn't was with Tom, apparently.

As Tom headed back to his ranch truck, Ashley pulled away.

Ethan waited until Tom had turned in the opposite direction before he followed the red sports car.

THE WAY BULL had run her off, Nettie suspected he'd been afraid Charlotte was going to tell her something. Not one to give up, Nettie decided to try a different tactic. If Pam had been sick and dying, there was the chance that she would have had to seek medical attention while she was in town.

Nettie had several friends at the hospital, but her friend Linda was always reliable when it came to dispensing information.

Also Linda had two sisters, both in health care. Each worked for a local doctor, while Linda worked at the hospital. Between the three women, Nettie was betting she would be able to find out if Pam Chandler had seen a doctor in Big Timber.

Nettie drove to the city park and put in the call instead of stopping by the hospital.

"You do realize that medical records are confidential," Linda said when Nettie reached her. "I don't want to get my sisters fired."

"I just need to know if Pam Chandler saw a doctor while she was in town," Nettie said, even though that wasn't all she wanted to know and she figured Linda knew it.

"I'll see what I can find out."

Linda called back five minutes later. Nettie could hear traffic in the background and figured Linda was outside smoking taking her break.

"Pam Chandler," Linda said. "Is that the dead woman they found on the sheriff's property?"

Nettie knew she would have to give some to get some, and by now most of the details were probably all over the county anyway. "She was shot, the gun apparently emptied into her body. She's been dead for months. According to what I heard, she was probably killed right after she tried to run me down on the main drag of Beartooth."

Those were things Linda apparently hadn't heard. Her friend let out a surprised sound as she exhaled smoke. "You were right. She saw a doctor. I won't say who."

"What I need to know is if she was dying."

Linda was quiet for a moment. "Did Frank kill her? Not that anyone would blame him, given what I heard about her."

"No. She must have had someone kill her to frame him—if I'm right and she was dying."

Linda took a drag on her cigarette, blowing it out in a long breath before she said, "She wasn't dying. She was pregnant."

"Pregnant?" It took a lot to shock Nettie, and her friend Linda knew it.

That was why she laughed. "Didn't expect that, did you?"

"Not in a million years. Who was the father?"

"Your guess is as good as mine. Wasn't she seeing Judge Bull Westfall's grandson, Billy?"

"He's just a boy."

"Thirty. And what was Pam? Forty? The sheriff robbed the cradle when he married *her*. Why wasn't it all right for her to rob the cradle with Billy?"

Nettie was speechless. She'd been so sure Pam was dying. Instead she must have had a horrible case of morning sickness that had left her looking thin and ill.

"Are you sure Frank didn't kill her when he found out she was pregnant with Billy's baby?" Linda joked.

"He didn't kill her. But I'm going to find out who did."

"You?" Her friend sounded surprised. Lynette could hear her crushing her cigarette stub under the sole of her shoe. "Couldn't that be dangerous?" Linda was actually a worse gossip than Nettie.

Word would now be all over the county that she was nosing into the murder. How long would it take before everyone knew that Pam had been pregnant? she wondered. If Pam had been killed by her lover, then Nettie doubted he wanted that news to come out, either.

It gave her only a moment's pause. Maybe it would help flush out the killer. Anyone who knew her would know she was merciless when it came to finding out people's secrets.

She thanked Linda and called Frank. When he didn't answer, she left him a message that he needed to call her. She wasn't dispensing this news on an answering machine.

"Snow." Tessa said it with a kind of awe that made Dillon glance over at her in surprise. He was thankful for the change of subject, but not pleased to see it was snowing. As he watched the huge, lacy flakes sailing into the windshield, all he could think of was what a pain it would be driving back if the snow started to stick on the highway.

"Have you never seen snow before?" he asked Tessa with new wonderment as he saw the delight on her face.

"It's so…beautiful."

He laughed as she whirred down her window and stuck her hand out.

"It won't stop, will it?" she asked. "I mean, will it be on the ground in the morning?"

"More than likely, given the way it's coming down."

Tessa looked happier than he'd seen her. He looked out at the snow, now hoping it did stick.

They had no trouble finding the Roundup Bar. Dillon ran in and left Tessa in the truck with the engine and heater going. Unfortunately, he was told that Tom Grady was in earlier, but he'd left and they didn't know if he would be back.

Dillon found a motel within a block of the bar and got two rooms. After they'd freshened up, they walked across the street to a small café and had dinner.

From the front window, Dillon could see the front of the bar through the falling snow. The spring storm had turned into a blizzard.

"The snow is sticking," he told Tessa as he watched the flakes beginning to build up on the pickups parked on the street. Like most small Western towns, the majority of the vehicles were pickups.

Tessa looked pleased. He'd seen her staring outside. Several times, she'd winced as if in pain.

"Are you all right?" he asked, suddenly worried.

"Fine. She's just really kicking up a storm tonight."

They finished their meal and Dillon suggested Tessa go on back to the motel. "There is no reason for you to be out in this storm." He thought she might put up a fight, but to his surprise, she agreed.

"But if you talk to Tom, you'll let me know when you get back to your room?"

He said he would.

They bundled up at the café door after he'd paid for their meals, then stepped out into the whirling snow. This time of year, the flakes were wet and heavy. They stuck to Tessa's eyelashes as she blinked up at the dizzying snowfall.

He laughed when he saw her catch a snowflake on her tongue and smile, as excited and happy as a child. "I think I'll walk you back."

"Don't be silly. I'll be fine." She pulled the coat he'd lent her around her. It was actually big enough to cover both her and the baby she was carrying. She patted her shoulder bag, reminding him of the .45 inside. Then she grinned at him and started across the empty street, practically skipping through the fallen snow.

He smiled to himself, warmed by the sight of her, and felt a tug on his heartstrings. *Don't go falling for her,* he warned himself.

CHAPTER SIXTEEN

BILLY WESTFALL? WAS it possible he was the father of Pam's baby? As it was, Frank suspected Billy as being Pam's accomplice the night he was attacked, so it didn't seem that far-fetched.

Nettie had known Billy since he was a boy. He'd always been an arrogant little snot, especially when he'd worked as a deputy at the county sheriff's department. He'd been too good-looking for his own good and had played on that. After Billy quit and Frank wouldn't let him back as a deputy, Billy had opened Westfall Investigations in downtown Big Timber, over a Western-clothing store.

Nettie found the door marked Westfall Investigations and stepped through to find herself at the bottom of a flight of steep stairs. Her years of working the store and being on her feet had kept her in shape.

She was only a little winded by the time she reached the top of the creaking stairs. The steps continued on up another flight to what apparently were apartments. From the landing, she stepped into a small space that opened on a hallway. There were four offices with doors in the hallway. All but one was empty, and that one was only a few short steps off the landing.

Westfall Investigations faced the main street. She didn't bother to knock, just tried the knob. When it turned in her hand, she pushed and stepped in.

Billy was asleep in his chair, head thrown back, mouth open, his boots on his nearly empty large metal desk. The office was sparsely furnished. Other than the used metal desk and the old oak office chair Billy was sleeping in, there was a tall gray metal file cabinet that had seen better days, and two orange plastic chairs for clients.

On one wall, there was a large framed photograph of Billy in his sheriff's deputy uniform up in the Crazies. Nettie stared at it for a moment before turning away in disgust at the smug look on Billy's face.

He hadn't moved since she'd entered the room. Other than his breathing, the only sound in the room was from the old metal blinds. A spring breeze coming through the open window behind him had the blinds tapping gently on the glass in a soothing rhythm.

Nettie let go of the old wooden door. The breeze caught it, just as she knew it would. It slammed with a resounding bang.

At the boom of the slamming door, Billy let out a snort and almost went over backward through the large window behind him. He jerked up, his boots hitting the floor with a thud. He blinked, saw her and scowled. "What do *you* want?" he demanded.

"Are you this rude with all your clients?"

Billy sat up straighter. "My *clients* call for an appointment."

She smiled at that. "Well, if you'd prefer to get back to your nap." She turned toward the door.

"Since you're already here…"

She smiled to herself before she turned back to him. Word around town had been that if Billy's new profession didn't pan out soon he would be out of business, since his grandfather, Judge Bull Westfall, wasn't footing the bill any longer. It amazed her that he'd managed to stay in business this long. She suspected that was Bull's doing.

Billy waved her into one of the plastic chairs. Clearly he had no secretary.

"So what's this about?" He eyed her skeptically. "You aren't here about the sheriff, are you?"

She wanted to wipe that smirk off his face, and hopefully she would get the chance. "Frank? No." She looked away. Billy wasn't quick on the upswing, but he got it this time.

"What? You and the lawman are on the outs since you found out he's a *murderer?*" He couldn't have sounded happier.

"I don't want to talk about it." She frowned. "You look like the cat dragged you in. Oh, I forgot, there was a death in the family."

Billy frowned.

"I heard you and Pam Chandler were very… close."

He scowled at her. "I don't talk about my clients."

"Pam was a *client?*"

He shifted in his seat. "Is there a reason you're here?"

"There's someone I need you to investigate."

"Who would that be?" he asked suspiciously.

On the way here, she'd thought about the best way to approach this, knowing he *would* be suspicious of her. So she'd gone with the obvious—her nosy nature, the reason a lot of people called her Nosy Nettie behind her back.

"The new waitress at the Branding Iron Café in Beartooth," Nettie said.

That surprised him, just as she'd expected it would.

"You know Bethany Reynolds had her baby and is now a stay-at-home mom," she said. "So Kate hired this new waitress who no one knows anything about."

Billy still looked surprised about her request. Nettie felt a little guilty. Not for lying to Billy. But for having the new waitress investigated.

But she needed to get Billy to trust her before she could find out what his connection was with Pam. He'd said she was a client. That meant there should be something in that old file cabinet off to her left. Nettie was convinced that if she could find the father of Pam's baby, she would find Pam's killer and prove Frank was innocent.

"What do you know about her?" he asked, sitting

up to retrieve a pen. From inside his top desk drawer he pulled out a new yellow notepad.

"That's just it—I don't know anything about her except her name is Callie. Doesn't even sound like a real name to me." She watched him carefully print the words *Callie, Branding Iron*. Then he looked up. "What do you want to know?"

"Whatever you can find out discreetly. I don't want it getting all over the county that I was checking up on her."

"Hey, I'm a professional."

Right. She stood.

"Don't you want to know what I charge?"

"Too much, I'm sure."

He smiled at that. "I'll need two hundred dollars up front."

She pulled out a checkbook, wrote him a check for one hundred dollars. "Come up with something and I'll pay the rest."

"She might not have anything to hide."

Nettie certainly hoped not. She'd picked the new waitress because she suspected she didn't. Billy would come back with a simple background—if he was capable of doing even that.

As she laid the check on the desk in front of him, she glanced toward the filing cabinet again. It didn't look as if it still locked. She suspected Billy had so few clients he probably didn't even know where the key was, if it *did* lock.

"You know how to reach me, but I think it might

be best if I gave you my cell phone number." Nettie took his pen from him and wrote her number on the yellow notepad.

"You'll be hearing from me," he said.

She'd gotten what she'd come for—a good look at his office and the door into it. She would be back— just not when Billy was around.

Nettie was halfway down the stairs when the door at the bottom banged open and Judge Bull Westfall appeared. At first she thought he'd followed her as he stormed up the stairs.

Bull's real name was William. He'd gotten the nickname because of his short stature combined with his bull-like build. Bald, he reminded Nettie of a bullet.

The bullet was headed right for her. But to her surprise, he climbed past her as if he hadn't even noticed her on the stairs. She heard him storm into his grandson's office. At the sound of the raised voices, Nettie considered reclimbing the creaky stairs so she could hear what the ruckus was about. But as it turned out, the trip would have been a waste of time.

She caught only snatches of the conversation before Bull suddenly appeared at the top of the landing. A few seconds later, he lumbered past her and out the door into the street. Nettie had gotten only a passing glimpse of the judge. His face had been flushed red and he'd been breathing hard, clearly furious. But his last words to his grandson still echoed in her ears.

*You stupid little fool. You keep your mouth shut,
or so help me, I'll kill you.*

LYNETTE HAD LEFT Frank a message to call, but he
hadn't been able to reach her all afternoon at the
store. Worried, on his way back from visiting his
daughter, he drove to Beartooth rather than going
straight to his ranch.

In its heyday in the late 1800s, the old mining
town had been a rip-roaring wild place. With the
discovery of gold in the Crazy Mountains behind it,
the town had grown rapidly. Early residents had built
in the shadow of the mountains where Big Timber
Creek wound through the pines. They'd constructed
substantial stone-and-log buildings, opening a bank,
a general store, a post office, garage, church, hotel,
and even a theater and a half dozen bars.

But when the gold ran out, people started leaving.

Now the narrow two-lane paved road into town
was empty—just as it was most days. Like a lot of
small Montana towns, Beartooth had died down to
what it was today, a near ghost town.

Right before the pavement ended, there was still
evidence of an old gas station with two pumps under
a leaning tin roof. Next to it, a classic auto garage
from a time when it didn't take a computer to work
on a car engine. The shells of old stone buildings
still stood in a line along the main drag, a reminder
of better times.

On each side of the creek, big houses had sprung

up during those boom times. Most were now deserted, standing empty like a lot of buildings in town, the window glass gone blank with dust or completely missing. Most everyone in the community now lived on nearby ranches and farms.

No one "passed through" Beartooth. If you kept going on up the road by what was left of the town, the pavement turned to gravel, which turned into jeep trails that wound up into the Crazies to old mining shacks or logging camps before dead-ending.

There was only one way out of Beartooth—back the way you came. Or in a pine box, as Lynette was fond of saying.

The only businesses still open were the Beartooth General Store, the Branding Iron Café, the Range Rider bar and the post office.

The one you could depend on being open seven days a week—after church on Sunday—was the Beartooth General Store. That was why Frank was shocked to find the closed sign on the front door.

He checked her house up on the mountain behind the store—no Lynette—before he went to the Branding Iron. The owner, Kate Lafond French, was sitting at one of the tables, making out her grocery list when he walked in.

"Have you seen Lynette?" he asked, unable to keep the worry out of his voice.

"Saw her leave earlier," Kate said without looking up.

"It is just so not like her."

Kate looked up then and frowned. "I'm sure she's fine. How are *you?*"

Word travels faster than a wildfire in this county. "Okay." He liked Kate. She was a hardworking, independent woman who hadn't had it easy. He was glad she'd settled here, even more glad that she'd found happiness with Jack French. Long after he and Lynette were gone, this community would live on now that younger couples were staying around.

"The reason I'm worried is that Lynette has it in her head to find out who killed my ex-wife."

"Oh, I can see where that would be cause for concern. Once Nettie gets her mind set…" She smiled. "I know how she is."

He laughed. "Yes, I guess you do." Lynette had been unrelenting when Kate had first come to Beartooth in her determination to find out what secrets the new café owner was hiding.

"Well, if you see her…"

"If it helps, she was headed toward Big Timber."

"Thanks." As he started to leave, Kate said, "I heard something interesting this morning. I don't normally listen to all the gossip that gets thrown around here, but…" She studied him a moment. "Your ex-wife, Pam Chandler? Didn't she befriend Judge Bull Westfall's sister?"

He nodded. "Charlotte Westfall." Bull had always been very protective of his sister. He'd actually supported his sister's decision to let Pam Chandler move in with her years ago. How ironic that he hadn't real-

ized just who he'd let move into his sister's house—
someone possibly more mentally unstable than
Charlotte.

"Well, someone at the bank apparently let the cat
out of the bag. It seems Charlotte was loaded, some
older rich husband? I heard the money is *gone*. Now,
mind you, this is just a rumor. But the talk is that
her account was cleaned out. I guess Bull went down
to the bank and raised holy hell, then stormed out."

"What does this have to do with my ex-wife?"
he asked.

"Seems Pam Chandler became Charlotte's new
power of attorney and absconded with the money
six months ago."

"When did Bull find out?" Frank asked, his pulse
a thunder in his ears.

"That's the question, isn't it?" Kate said with a
smile. "Did he know six months ago and only made
that recent scene at the bank because her body has
been found?" She shrugged. "I just thought you'd
like to know."

Frank understood exactly what she was saying.
If true, Judge Bull Westfall would have a motive for
murdering Pam Chandler.

To Nettie's surprise, Billy Westfall got back to her
more quickly than she'd anticipated.

"You might want to stop by my office," he said.
"I've got some news on the new waitress at the
Branding Iron."

"Can't you just tell me on the phone? I'm almost home. I don't really want to turn around and drive all the way back into town."

"Your choice."

"I can't make it this evening," she said. "I have a church meeting I can't miss." A little fib, one she thought she could be forgiven for, given that what she had planned later was much worse.

"Fine," he said, clearly disgruntled. "And I'll expect the rest of my retainer when I see you tomorrow after you close the store. You probably won't be surprised by what I found out. You wouldn't have asked me to check Callie Westfield out if you hadn't suspected I'd find something."

Nettie couldn't imagine that he'd found out anything of interest. She'd been so sure about the young waitress that she hadn't worried about using her to get into Billy's office. She had needed to check out the building so she'd know who would be there tonight. Also she'd gotten a good look at the filing cabinet, as well as Billy's office door. Both, according to the article she'd seen on the internet, were easy to get into.

"You're saying you *found* something? Something… good?"

"Something that will knock your old-lady nylons off."

"Don't push it, Billy."

"Well, don't sound so surprised. I'm actually good at this."

Nettie still couldn't believe it.

"Too bad you can't come to my office now. I guess you'll have to wait to find out what it is. Don't forget to bring my hundred bucks." He hung up.

ETHAN FOLLOWED ASHLEY'S little sports car to the edge of Greybull, where she drove into a gas station. It was one of those old filling stations that would smell like grease in the small office. A vending machine would have a few stale candy bars, and an old-fashioned pop machine would drop a can of cola for a few quarters. The rest of the building would be used for working on vehicles.

He pulled over down the street and watched as Ashley got out to pump her own gas. He stayed down in his seat where she couldn't see him as he noticed that she kept looking around. Tom must have warned her that he was in town looking for Luke.

Ethan thought about confronting her now. She was alone. She wouldn't have Tom to protect her. If he thought he could have bullied Luke's whereabouts out of her, he might have tried. But knowing Ashley, he decided to stay where he was. He was counting on her leading him to Luke.

She filled the car with gas and then went inside. A moment later, she came back out carrying a key on a piece of wood that looked a good foot long.

She made her way along the side of the gas station to the ladies' room and, after a short struggle with the key in the lock, disappeared inside.

Earlier, he'd thought she was leaving town. Now he wasn't so sure. With the snowstorm progressively getting worse, she would be a fool to chance leaving in that car without four-wheel drive.

But then again, it would depend on how badly she wanted out of town, he thought.

He glanced at his watch. She seemed to be staying in there a very long time, he realized.

As the gas station attendant came out and walked to Ashley's sports car, Ethan sat up straighter. The attendant, who looked to be in his late teens, was glancing around the same way Ashley had been earlier.

The kid hit the remote key, unlocked the car and slid behind the wheel.

Ethan glanced toward the ladies' bathroom. The door was still closed. Why would Ashley have given the attendant the key to her car? For a moment, he thought maybe she was going to have the tires changed or some work done. But the attendant didn't pull the car into the service bay. Instead, he drove around the opposite side of the station, out of sight.

He reappeared moments later to head back inside behind the counter.

Ethan jumped out and ran toward the station. He hadn't taken his eyes off the ladies' room, had he? Only for a few seconds, when his gaze had been on the attendant.

When he reached the door of the ladies' restroom, he tried the knob. It turned in his hand. As the door swung open, he caught that distinct smell of bathroom cleaner every old filling station used. The bathroom was empty. The key, still attached to the plank of wood, gleamed against the porcelain of the sink where Ashley had left it.

He didn't have to walk around the other side of the gas station to know that he would find Ashley and her car gone, but he did anyway, mentally kicking himself all the way.

There were tracks in the snow, but nothing else. As he walked back to his pickup, he considered trying to catch up to her. There were only three ways out of town, at least on paved highway. He couldn't be sure she'd even left town. Maybe she and Luke had a place in Greybull, but then what had she been doing staying in a motel?

Knowing Ashley, she could be anywhere right now. He'd just be spinning his wheels to try to find her in this storm. He couldn't believe he'd let someone like Ashley dupe him. He told himself he'd better step up his game or he was as good as dead.

CHAPTER SEVENTEEN

DILLON WAS SITTING at the end of the bar when Tom Grady walked in. He'd decided to hang out at the bar on a hunch that with the bad weather and Tom off for a few days, he'd turn back up. He recognized him at once from the description he'd gotten back at his office.

He watched the cowboy move down the bar to an empty stool. The place was dead this early in the evening and Dillon was glad of it as he picked up his beer and walked toward Tom.

He'd seen the man's expression when he'd come through the door. He'd looked upset. The bartender had slid a beer in front of Tom and left him alone. He had picked it up and downed most of the beer before he noticed Dillon, and looked both surprised and upset to see him.

"I thought you was leavin'," Tom Grady said, and took another drink of his beer. Wiping his mouth, he said, "I ain't got more to say than I did earlier, so you're wastin' your time, if that's why you're back."

Ethan had been here earlier? So he was in Greybull. They might even have passed each other on the highway. "I'm not Ethan."

Tom studied him for a moment. "Is that s'posed to be a joke or somethin'?"

"My name is Dillon Lawson. I'm looking for my brother. I take it you saw him today?"

Tom gave him a cold, dead stare in answer. Dillon hadn't worn his uniform, so dressed in jeans, boots and a Western shirt, he probably looked just like his brother. "Leave me alone, Ethan. I done told you everythin' I know."

Dillon pulled out his driver's license and the photo of him and Ethan when then they were young. "Ethan never mentioned me, huh?" He tried not to let it bother him that Ethan hadn't seemed to have mentioned that he had an identical twin to *anyone* he knew.

Tom glanced at the Montana driver's license, then the photo, then Dillon. He looked gobsmacked. "Are you kiddin' me?"

Dillon shook his head and signaled the bartender for two more beers. "Why don't we move over to a booth?" he said to Tom.

Once they were seated, two fresh beers in front of them, Dillon said, "It's urgent that I find Ethan. He was here earlier?" Tom nodded dumbly. "Do you know where he was going after he left?"

Tom shook his head. He still seemed in shock. There had always been people who had stared at him and Ethan when they were together as if they were an abomination, some oddity that shouldn't have been.

"You look so much like him. It's…eerie."

"Yeah," Dillon said. "We used to get that a lot. Maybe if you could tell me what the two of you talked about earlier…"

Tom picked up his beer and looked more close-mouthed than ever.

"I know about Halbrook Truman."

For the second time Tom looked shocked. "Who told ya?"

"Halbrook. He's still looking for all of you."

"Not me," Tom said. "I done made it right with him."

Dillon eyed the cowboy. "How did you do that?"

"Paid him back." Tom looked away.

Dillon had spent years interrogating guilty people. He knew all the signs. "You gave up the rest of them, so you must have known where they were." It wasn't a question.

Tom wiped his hand across his mouth as he shook his head and avoided Dillon's gaze. "I don't have to sit here—"

He started to rise from the booth, but Dillon grabbed his arm. From out of the corner of his eye, he saw that some cowboys had come in and were now watching the two of them, ready to jump in.

"Please," Dillon said, releasing him. "I just want to find my brother, but I have to know what's at stake here. What did you take other than the man's money and his fiancée?"

"Ashley came with us of her own accord," he said,

and eased back into his seat. "You leave her out of this. She don't want to go back to Halbrook."

He'd just bet she didn't. "Understand something. For the past year, I believed my brother was dead. Did he fake his death down in Arizona because of Halbrook?"

Tom looked trapped. "You really just wanna find your brother?"

Dillon nodded. "I could give a damn about the rest of it. But I have to know what's going on."

Tom turned his beer bottle in his fingers for a moment. Dillon didn't push him to talk, but waited as patiently as he could. He was anxious to get back to the motel and make sure Tessa was all right. But Tom Grady had the information they desperately needed, if they hoped to find Ethan and get his trouble away from Tessa and the baby. Dillon needed to know why he was on the run.

"Ethan told me Halbrook's men caught up to him and tried to kill him, somethin' about a speeding car going over some cliff."

So Ethan *hadn't* faked his death. He'd escaped death, and that was why he'd disappeared and become Ethan Cross before he met Tessa.

"So who *did* die in that car?" he asked, although he was pretty sure he already knew.

"Buck. Buck Morgan." Tom looked away.

"How could Ethan be sure it was Halbrook's men? I just find it hard to believe that even a man like Halbrook Truman thinks he can get away with murder.

Killing someone just because they ripped off his money—"

"It weren't just his money. Luke took his fiancée."

"And what else?" Dillon asked.

Tom looked away for a moment. "If you want to help your brother, then get the rifle Luke took back to Halbrook."

"The rifle?" He thought of the computer searches Tessa had found on her laptop. So they'd been right. "The old Henry?"

"You know about *that?*" Tom looked startled and upset. Clearly the rifle was a secret they had kept among them. Why was that?

"So where is this rifle? Does Luke have it? You must know where he is. Or Ashley?"

Tom stood up abruptly. His half-empty beer bottle rocked on the table for a few moments before it settled back down again. "I don't want nothin' to do with this. I done what I had to." He looked up then, and Dillon saw guilt in the man's gaze. Tom swallowed. "I shoulda never gotten involved. I just wanna be left alone."

Dillon watched him go back to the bar, taking up a stool near the cowboys who'd come in. They were still watching Dillon with suspicion.

He pushed his untouched beer away, left a tip and got up to leave. As he exited the bar, he was thinking about the look in Tom Grady's eyes. What was so special about this rifle that it had them all running so scared?

Why *had* Tom gotten involved? Not for the money.

It struck him that it had been the woman. The guilt he'd seen in the man's eyes and the pain… Both could have been from ratting out the others, but Dillon suspected it had more to do with Tom's feelings for Ashley Rene Clarkson.

As Dillon stepped outside into the falling snow and started down the street, he heard the bar door open behind him. He didn't hear the men coming because of the snow blanketing the sidewalk, but he sensed them and was ready when the three cowboys jumped him.

FRANK CALLED HIS lawyer from his truck parked in front of the Beartooth General Store. There was still no sign of Lynette.

"Have you heard the rumors about Pam swindling Charlotte Westfall out of all her money?" he asked when Marsha answered.

"I have."

"So if it's true, where is the money now that Pam is dead?"

"I'm trying to find out if she left a will, if the rumors are true and if Bull Westfall has a motive for murder," Marsha said. "How is your daughter?"

He wished he knew the answer to that. Again he was reminded of the moment when she'd turned to smile at him. He shivered. "I saw her. You heard her trial has been scheduled for the end of the year."

"I heard. Frank, I'm getting another call. I'll

get back to you when I know something definite. Meanwhile…"

"I know the drill. Trust me, I'm staying out of it." He could hear her skepticism just before she hung up. He had only barely broken the connection when he saw Lynette drive up.

She didn't notice him at first, giving him a few moments to study her. She looked like the cat who'd eaten the canary. He groaned as he got out of his truck and walked toward her.

"What have you been up to?" he asked.

Lynette smiled. "What makes you think—"

She looked so darned cute, her face a little flushed, her eyes bright. Impulsively, he looped his arm around her waist and pulled her to him for a kiss.

"Whew," she said when he let her go. "Whatever I'm up to I'm going to do it more often if that's the response I get. And right here on the main drag of Beartooth. Really, Frank."

He looked around, surprised by his own actions. Across the street at the café, Kate was smiling at them from the front window. "We should probably step inside the store."

Lynette laughed as she breezed by him and up the steps. He followed. Inside the cool, dim darkness of the store, he thought about kissing her again. He thought about doing a whole lot more than that.

"I have news," she said as she turned on the lights and flipped the store sign to Open. "Pam wasn't sick or dying. She was *pregnant*."

He thought he must have heard her wrong. *"What? Who?"*

"That I don't know yet. I visited Charlotte Westfall earlier. That woman is nuttier than a peanut log. I didn't get anything good out of her, but guess who showed up about thirty minutes after he'd left? Bull. He was in a mood."

Frank was still thrown by Lynette's announcement of Pam's pregnancy. But the word *Bull* caught his attention. "If your grapevine is correct, the reason he was in a mood, as you put it, is that he'd just found out that Pam had fleeced his sister out of all her money." He told her about the rumored scene at the bank. "Bull probably thought you'd already heard and were there to get the dirt from his sister."

"That gives Bull a motive for killing Pam."

Frank shook his head. "I can't see Bull killing anyone."

"You didn't see how angry he was."

"But if he just found out today—"

"Did he?" Lynette grinned. "Or did he just make that show at the bank to make it look as if he'd just learned today? Maybe he was furious over something else. I saw him again at Billy's. He stormed past me as if he didn't even see me. He threatened to kill Billy if he talked."

"What?" He was having a hard time believing this. "Talked about what?"

She shrugged. "I should probably tell you what else I'm planning to do." She started, but he stopped her.

"Lynette, I'm going to pretend I didn't hear you say you were going to commit a felony. I might be suspended right now, but—"

"I don't know what you're talking about," she said, and grinned.

He groaned. "You're going to be the death of me."

"I hope not," she said, moving closer. "About that kiss earlier…." She was only a breath away when the bell over the front door of the store jangled and they were forced to step apart.

Frank wondered if something would always keep them apart. It wasn't a thought that settled well. Once he was cleared of Pam's murder… But what if her frame-up was too solid? What if she would win in the end and manage to see that he and Lynette never got their happy ending?

Right now, though, he was more worried about Lynette. The way she was going, she could get herself killed.

TESSA HAD TRIED to stay in her motel room, but the baby kept kicking and she couldn't find anything on the television to hold her attention.

She had stood at the window to watch the falling snow for a long time. It enchanted her. As she placed a hand over the baby growing inside her, she made a promise that her daughter wouldn't go thirty years before seeing snow.

The white stuff fell in huge lacy flakes that obliterated everything. She could barely see across the street. Dillon had told her to wait in her room, but she felt antsy after the long car ride and worried about what was happening at the bar. Did Tom Grady know where Ethan was? Would he tell Dillon? Maybe Tom hadn't even shown up. Maybe Dillon was still waiting for him.

She couldn't stand another moment of not knowing what was going on. Grabbing her coat, her purse and the motel room key, she stepped out into the falling snow. It whirled around her as she walked down the block toward the Roundup Bar.

Tessa felt anxious and wished she hadn't involved Dillon in this. If she had just stayed in California and left well enough alone… But then Dillon would have gone on believing his brother was dead. Maybe that would have been a blessing, under the circumstances.

Except it wouldn't have helped keep her and the baby safe. Ethan's trouble was now hers.

But her heart went out to Dillon. It was bad enough that what they had uncovered had managed to shed more light on Ethan's total disregard for anyone but himself. She hadn't needed to hear more disappointing things about him. She could imagine how hard it had been on his identical twin, especially since part of Dillon still blamed himself for the way his brother had turned out.

What had Ethan gotten himself into this time? If Dillon was right and Halbrook was behind all of this, then it was bad. She'd sensed a darkness in Halbrook Truman when she'd been in his presence.

The man was dangerous, but she suspected Ethan already knew that. Halbrook was still looking for him. What if he found him? Ethan could already be dead by now.

That thought made her sad. She had loved Ethan. She would love their child until the day she died. But it was Dillon she worried about now. Ethan had made the trouble he was in. What she couldn't bear was the thought that if something had already happened to Ethan, Dillon would have to go through the grieving process again—and all because of her.

As she neared the bar, she saw what appeared to be four men scuffling. Her heart leaped to her throat when she recognized Dillon in the middle of it.

He was holding his own against the three men— but she could see that it wouldn't be for long. Two more cowboys had just come out of the bar and were moving in Dillon's direction.

"Stop!" she called out, but none of them paid her any mind. Reaching into her purse, she pulled out the .45.

"Stop!" Tessa called again, to no avail. She could see that Dillon was starting to tire and taking more blows. Once those other two cowboys reached them…

She pointed the gun at the sky and pulled the trigger. The report sounded like a cannon going off on the quiet, snowy street.

The sudden loud report got their attention. They didn't freeze, though, until she leveled the weapon in the direction of the cowboys Dillon had been fighting.

"Get out of here while you still can," she said as she moved closer. "And yes, I do know how to shoot this, and with deadeye accuracy," she added when she saw them considering trying to take the gun from her. They'd had just enough to drink that they wanted to try. There was obviously a lot more of them than her and Dillon.

She fired another shot into the air, then pointed the gun again at the man she suspected was the ringleader. The two who'd just come out backed away first. The other three took their time, several stooping to the snow to pick up their Western hats, which they'd lost during the fight.

"You want to press charges against any of these men, Undersheriff Lawson?" she asked Dillon loud enough for the men to hear.

They all looked surprised and moved a little faster off into the storm.

It wasn't until they'd disappeared back into the bar that she turned to Dillon. She saw that he was hurt, but trying hard to hide it. She watched him wince as he bent to pick up his hat from the snowy ground.

"Are you all right?" Her voice broke as she rushed to him. His right eye was already swelling shut and his lip was bleeding.

"I'm fine. You shouldn't be out in this weather."

"They could have killed you."

"I don't think they would have gone that far." He

met her gaze. "But thanks for showing up when you did."

"I didn't like the odds of five against one. You're hurt. Come on, let's get you back to the motel."

She put her arm around him, noticing that he was limping. "What happened? Did you get to talk to Tom Grady?" she asked as they moved through the storm.

"I'll tell you all about it," he said. "You're soaked to the skin." He touched her hair, now caked with snow, the look in his eyes almost her undoing.

At the motel, Dillon got his first-aid kit from his SUV, and Tessa ushered him into her room. She could see that he was favoring his ribs along with his right leg.

"Sit," she ordered, and he lowered himself to the edge of her bed. "Are you sure we shouldn't take you to the emergency room?" she asked as she opened the first-aid kit.

He smiled up at her. "I'll be fine. I've been in worse fights over my brother."

She met his gaze and saw that his greatest pain wasn't physical. She again wished she'd stayed in California. Had she never come looking for Ethan, Dillon wouldn't have ever had to learn the truth about his brother. He'd already buried his twin, done his grieving and moved on. Until she'd shown up.

"I'm so sorry I got you into this," she said, close to tears as she sat down on the edge of the bed next to him. "You could have been killed."

"Not without taking out a few of them," he said as he took the first-aid kit from her. "I'm okay. Anyway, I'm the one who is supposed to be taking care of you, not the other way around."

She shook her head and rose from the bed, more angry with Ethan than ever. She feared Dillon was right and that Ethan had purposely left that photograph for her. He would have known that Dillon would take care of her. What the fool didn't understand was that it was the last thing she wanted.

"I'm not your responsibility," she snapped, her back to him. "And your brother had no right sending me to you, if that's what he did."

"We're *family*. Don't you know how much I care about you and the baby?" His voice broke.

The pain she heard made her quickly wipe her tears. She turned to see him trying to wrap his ribs by himself.

"Here, let me do that," she said, and stepped to him, taking the tape from his hand. He had removed his Western shirt. His suntanned chest rippled with muscles. No wonder he'd been able to hold off the men who'd jumped him.

"Why didn't you tell them you were an under-sheriff?" she demanded as she finished wrapping his ribs, trying hard not to hurt him any more than he already was.

"I have no authority down here," he said between gasps.

"Still, they probably would have stopped before they broke your ribs."

"They aren't broken. Maybe cracked. Probably just bruised." He smiled at her and her eyes filled with tears. "Come on, I'm fine. Really."

"You're limping."

"Just trying to get a little sympathy from you."

She shook her head. "You can't even admit that you're hurt." She saw the truth then and let out a cry of indignation. "You *wanted* to fight them, *needed* to fight them." She would never understand men.

He was shaking his head, but she could see it was true. He was angry at his brother, frustrated that Ethan had dumped a pregnant woman on him and he had wanted to take it out on those men when they came after him.

She said as much to him.

He didn't deny anything except the part about her being dumped on him. "Tessa, you and that baby are the best thing that has happened to me in a long time."

He looked embarrassed by his words and the emotion she heard behind them.

"You didn't deserve to get hurt like this," she said, feeling her own well of emotion. "You can't keep blaming yourself for the way Ethan turned out," she said, but she could see that her words fell on deaf ears. "Here, take a couple of these." She handed him the pain pills and started to go for a glass of water.

He took the pills and swallowed them dry before she could move.

He reached for his shirt, but she took it from him.

"Let me wash out the blood," she said, and hurried into the bathroom. She turned on the water, letting it run. Her fingers gently rubbed the soft fabric of his shirt. It smelled like him, a masculine, outdoorsy scent with only a hint of perspiration. A deadly combination when coupled with the memory of him shirtless on her motel bed.

As she raised her gaze to the mirror over the sink, she saw that her cheeks were flushed, her eyes too bright. She knew that look and hurriedly put down Dillon's shirt to splash fresh water on her face before she plugged the sink and washed the blood from his shirt.

What was it about Dillon? There was something so guileless about him. Ethan, on the other hand, hid everything, maybe especially his emotions—if he had any. She thought of him as being broken, while his brother was…wounded, making her want to protect him the way he tried to protect her.

She smiled at the thought. Wasn't it just as possible that, if Ethan had really left the photo so she would find Dillon, it wasn't for his twin to take care of her but just the opposite? That was assuming Ethan had a heart. Or gave a damn.

Hanging the shirt over the shower rod, she went back into the other room to find Dillon asleep on her bed. He'd lain over at the end of the bed as if to rest, waiting for the pain pills to kick in, and was out like a light.

Tessa moved to him and pulled off his boots. He stirred enough that she managed to get him higher in the bed and to one side. She watched him sleep for a moment before she turned out the light and climbed in next to him.

As she lay there, she wished she'd met Dillon first. Wishing, though, didn't change anything— she'd learned that as a child. And maybe she wouldn't have appreciated Dillon without first knowing his brother. Crazy thoughts, she admitted.

The motel room grew quiet except for Dillon's soft breaths. Even the baby had settled down after spending much of day moving around. Through a crack in the curtains, Tessa watched the snow falling outside and thought of the promises she'd made her daughter.

As she closed her eyes, she prayed that she would be able to keep those promises.

CHAPTER EIGHTEEN

NETTIE HAD SET her alarm, determined to move fast on what Frank had called her "plan to commit a felony." Fortunately she hadn't told him when she was going to do the deed. The alarm went off a little after midnight. Sitting up, she hit the clock to stop the annoying sound. For years she'd gotten up without an alarm. Every morning at just a little after six, her eyes snapped open and she was ready for the day.

Her ex-husband, Bob, had been one of those moody morning people. She'd been glad to escape to the store so he didn't ruin every morning for her.

Earlier tonight, she'd fallen asleep fully clothed, dressed all in black, including an old hoodie Bob had left behind. As she exited the house, she felt like a cat burglar. She just hoped it made her invisible once she got to Big Timber.

She'd packed last night, putting the tools she thought she might need into her SUV. Being her first breaking and entering, she had probably brought too much.

Sliding behind the wheel, she went over her plan, hoping luck would be with her. She couldn't blame Frank for not wanting to hear about it. He'd been a lawman too long to understand that certain instances required bending the rules.

"When are you planning to do this?" he'd asked before he'd left.

She'd shrugged. "You think it's a terrible idea, don't you?"

He'd given her one of his looks in answer.

"Yeah, it was a crazy thought." She'd left it at that, not that she thought she'd fooled Frank. He knew her too well. But he hadn't pressed it.

She figured what he didn't know wouldn't hurt him. If she got caught... Well, that would be another story.

The twenty-mile drive into town didn't take long. Just as she'd hoped, Big Timber was dead. All but one of the bars had already closed, since it was a weekday and there wasn't much happening.

She knew better than to park along the main street. Or even worse, right in front of Billy Westfall's P.I. office. She drove up the street three blocks, turned right and drove back toward Billy's office building. She had considered parking in the alley behind it, but she had a feeling that the cops probably watched for just that sort of thing behind local businesses.

She parked instead across the street from some houses, where there were other cars around. For a moment, she sat watching the street. It was deathly quiet, like any small Western town this time of night.

Getting out, she withdrew the large shoulder bag

she'd put the tools in. She'd gone online and typed in *how to break into anything,* so she was pretty sure she had the necessary tools—and then some.

As she walked to the corner, she thought about how long it had been since she'd stayed up after midnight, and recalled a night not all that long ago. She and a man had shut down the Range Rider in Beartooth. The memory had once been a good one. It wasn't anymore, not since she'd learned the truth about the man. Frank might be right about her picking the wrong men. She'd done it twice so far.

She shook her head at her own gullibility as she neared the alley. When she'd hired Billy, she'd also checked the back door of the building and found it to be open, since it was also access to several apartments on the third floor.

Just like that day, Nettie found the back door into the building unlocked. This was Montana. Any other place and the door would have been locked and there would have been bars on the windows.

She stepped into the dimly lit hallway and shifted the heavy bag of tools to her other shoulder, the tools tinkling softly. There was no sound except for the creak of floorboards under her feet as she made her way down the hall to the stairs.

The stairs seemed steeper than they had earlier. She'd been happy to find that the other offices on Billy's floor had appeared empty. She recalled seeing several with for-rent signs on their doors.

At the top of the stairs, Nettie had to stop to catch

her breath. Again she shifted the bag of tools, careful not to clang them against anything. The stairs continued up to the apartments overhead. All was quiet up there as well, it seemed.

Once she caught her breath, she stood listening. Not a sound. As she stepped into the hallway, she was relieved to see, through the crack under the door, that no light was on in Billy's office. Not that she really thought he might be working this late.

Nettie inched across the creaking floorboards to his door. The hall light was so small and dim that it was too dark to work without her flashlight. She pulled it out and shone it on the lock—and felt a start.

The internet directions required using a pry bar between the door and jamb next to the doorknob. Nettie had scoped out the lock when she'd been here before and had seen that it was old and should be easy to break into.

What she hadn't counted on was the door being partially ajar. She pointed her flashlight at the floor and gently pushed with two fingers.

The door swung open with a groan that made her teeth ache. Everyone in the county must have heard that, she thought.

The room was pitch-black—just like the night. She angled the flashlight into the near-empty space and almost jumped out of her sneakers.

NETTIE FROZE WHEN she spotted the body in the chair behind the large desk.

Billy Westfall was lying back in his office chair, his boots on his desk, his hat over his face just as he had been the last time she was here. Only this time, he looked dead. Her heart was beating so hard she didn't hear the noise at first.

Drunken snores. She realized they were emanating from beneath his cowboy hat. The man had almost given her a heart attack.

She stared at him, half expecting him to wake up any moment and catch her standing there holding a flashlight in one hand and pry bar in the other.

But after a few moments, her heart rate dropped a little and she quit trembling so hard. She'd come too far to quit now. Cautiously, she shone the flashlight toward the file cabinet. She knew it would be worse than risky, but she put the pry bar back in her shoulder bag without jangling the tools too much and, keeping the flashlight beam low, edged forward.

Billy continued to snore as she carefully drew open the middle drawer, one that she could reach the easiest. It was filled with office supplies: pens, scratch pads, copy paper, new yellow writing pads, standard invoices and envelopes.

She gently shoved it closed and reached for the next one below it. This one proved to be empty. So did the bottom one.

Billy shifted slightly, making his office chair squeak.

Nettie froze again, holding her breath until she had no choice but to let it out. She didn't dare turn to look at him. A few moments later, he began to snore again and she tried to relax.

Pulling out the top drawer, she had to stand on her tiptoes to see inside. There was a whole box of unused new file folders, but in front of them she saw some with names on them.

He'd apparently had more cases than she'd thought. As she sorted through a dozen or so, she recognized most of the names on the labels. Her curiosity was almost her undoing. Each little file had some secret pertaining to these people she apparently knew nothing about.

People wouldn't have hired Billy Westfall unless they were desperate. So what had they come to him about? she wondered.

Billy's office chair squeaked again. This time the quiet lasted longer. When he finally began to snore again, she hurriedly found the file she'd come for. It was plainly marked Pam Chandler.

She hadn't seen one on Callie Westfield, the new waitress at the Branding Iron. Billy probably hadn't started one yet.

She did wonder, though, what Billy had found. Knowing him, it was nothing.

She had planned to photograph the contents of Pam's file and leave it where she'd found it. But Billy had changed those plans. What was he doing here anyway? Was it possible he was living in his office?

She was debating whether she should just take the contents or take the whole file. It felt as if there was hardly anything in it, but she couldn't check and still hold the flashlight.

As she turned, deciding to take the whole file, she looked on his desk, thinking what he'd found out about Callie might be there.

She stepped closer. There were more papers on his desk than there had been when she'd visited his office earlier. On top of the papers was an envelope that appeared to have been written before he'd fallen into a drunken sleep. Nettie stepped even closer, then froze when she saw what Billy had scrawled across the envelope.

To Be Read in Case of My Death.

His name was signed under that.

A bit dramatic, even for Billy. He'd probably written it while drunk, but still, was he worried someone was going to kill him? His grandfather had threatened him, true enough. But then anyone who knew Billy Westfall for very long wanted to kill him.

What was inside the envelope? Or had Billy only gotten as far as it before he'd passed out?

She stepped a little closer. A yellow notepad was next to the envelope and a pen. She picked up the pen and gently lifted the edge of the envelope. Sealed.

What if there was a confession in there? Billy might have been the last person to see Pam Chandler alive. What if he'd confessed to killing her and the baby she was carrying?

Nettie stared at the envelope. She knew she

shouldn't take it. But then again... She quickly scooped it up and dropped it into her bag.

Billy stirred. She took a slow-motion step back, then another, before running into the file cabinet. Billy made some piglike sounds, and for a moment she thought he would open his eyes and sense her standing there.

He began to snore again.

Letting out the breath she'd been holding, Nettie started for the door. All she wanted was to get out of there. She left Billy's door ajar—just as she'd found it—and started for the landing, when she heard someone coming up the stairs.

Nettie realized that she hadn't heard the front door open and close. Whoever it was had come in the back—just as she had. She told herself it could be one of the renters from upstairs coming in late.

She tucked the file in her shoulder bag and doused the flashlight. Whoever was coming up the steps had slowed. She looked around for a place to hide until the person passed, but finding none, she had to sneak farther down the hall of empty office spaces.

One door was set back a couple feet. She stepped into that small alcove and pressed herself against the wall. She couldn't wait to get home and look through the file on Pam Chandler. There had to be something in it that would save Frank. There just had to be.

The footsteps resumed, the sound echoing softly through the old building. The climber had reached the second-floor landing. She waited for him to continue on up the stairs to the apartments. She just assumed it was a him because of his heavy tread.

To her surprise and panic, he didn't start up the next flight of stairs. Instead, he turned into the hallway where she was hidden.

Nettie's heart caught in her throat. Was it one of the cops checking the building? Had someone seen her enter? Or had the law officer seen her flashlight beam in Billy's office? She should have closed the blinds. But then she would have awakened Billy for sure.

She pressed herself against the wall, thankful right then that she wasn't a large woman.

Just when she thought about pulling out the hammer she'd brought, she heard the footfalls turn toward Billy's office. The door groaned open. Billy must have heard it, too, because his boots came off his desk and hit the floor with a thud.

"What the hell?" he bellowed, no doubt startled to wake up and find someone standing in his office. The man would have been silhouetted against the faint light in this part of the hallway.

The overhead light in Billy's office snapped on suddenly. The golden sheen raced along the old wooden floored hallway within feet of her, the shadows fighting it back.

"Oh, it's just you," Billy said. "What are you doing here?"

The man said something low that Nettie couldn't hear.

"So what if I'm drunk? What's it to you?" he asked belligerently.

Another quiet exchange then Billy's anxious tone. "Leave me the hell alone. You've done enough damage. Don't you think I know that you killed her?"

"Keep your voice down," the man said, his words a harsh whisper.

"Why? Pretty soon the whole world is going to know. I'm going to tell them." The scrape of boot heels, the creak of Billy's office chair. "Get your hands off me! If anything happens to me, I wrote down everything. Everyone is going to know. You're going to prison."

Nettie listened in alarm at what sounded like a struggle. The sound of glass shattering made her jump, but nothing like the shriek as someone went out the window. What followed was dead silence.

The silence ended a few minutes later as footfalls were heard upstairs in one of the apartments.

All Nettie could think was that she had to get out of there. But the only way was past Billy's office, and unless she was mistaken, the killer was still in it.

She could hear him rummaging around—looking for the evidence Billy said he was leaving? Or Pam's file? That was who Billy had been talking about when he'd accused the man of murder, wasn't it?

With a start, she remembered the letter she'd picked up off Billy's desk. Nettie began to shake. She tried to hold her breath but couldn't as she heard the banging of the file cabinet drawers. The man was hurriedly searching the office. He continued to bang drawers, first the metal file cabinet, then what sounded like the drawers of Billy's desk.

In the distance, she thought she heard the sound of a siren. The man in Billy's office let out an oath. The light went out. She blinked in the sudden dark of the hall and waited for the sound of his tread, praying he didn't come down the hallway. There was no way he wouldn't see her if he did. Still, she pressed her body tighter to the wall. Her shoulder bag, with the tools she hadn't even needed, thumped against the wall and she thought her heart would stop cold.

The man started down the hall in her direction.

Her breath caught in a painful lump in her chest. She shut her eyes, squeezing them tight, and prayed. This was it, Nettie thought. There was no doubt in her mind that whoever this man was, he'd just thrown Billy out the second-story window. If he'd killed Billy, he would kill her, as well. Whatever he'd been looking for, he hadn't found it. She thought of the file and letter in her bag and almost wet her pants.

The man had taken four steps down the hall in her direction when there was another thud, this one overhead and duller than when her bag had accidently bumped the wall. He took another step.

The sound of the siren was growing closer and the crash of Billy going out the broken window had awakened someone upstairs. She heard voices upstairs and a door open and close. She thought about trying to get the hammer out of her bag, but what would be the point? The man would probably just take it away from her and kill her with it.

His footfalls suddenly retreated back down the hallway. She heard him on the stairs and then she heard nothing.

Nettie didn't know how long she stood pressed to the wall, trembling like a wet cat. She didn't want to move, but she knew she couldn't stay where she was.

Ratcheting up her nerve, she moved cautiously down the hallway. She'd already decided that if she ran into the killer, she would throw the bag of tools at him and scream bloody murder, not that it would probably save her.

Billy's office door stood open. She could see the shine of broken glass scattered on the floor from the gaping hole left in large old window behind his desk. She hurried down the stairs, turned at the bottom and practically ran down the hallway to the alley.

Once outside, she slowed to catch her breath. A sheriff's office car sped past on the street at the end of the alley, its lights flashing and siren blaring. Nettie kept walking.

FRANK CURRY GOT the call after midnight. He sat up, instantly afraid. It had been hard enough getting to sleep, wondering what Nettie had planned—and knowing whatever it was, nothing he could say could keep her from going through with it.

Bad news always came in the middle of the night, he thought as he picked up the receiver. "Hello?"

"This is Nurse Draper at the state hospital." He recalled her as being a large, kind woman.

Tiffany. Why else would the nurse be calling this late? "What's wrong?" He could hear it in her voice. His heart was pounding as he sat all the way up and braced himself.

"I'm afraid your daughter has escaped."

"Escaped?"

"As part of our protocol, we are required to call the parent."

He turned on the lamp beside his bed. Where would Tiffany go? All that hatred, there was only one place she would go, he thought. "How long has she been gone?"

"Less than hour. We are checking the grounds now."

"I'm on my way."

"There really isn't any reason for you to—"

"I'm coming up there to help look for her," he said as he started to hang up.

"Wait a minute, Mr. Curry. I just got word. They've found her."

He heard the relief in the nurse's voice. "Is she all right?" he asked, his voice cracking.

"She appears to be unharmed."

"I want to see her."

"I'm afraid that won't be possible. Tiffany injured several people before she got out of the facility. She will be put under suicide watch for the next forty-eight hours until the investigation is complete."

Frank swore silently. "The people she injured, are they—"

"They've both been taken to the hospital in Anaconda. I'm sorry, but…it's bad."

"I'm coming up there anyway," he said, and hung up. He sat for a moment on the edge of the bed. He'd never felt this helpless or this alone. He dialed Nettie's number, but hung up after four rings. Maybe she was home but had either turned off her phone or was a sound sleeper. He realized he didn't know anything about her sleep habits. That thought made him sadder than he already was.

"Tiffany, why?" he said under his breath.

He knew why. His daughter was sick. But worse was the thought that she might never be well. Nor might never be allowed to leave the mental hospital now, after what she'd done.

CHAPTER NINETEEN

NETTIE HAD CALLED Frank the moment she'd left Big Timber. She'd had to pull over in a wide spot, she'd been trembling so hard. She'd even considered stopping by his house. But she'd known that she needed to get her head on straight first. It wasn't as if she didn't know how Frank was going to react.

She could be an accessory to murder, or worse.

When she'd reached her SUV, she'd loaded her shoulder bag with the tools, then driven around the block. A crowd had gathered in front of Billy's building, along with several more sheriff's department rigs. On the second floor, she could make out the dark hole in the window where Billy had fallen from.

As she'd driven by, she'd seen the body covered on the sidewalk, broken glass all around it.

She'd never needed Frank's strong arms around her as much as she did tonight, but she knew she couldn't involve him in this. While he wasn't technically sheriff right now, pending the investigation, he was still a lawman through and through. She couldn't believe he was accused of murdering his ex-wife and looking at possibly spending the rest of his life in prison—if not getting a death sentence.

Just the thought terrified her and helped convince her that what she'd done tonight wasn't so awful after all.

Frank hadn't answered his phone and she hadn't left a message. When she'd arrived home just before daybreak, she'd been dying to get into the file and see what in it might be worth murdering Billy—not to mention opening the envelope Billy had left in case of his death.

More than ever he must have realized someone wanted him dead. But who? It had to be in the envelope.

She'd started to rip it open, but she could hear Frank telling her that what she had was now evidence in a second murder—Billy's. She'd decided she needed a clearer head, so maybe if she lay down for a little while… Exhausted from the night's ordeal and the hour, she'd put the file and letter in a safe place and had fallen into a deep, troubled sleep.

"FRANK? WHERE ARE you?"

"I'm at the state mental hospital. Tiffany tried to escape last night. She injured two of the hospital personnel."

"I'm so sorry," Deputy Bentley Jamison said.

"What's wrong?" His first thought was Lynette.

"It's Billy Westfall. He committed suicide last night. Alcohol was involved, according to the coroner. He took a nosedive out his office window."

Frank had been so sure that Billy had killed Pam,

that the two of them had been in on this plot to frame him since the get-go, that he was shocked to hear Billy was dead. He thought about what Lynette had told him about Pam being pregnant. Could Billy have been that despondent over her death?

"You're sure he killed himself?"

"Certainly looks that way. You have a reason to suspect that wasn't the case?"

"What?"

"When was the last time you saw William Westfall?"

"Billy? It's been months. Bentley, I had nothing to do with this."

"You had said you thought Billy was working with your ex-wife."

Frank laughed. "I said a lot of things. But I can assure you that even if that was true, I didn't kill him." He frowned. "Billy was annoying as all get-out, but I still can't imagine why anyone would kill him."

A thought hit him like a brick. Lynette. He'd been unable to reach her last night when he'd called after midnight. He'd warned her about investigating Pam's murder. Now he was even more worried, since Billy Westfall had been on her list of suspects and she'd mentioned something about going on the internet to find out how to break into buildings.

"Frank, I hate to ask."

For a moment, he'd forgotten he was talking to the investigating officer in Pam's murder. He realized belatedly why Bentley had called him. "You want to know where I was last night." He swore softly under his breath. For a while he'd also forgotten that he was the number-one suspect.

"I have to ask," Jamison said.

"I got the call from the hospital around midnight and left right away for the hospital. I can substantiate the call and what time I filled up with gas near Three Forks. Before that I was alone at the ranch." Not entirely alone. Four crows had been on the telephone line as he was leaving.

"Okay."

"What time did he die?" Frank asked, wondering if his alibi cleared him or if he was looking at a possible second murder rap.

"Close to 1:00 a.m."

He breathed a sigh of relief. "Any idea why he might have jumped?"

"We believe he had started to write a suicide note."

Frank heard the deputy hesitate. "What?"

"He'd started a note to you. Any idea what that might have been about?"

"He must have felt guilty for setting me up for Pam's murder," Frank said, although he doubted that had been the case. Billy Westfall wasn't capable of guilt.

All of a sudden Frank was anxious to talk to Lynette. He could just see her standing over Billy with a gun, demanding he write a confession. But if he refused, she wouldn't have thrown him out a window, would she?

Luke had needed to get to Ashley so she could tell him what she'd done with the rifle. But when he'd looked outside, he'd realized he didn't want to drive out of the Big Horn Mountains in a snowstorm at night.

Anyway, let Ashley squirm a little. It would be good for her. He knew he was being a jerk. Ashley had sounded panicked on the phone when she'd called him yesterday evening, making him wonder what he might be walking into. If it had been a trap, it was one that at least hadn't gotten sprung on him last night in the dark.

This morning, even though it was still snowing, he felt more prepared to handle whatever the woman had in store for him. He still couldn't get it out of his head—she'd gone to see *Tom*. Luke hadn't even known that she and Tom had kept in touch. It made him nervous. He knew how Tom felt about Ashley. Hell, anyone who'd seen him look at her with those big sad eyes knew he'd been mooning over her since the beginning.

Which meant Tom would sell him down the river if he thought he had a chance with the woman. The motel in Greybull definitely might be a trap. Halbrook's men could be waiting to take him out.

He'd called Ashley back when the blizzard had blown in and told her he didn't know when he would make it to Greybull, but that he was definitely coming and to wait for him no matter what.

That, he figured, should take care of Halbrook's

men. If it was a trap, let them sit for hours waiting in a snowstorm. This morning after the snowplows had run, he'd driven down Alternate Highway 14 toward Greybull, hoping Ashley hadn't betrayed him.

Ashley had sounded better when he'd talked to her the second time. He'd almost wondered if she'd changed her mind about wanting to come back to him. Or maybe about setting him up?

Something had changed, that much was clear. He just had to wonder what—other than the motel. She'd moved to one called Sleepy Rest.

Under other circumstances, there was no way he would have driven to Greybull after her. But last night he'd searched for the rifle everywhere he could imagine she might have hidden it. Since there were a dozen old cabins, not to mention the massive barn, the hiding places were unlimited. Wherever she'd hidden the rifle, if she was telling the truth, he couldn't find it. He needed her to tell him— no, she'd have to show him where it was, since he couldn't trust the woman as far as he could throw her. His inability to find the rifle meant that the two of them would be crossing paths again. She was smart enough to know that.

"Just hang tough," he'd told her. "I'll be there soon, so don't leave. Sleepy Rest Motel, right?"

"Right." She'd been either lying or in a hurry to get off the phone so she could make another call.

He couldn't be sure she would even still be in Greybull.

After he'd hung up, he'd cursed Ashley, the weather and his own stupidity for getting involved with her in the beginning. He had to remind himself that he had needed her to get into Hal's safe.

But he hadn't needed her after that. That was when he should have let Tom Grady have her. It would have saved him a lot of grief.

It was all water under the bridge, he told himself now as he neared the outskirts of Greybull, Wyoming. Ashley was coming back with him—at least until he had the rifle again. After that... Well, she was all Tom Grady's. She probably had already been Tom's. That thought enraged him. If he ever saw Tom Grady again...

DILLON WOKE, AND for a moment he didn't know where he was. Definitely not in his house on the ranch. He could hear water running and someone singing.

He opened his eyes. The motel room came into view and he tried to sit up, but quickly changed his mind. His ribs hurts like hell, reminding him of what had happened last night, including the cool, silken feel of Tessa's fingers as she'd bandaged him.

After a moment, he managed to swing his legs off the side of the bed and push himself into a sitting position. He was pretty sure his ribs were only bruised—possibly a couple were cracked, but not broken. Like the rest of his body, they hurt like the devil.

Two things hit him once he sat up. He was dressed in only his jeans, and he was still in Tessa's room. Apparently he'd fallen asleep after taking the pain pills. He didn't remember falling asleep, let alone taking off his boots. That must have been Tessa's doing.

The singing was coming from the bathroom. Tessa. He smiled at the sound and had a sudden image of her in the shower. He felt himself flush with the heat of it. She couldn't have been more beautiful than she was now. Pregnancy made her seem to light up from within. He could tell that she felt awkward, embarrassed by how big she was. She had no idea that it made her even more appealing. There was a softness in her expression, a brightness in her blue eyes, a sweet innocence in the way she placed her hands over her stomach and smiled excitedly when her baby moved.

The singing stopped. So did the sound of the running water.

Dillon shook his head as he remembered Tessa appearing out of the storm with the .45. The woman had fired off two shots on the main drag of Greybull like some Old West heroine. It was a wonder she hadn't gotten arrested. That they both hadn't.

She came out of the bathroom and seemed surprised to see him sitting on the edge of the bed. Her hair was still wet and fell to below her shoulders.

She'd dressed in a turquoise maternity blouse that brought out the blue of her eyes. The dark jean leggings ended at her ankles. Her feet were bare. Her toenails, he saw, were painted a pale pink. There was something almost too intimate about that and he quickly looked away.

"Are you all right?" she asked, frowning with concern as she moved to him.

"Better, thank you," he said as he struggled to pull on his boots.

"Your shirt isn't quite dry. I could make some coffee…."

He shook his head and pushed to his feet, trying hard not to grimace. He might very well owe her his life. He'd been a damned fool last night. She'd been right about him wanting to fight. At first it had felt good. He shuddered inwardly at the thought of what kind of shape he would have been in last night if she hadn't shown up when she had.

But her concern—that was all it was, he told himself—made him uncomfortable. Sometimes he forgot his place, forgot that she was carrying his brother's baby.

"I'm fine," he said. "I have a shirt in my room I can wear. We should probably get something to eat."

"You're not fine. Your eye looks as if it hurts, and I can tell your ribs do." She moved next to him, now so close he could smell the fresh scent of soap on her flushed skin. He looked into her eyes and felt as if he'd jumped off a high cliff into a shimmering sea. His breath caught and when he tried to swallow, he couldn't.

"Dillon." His name on her lips was his undoing.

His gaze went to her mouth, a full mouth as lush as her body. Her lips parted as if she could read his expression, see in his eyes how badly he wanted to kiss her at that moment.

He knew it was wrong. Not just the overwhelming desire to kiss her. He wanted more than that. He started to step away from her, forgetting his right leg was weak from being kicked in the knee last night. He stumbled and it was her arms that caught *him*. His gaze shot to hers. Before he could stop himself, he leaned down and touched his lips to hers.

He heard her intake of breath, felt her tremble, and then his hands were cupping her face. Her lips parted and he found himself lost in her. The kiss, at first almost innocent, deepened, rising with the same dizzying speed as his desire. For a moment, he felt blinded by it, like a flash of light that blurred everything.

But like a flash of sudden light, sight finally returns, often with a sense of being clearer than before.

He hadn't wanted to just kiss Tessa. He wanted her. He wanted this baby. He…he wanted his brother's woman.

That thought hit him like a bucket of ice water. He let go of her and stumbled back. "No," he said, shaking his head. "No."

TESSA REACHED FOR him, but he stepped back.

"I'm sorry," he said, looking as off-balance and shaken as she felt. "That won't happen again."

"If this is about your brother…"

He laughed. "How could it *not* be about my brother?" He shook his head and looked around for his shirt, as if he'd forgotten that she'd told him it was still damp.

"When I kissed you, I wasn't kissing Ethan."

"You're in love with my brother. You're having *his* baby." Dillon's voice broke with emotion as he took another step back as if needing to distance himself from her.

"I *was* in love with Ethan. Or the man he said he wanted to be. But, Dillon, that was months ago."

"You're carrying *his* baby."

"Yes," she said, putting her hand over her stomach. She felt her daughter moving just under her skin, something so miraculous that it left her in awe. "But Ethan is never going to be the father."

He looked confused. "You came all this way looking for him, hoping that when you found him—"

So Dillon had seen that. Over a few short days, he seemed to know her better than Ethan ever had. "Yes, I'd hoped that he would take one look at me and realize he couldn't walk away from us." She shook her head. "But the truth is, I knew in my heart I would be raising my daughter alone. I just wanted to offer him the chance to be a father to my daughter. I didn't want her to be robbed of that." Tears choked her last words. She cleared her throat. "But after what we've learned about him, I can't even trust him with our daughter. I certainly would never trust him again with my heart."

Dillon shook his head. "You can say that now, but once you see him... We should get going."

As he started past her, she reached for him, but her fingers only brushed his bare arm. Still, she felt her own skin ripple with gooseflesh. Her blood was still pumping hard from the kiss. There had been no confusing his kiss with Ethan's. The two men may look alike, but that was where the similarities ended.

"Dillon, please," Tessa said, but he stepped to the bathroom, grabbed his shirt and shrugged it on as he moved toward the door, running away, not unlike his brother had.

Tessa fought tears, chastising herself. Was she letting her emotions run away with her, as well? It didn't matter. Dillon would always think she wanted his brother, not him. Had that been the case with Elizabeth? She feared it had. It would explain why Dillon, at thirty-six, lived alone.

THE COLD MORNING air was just what Dillon needed. He shivered. But his shirt, even damp, was better than no shirt at all, and he'd had to get out of that room, away from Tessa.

He hurried toward his room. What the hell had he been thinking, kissing her? Mentally he kicked himself all the way to his room. He hurt all over from the attack last night, but that was nothing compared to the ache in his chest. Inside the motel room, he stood for a moment as he tried to regain control. This wasn't like him. But then again, he'd never found himself in such an unbearable situation.

The kiss had knocked him to his knees. His heart was still pounding. The feel of her in his arms— But it was the realization that made him hurt inside. He wanted his brother's woman. History was repeating itself.

He shoved the thought away the same way he had her and instantly regretted the abrupt way he'd ended things. He thought of Elizabeth. This wasn't the first time he and Ethan had fallen for the same woman. It wasn't going to happen again.

Dressing quickly, he packed, then took his bag out to the SUV and started the engine. While the heater warmed the interior, he cleaned the snow from the windshield. As much as it hurt to move, it felt good to have something to do. He had to end this, and the only way was to find Ethan, clean up whatever mess he'd made of his life and cut them both loose.

As he saw Tessa come out of her motel room, he realized how impossible that was going to be. That baby was still his niece. Yes, his niece, he reminded himself. Ethan's child. As long as he remembered that…

He hurried over to load her small overnight bag into the back of the SUV. He watched her climb awkwardly into the rig. As he slid behind the wheel, he said, "I'm sorry about earlier."

She said nothing. A lump formed in his throat as

he looked over at her. Ethan had once said he hated having an identical twin. That he felt cheated out of his own identity. "I have to share my birthday every year," he'd complained, only to anger their father, who called him an ingrate and threatened to backhand him.

Dillon had never understood that feeling more than at this moment.

Out of the corner of his eyes, he saw Tessa tense and clutch her stomach.

"Is it the baby?" he asked alarmed.

She shook her head and eased back into the seat, pulling on the seat belt. But he could tell that last kick had her worrying that the baby might be coming too soon.

He wanted to place his hand over hers because he desperately wanted to again feel that life growing inside her. He needed the reminder that it was Ethan's child, Ethan's woman carrying it.

He started the engine, ignoring his own pains. When he caught a glimpse of himself in the mirror, he was shocked by how bad he looked. His right eye was still slightly swollen and very black-and-blue. Between that, his cut lip, his hurt ribs and the pain in his one leg, he was a mess. Not exactly the man anyone would pick to send Tessa to for protection.

Where are you, Ethan? Are you watching me right now? Show yourself, you bastard. Let's end this once and for all.

Ethan didn't appear, not that Dillon had expected

him to. He turned to Tessa. "I'm sorry about the way I reacted in there—"

"It's all right. I get it."

He doubted she did. From her tone, he could tell she was hurt. It was the last thing he wanted, but there was no fixing it. All he could do was find Ethan, get him out of whatever hot water he'd gotten himself into and give his brother a chance to be a husband and father to Tessa.

Just the thought made him ache. They would probably go back to Southern California. They would have no reason to stay in Montana. He thought of his house. He'd never minded living alone. But now, when he thought of it, he saw Tessa dancing in the kitchen, her eyes closed, her arms out and him stepping into them. She would always be there, her memory lingering like a melody he couldn't get out of his head.

CHAPTER TWENTY

NETTIE WOKE TO pouring rain. She saw on the television weather report that it was snowing in the mountains to the south of town, all the way to Colorado. *Better rain than snow,* she thought as she stumbled out of bed, surprised she'd fallen asleep in her clothes.

It all came back to her in a staggering flash of memory. She padded into the kitchen and made a pot of coffee before she tried to call Frank again. The reception was terrible because of the rain and wind outside. She left another message and poured herself a cup of coffee.

She got out the file and envelope she'd hidden the night before and laid them on the kitchen table, unopened. For a few moments, she merely stared at them.

The word *evidence* kept flashing in her mind. She'd taken valuable evidence. Clearly Billy had been afraid someone was going to try to kill him. Now someone had.

Would Billy name the man who had thrown him out the window? Was it inside this envelope? Or was there something in it that would incriminate Frank even more? Wasn't it possible Pam Chandler wasn't finished with her ex-husband even yet?

Nettie swallowed and picked up the envelope. Her first instinct was to tear into it. Instead, she rose and put the kettle on.

She forced herself to wait until the water boiled before she went back to the table. Carefully, she steamed open the envelope. Her hands were shaking as she gently lifted out the folded sheet of yellow notepad paper.

She unfolded it carefully and tried to read what was written on the paper in Billy's nearly illegible scrawl.

If I end up dead...

The rest of it was gibberish, but one of the words could have been Frank. Nettie balled the paper up and tossed it into the fireplace, even though no flame burned there. She wadded up the envelope, angry enough to spit nails.

After she'd put a match to both pieces of paper, she picked up the file, afraid what she would find inside it. She was even more disappointed to find there was nothing she and Frank didn't already know in the file. She'd risked her life, and for what?

She couldn't get the memory out of her mind of the heavy footfalls she'd heard last night. Thank goodness she hadn't called the sheriff's office and reported the murder from Billy's office. If she had left the envelope where she'd found it and told Deputy Jamison about the heavy footsteps...

Now if only she would hear from Frank. She tried his home phone, then his cell. Both went to voice mail. She left another message for him to call.

As much as she hated it, she had no choice but to go to work. Hopefully, it would keep her mind off everything until she heard from Frank.

More than ever, she needed his arms around her.

OVER BREAKFAST, DILLON told Tessa what he'd learned from Tom the night before. Things had been awkward at first between them. But neither mentioned the kiss, and by the time their omelets arrived, he felt the tension evaporate, even if the kiss was far from forgotten.

"He *told* you that he gave up Ethan?" Tessa cried, almost dropping her forkful of eggs.

"In so many words. He returned his share of the robbery money, but couldn't return apparently the one thing Halbrook would kill for to get back—an antique Henry rifle that had belonged to his great-grandfather."

Tessa's head came up. "The rifle Ethan was looking for."

"It seems Ethan wasn't interested in buying it. He must have figured that Luke would eventually try to sell it, and when he did…"

"He would find Luke." She looked thoughtful as she nibbled at a piece of her toast. "What do you think Ethan planned do when he found Luke and the rifle?"

"That is the sixty-four-million-dollar question, isn't it? If he was smart, he would give it back to Halbrook. Not that it might make a difference at this point."

Tessa shook her head. "Halbrook tried to kill Ethan?"

"That's what Ethan told Tom."

"How can the man get away with that?"

"Halbrook won't get *his* hands dirty. He'll hire it done and probably get away with it, since there are only a handful of us who even know about the missing rifle apparently."

"Do you think Tom knows where Luke is?" She'd made short order of her breakfast. He was glad what he'd told her hadn't ruined her appetite.

"I suspect he does. I think he's been in contact with Ashley. He's very protective of her for a man who claims he hasn't seen her since the three parted ways almost a year ago." He met her gaze across the table. "But Tom did say he saw Ethan yesterday."

She nodded as if the news didn't come as a shock.

He waited for a reaction, but got none.

"I knew he was looking for Luke and Ashley," she said after a moment. "I just didn't know why. I found some searches on my laptop he did."

Dillon wished she'd told him that before, but he couldn't blame her. She must have thought Ethan was going back to his old ways with his former cohorts—including Ashley.

"Tom said he told Ethan the same thing he told me," Dillon said. "Basically nothing."

She nodded and looked out the café window. He followed her gaze and saw Tom Grady pull up across the street and get out of his pickup. Tom looked in their direction, and then started across the street.

The snow had stopped sometime last night after dumping more than eight inches. Fortunately the plows had come out early and cleared most of the snow off the main street, but left a pile right down the middle of the street that had turned to slush.

Dillon watched Tom wade through the melting snow as he made a beeline for them. "Maybe Tom changed his mind about talking to us," he said as he motioned to the tall, thin cowboy.

The truck came out of nowhere. Dillon heard the growl of the engine. So did Tom. He looked in the direction of the sound, stopping in the middle of the street. Dillon saw Tom's expression and was on his feet, pushing away from the table before running for the café door. He reached it only a second before a dark-colored pickup careened into Tom.

The cowboy's body rose into the air as the pickup roared past. By the time Tom hit the pavement, the truck was gone.

Dillon hurried out of the café and into the street to him, dropping down beside the wrangler's broken body. "Tom?" Behind him he heard Tessa calling 911 on her cell phone. Several other people had come out into the street to offer help. "Can you hear me?"

Tom's eyelids fluttered. He made a guttural sound.

"Don't try to talk," Dillon said. "An ambulance is on the way." He pulled back a little to look down the street, thinking he already heard the sound of a siren headed this way. Another joy of a small town.

Tom grabbed his jacket sleeve and pulled him closer. The cowboy's lips moved. Only a breath of sound came out. Dillon leaned closer.

"Luke."

"It's all right, Tom. Just try to lie still."

But the man's lips were moving again and the fingers clutching Dillon's coat were insistent. "Tomahawk."

"Tomahawk?" Dillon repeated. The word meant nothing to him. He looked into Tom's face.

"Tomahawk…Lodge." Tom's eyelids fluttered then closed as the sound of sirens filled the air. The fingers gripping Dillon's coat loosened and dropped to the pavement as two EMTs hurried to Tom's side.

But Dillon could see they were too late. Tom Grady was gone.

TESSA STOOD SHIVERING at the edge of the street, too shocked to move as she watched Dillon help the EMTs load the stretcher in the back of the ambulance. She'd seen it all from the café window before she'd raced outside behind Dillon. The pickup had purposely run down Tom Grady in broad daylight.

She shivered again as she recalled the man in the pickup who'd come to Dillon's ranch that day looking for her. She couldn't be sure it was the same truck—all she'd gotten was a glimpse—but what would the man who'd come out to the ranch have done if he'd found her?

"Tessa?"

She blinked. She'd been so lost in thought that she hadn't seen Dillon join her. She'd been only vaguely aware of him talking to the police just moments before.

"You're freezing," he said, and put an arm around her as he ushered her back inside the café. "I need to pay for our breakfast," he said, leaving her just inside the door. He seemed hesitant even to walk a few feet away. "Are you all right?"

She nodded, knowing she must be wide-eyed. She was trembling from the shock and the cold and...

"Here, sit down for a moment." He helped her into a chair at the table they had vacated earlier. She hadn't even realized that her knees were giving way.

"Thank you." She caught his hand as he started to walk away. Her gaze met his. He stood waiting expectantly for whatever else she wanted to say. But there were no words for what she was feeling. "Thank you," she repeated.

He touched her cheek with the rough pads of his fingertips and smiled down at her. "Drink a little of this." He handed her her water glass from earlier.

She clutched it in both hands and nodded. As he moved away, she lifted it to her lips and took a drink. Tears sprang to her eyes, blurring the interior of the café. She turned away, not wanting anyone to see her crying, though there was hardly anyone in the café. She couldn't even be sure who she was crying for. That poor cowboy who'd just been killed? Or Ethan, who was neck deep in all this mess, and his brother, who she'd dragged in, as well? Or was she crying for herself and her baby?

Wiping hastily at her tears, she tried to pull herself together. Behind her, Dillon was paying their bill and asking the waitress if she knew of a place called the Tomahawk Lodge.

LUKE'S CELL RANG, making him start. It was the last thing he needed right now, he thought as he pulled down a side street, weaving his way away from the main drag of Greybull and the sound of sirens.

He saw that it was Ashley calling again and was in no mood for her right now. For a moment he thought about not taking it. He was pretty sure she was merely getting antsy and wondering where he was.

He'd let her wait, telling himself he needed a little time to calm down. His hands were shaking, his heart pounding. With relief, the phone quit ringing. He took a breath and told himself everything was going to be fine. Unfortunately, he doubted that.

His phone rang again. "What?" he barked into the phone as he checked his rearview mirror and took another side street.

"Luke?"

"Isn't that who you called?" Instantly, he was

angry. Had she been trying to call Tom instead? He was already regretting coming to get her. The woman made him crazy. To hell with taking her back with him. He would wrap his fingers around her skinny throat and squeeze the whereabouts of the rifle from her and then leave her high and dry. He was over her.

He realized she was crying into the phone. "What now?" he said with an irritated sigh. This woman was going to get him killed.

"They killed him."

Luke slowed, took a right, then a left and pulled over at the curb in front of an empty house.

"Stop blubbering," he snapped. "What are you talking about?"

"Tom. Just a few minutes ago. A hit-and-run right on the main street of Greybull."

Luke closed his eyes for moment. "He's dead? Maybe it was just an accident. You don't know for certain— Wait a minute. How do you know? Did you *see* it?" His heart hammered so hard he had trouble catching his breath.

"I got hungry and I went uptown."

He gritted his teeth. "I told you to stay at the motel."

"Tom knew they were going to get him. This undersheriff out of Montana asked him about Halbrook." More crying. "He told Tom that he was looking for Ethan. He had this pregnant woman with him." Sniffing and crying and nose blowing. "Tom said the lawman knew about the rifle."

Luke wondered if things could get worse. "So you *saw* it happen?"

"No. I got there just after."

He tried to breathe easier. "Where are you?"

"I'm back at the motel." She gave him the directions and started crying again. "We have to give the rifle—"

Luke snapped the phone shut and tossed it into the seat next to him as he pulled out onto the street. He knew what he had to do, starting with getting his hands around Ashley Rene Clarkson's pretty little neck. He was in so deep now, what would it matter if he killed her? Anyway, this was all her fault.

TESSA FOUND HERSELF staring out at the street where several police cars were now parked. She could see officers questioning people.

She swallowed the last of the tears as she thought of Ethan and what he had gotten her and their baby into. The anger helped dry her tears and strengthen her resolve. All this over some old rifle?

Or was there more? Something else that, if they kept looking for Ethan, would be dropped on them like a bomb?

That was when she saw him. He stood back in the shadows of the building across the street, his old black Stetson pulled low, but she would have recognized him anywhere because of the way he stood, the way he moved.

She struggled to her feet, knocking over the glass

of water she'd left too close to the edge of the table. Already off-balance from being so pregnant, she stumbled from getting up so quickly. As she began to fall, she grabbed for something to stop her.

"Tessa?" Dillon cried in alarm as he caught her, and not for the first time.

She leaned into him as she got her feet under her and looked across the street. Ethan met her gaze for just a split second and then he was gone.

"I'M TAKING YOU to the hospital," Dillon said as he helped Tessa back into her chair at the table. "I want a doctor to check you over."

"No, I'm fine."

"You're not fine. Tessa, you're as white as a sheet." He saw her struggle to keep from crying and realized what a fool he was. She'd just witnessed a man being killed. "I'm so sorry you had to see that. Of course you're upset."

"I am." She took a deep breath and let it out slowly as she met his gaze. "But it wasn't just that." He felt himself stiffen as if anticipating a blow. If she said the kiss— "I saw Ethan."

"What?" His gaze made a sweep of the street before it returned to her. *"Where?"*

"He was standing across the street in the shadows."

"You're sure it was him?"

"It was Ethan. The moment he realized I'd seen him, he was gone." She looked away and he felt a stab of jealousy as he recalled the way she'd leaped up from the table and almost fallen in her haste.

Damn Ethan. He'd sent this woman and her baby to him, knowing big brother Dillon—Dillon had been born seven minutes before Ethan—would take care them. Dillon had spent years getting his brother out of trouble and blaming himself when he couldn't save Ethan in the end.

"Well, we knew he was in town. At least he was yesterday," he said, trying to hide the anger and pain he felt. But now Tom Grady was dead, run down in the street. Surely Ethan hadn't— He shoved the thought away, refusing to believe it.

"I heard you asking about the Tomahawk Lodge," Tessa said.

He looked at her, surprised. He'd thought when she turned away that she had done so because she was close to tears. But he saw that she was dry-eyed. The only thing burning in all that blue seemed to be steely determination.

"I think that's where we'll find Luke."

"If Luke has the rifle, then that is where Ethan will be headed. Where is this lodge?" she asked.

"In the mountains off Alternate Highway 14. I guess there are some old cabins up there in a remote spot, very isolated."

"The perfect place to hide," Tessa said.

"I don't think that is where Ethan has been stay-ing," Dillon said. "The waitress told me that the lodge hasn't been opened in years—not since Jed Blackwell died."

"Blackwell," Tessa repeated. "A relative of Luke's?"

"That would be my guess."

"Ethan must not have known about it, or he wouldn't have been trying to find out from Tom Grady where Luke was," she said. "Still, if we find the rifle, then Ethan will find us, right? So we're going to this lodge."

He cleared his throat. "I think after what happened today there is no doubt about how dangerous this is—"

"If you are going to try to talk me out of going with you, you can save your breath. I'm the one who got you into this—"

"Ethan is my brother."

"Yes," she said. "Because of Ethan, we are both involved. I'm not bringing my baby into this world until this is resolved."

He wasn't sure she would have a choice, but kept his mouth shut.

"The only way that is going to happen is if we can find Luke, find this rifle and Ethan and end this once and for all. I won't feel safe until that happens." Her gaze locked with his. "After today, do you have any doubt that if Halbrook Truman is behind this, he wouldn't use me or my child to get his revenge against Ethan?"

Dillon had already thought of that. He blamed himself for taking Tessa with him to the Double T-

Bar-Diamond in the first place. He'd had no idea what they were walking into. Not that he could have kept her away from Halbrook, he reminded himself. She'd been determined to go there anyway.

But she was right. They were now both involved. Both had unresolved reasons for wanting to find his brother.

Dillon considered what to do, knowing that Tessa would find a way to Tomahawk Lodge on her own if he didn't take her. He would just have to make sure she was safe. He thought about last night and the fact that she'd been the one to save him. He hadn't known just how dangerous this would be, and he wasn't in great shape to do much saving.

"If what you told me about Tom was true, then there is only one reason they would decide to kill him," Tessa said. "He didn't have any more information to offer."

He looked at her. "We have to assume, then, that he told Halbrook where to find Luke and Ashley and the rifle."

She nodded. "And told them that Ethan was also in town, as well as the two of us."

Dillon felt his heart drop as he realized she was right. Tom had given them *all* up.

CHAPTER TWENTY-ONE

WHEN ETHAN REACHED his pickup and parked on a side street, he sat for a moment, feeling as if he'd been head butted by a Brahma bull. Tessa. He lay over his steering wheel, fighting the pain. Seeing her like that, so pregnant. He cursed himself for getting involved with her. Had he really thought he could change himself—let alone the past?

He sat up and pushed back his hat. He couldn't think about any of that now. Not the look on her face when their eyes had met. Or the way his brother had been the one there to catch her. He smiled even though it hurt. Hadn't he known Dillon would take care of her? So why didn't that give him the peace of mind he'd hoped it would?

Because as messed up and dangerous as the past had become, Ethan wasn't sure even Dillon could protect Tessa and the baby now. He was still reeling from finding out that Tom Grady was dead.

So what were Dillon and Tessa doing here in Greybull? Ethan swore. He should have known Dillon would try to find him. He hadn't thought that part out. As usual, he hadn't considered the consequences of his actions. He'd thought with Tessa that pregnant, Dillon would keep her on the ranch, safe.

Then again, he also hadn't considered how determined Tessa could be. Another reason he had to find Luke and put a stop to this before Tessa and the baby got hurt. He was depending on Dillon. His brother had always been there for him. Ethan couldn't bear the thought that he might get them all killed because of some stupid thing he'd done.

He shifted his pickup into gear and was about to pull out when he glanced in his side mirror and saw a pickup headed his way. His pulse began to pound. For a moment he couldn't believe his eyes.

As the dark brown pickup came nearer, he turned his face away, letting Luke drive on by. Ethan sat for a moment, heart pounding. The left headlight was smashed and there was something dark smeared on the dented bumper of Luke's pickup.

Ethan let out a curse. *What the hell, Luke?*

He waited a few moments to let Luke get a little bit ahead of him. Then he followed, suddenly even more afraid how this was all going to end.

TESSA EXCUSED HERSELF to go to the ladies' room down the hall at the back of the café.

Dillon finished his coffee, then watched the snow continue to drift down outside. He was still shaken after witnessing the hit-and-run. Tom Grady was dead. But at least Ethan was still alive—or had been when Tessa had seen him minutes ago.

"Ethan, where are you? What kind of game are you playing?" he asked under his breath, then glanced at his watch, realizing Tessa had been gone for a long while. He'd seen her holding her stomach. She'd said it was just the baby kicking, but he suspected this baby might be coming sooner than she'd hoped. The last thing he should do was take her up to some closed mountain resort miles from a hospital.

He got up, left a tip then when there was still no Tessa, he walked down the hallway toward the ladies' restroom.

People had come and gone earlier while they'd been eating, but after the hit-and-run the place had cleared out quickly. Now it was pretty much deserted. He tapped on the bathroom door marked Women.

"Tessa?" He tried the door. Unlocked. His heart began to pound even before he turned the knob to find the small single commode bathroom empty. "What the—"

His cell phone rang. He was headed back into the café, thinking he must have somehow missed her, as he dug out his phone.

He saw at a glance that Tessa wasn't in the café. He spun on his heel and headed for the back door, his mind racing. Why would she have left? He flipped open his phone as it rang again, thinking it must be Tessa.

"Hello?" he said as he pushed the back door open and stared out into the storm. There were two sets of tracks in the new-fallen snow and one set of tire tracks close to the door.

His pulse was pounding now. "Hello?" he repeated into the phone.

"Is this Dillon Lawson?" asked a male voice.

He froze. "Who wants to know?"

"We have your brother's pregnant girlfriend. We're willing to make a trade. Her for your brother and a package. Your brother will know about it."

His heart dropped like stone down a well. "I don't know where my brother is, and that woman isn't his girlfriend. Not only that, she could have that baby at any time."

"I suggest you find your brother quickly, then. We'll call back." The line went dead.

LUKE TOOK THE back streets to the ratty motel where Ashley had said he would find her. He checked his rearview mirror and saw an SUV behind him. It had been following him for a few blocks now. He drove past the motel, took a right and pulled over in front of a large old Victorian house.

The SUV cruised past on the street he'd been on, an old pickup behind it. Luke waited for a few moments. He figured by now Ashley would be pacing the floor and furious. No more furious than he was as he pulled out, circled the block and parked on the street rather than pulling into the motel lot.

Again he sat for a few minutes, watching the motel office and the parking lot. There were only three vehicles parked out front, all pickups. So where was Ashley's red sports car?

He glanced down the narrow residential street and saw the car parked a couple blocks away in front of a house. Could she be any more obvious with a car like that?

Luke had told her not to buy it. But she'd seemed to think if she didn't "invest" her share of the money they'd taken out of Halbrook's safe, Luke would eventually get it. Maybe she knew him better than he thought.

She'd said she was in unit number seven, the last one and the one he was closest to. He cut the engine and got out. Tom was dead. He still couldn't believe he'd done what he had. If Ashley hadn't come down here to see Tom…

Their numbers were dwindling, he realized, with Tom and Buck dead. Ashley must be scared out of her mind and ready to sell her soul to save herself. So he had no doubt she would sell him out, as well.

The motel lot, still covered in a thick blanket of snow, with more falling, was eerily quiet. As he moved through the storm, he looked for fresh tracks to her door and saw her high-heeled boot soles, leaving the motel and returning. No one else's.

Luke knocked at her door, just two short raps. Silence. He rapped again, thinking she might be in the shower. That would be just like her to wait until he was here to shower.

"Ash?" he said and tried the knob. Locked. "Ash!"

"You're leaving if I have to carry you out of here like a sack of potatoes."

"I'll scream," she threatened.

"Only once."

DILLON MADE THE call to Halbrook the moment he left the café. "Listen to me and listen well," he said when the rancher came on the line. "If anything happens to Tessa and her baby—"

"I don't know what you're talking about."

"But you do know who this is. And you know why I'm calling. Understand this, I'm as anxious to find my brother and your *property* so I can have you arrested for kidnapping and murder."

"Are you drunk?"

"Your man just ran down Tom Grady on the main street of Greybull, Wyoming. I witnessed it."

"What?"

"Tessa could have her baby at any time. You'd better pray nothing happens to her or that child or I will—"

"You really shouldn't be threatening people, *Deputy*. I can tell you're upset, but like I said, I have no idea what you are talking about. No one I hired killed *anyone*."

Dillon ignored the "deputy" jab. "Tell your men to take Tessa Winters to the local hospital. I'll get your rifle back." He heard Halbrook swear.

"Like I said, I have no idea what you're talking about."

He heard movement inside the room. The door opened a crack. One big overly made-up blue eye peered out at him.

"Take the damned chain off," he snapped irritably.

She closed the door, he heard the scrape of the chain and finally the door swung open.

He gave the room a quick glance before he pushed past her to check the bathroom. Empty. As he turned, he saw Ashley locking the door and putting the chain back on. Did she really think either would keep the men after them out of this room?

"What the hell is this all about, Ashley?" he demanded, furious with her for dragging him to Greybull and, worse, making him do something he thought himself incapable of doing, especially out of jealousy. Not to mention that the town was crawling with cops, as well as Halbrook's men. "Have you lost your mind?"

Big crocodile tears welled in her eyes. "Tom's dead."

"My point exactly. What are you doing here? What am I doing here? If you sold me out—"

"I wouldn't do that."

"But Tom would. You probably played right into his hand." He wanted to belt her one. This was all her fault. She stepped to him and put her arms around him, burying her face in his chest.

"I can't believe they killed Tom," she cried.

He shoved her away. "Get your things together. We have to get out of here."

She pouted as she began to slowly put her clothes into her suitcase. He pushed her aside, threw everything in and slammed the lid.

"Those clothes are going to be all wrinkled."

He looked at her as if he could strangle her. All that kept him from it was the fact that she was the only one who knew where she'd hidden the rifle. He went into the bathroom and dumped everything into her makeup bag. It was heavier than her suitcase.

"You really don't have to wear all this crap on your face," he said as he took both bags to the door. "Come on. We're leaving your car here. You can ride with me."

"What makes you think I would go anywhere with you, the way you treat me?" she demanded.

He turned to look at her. She stood, defiance burning in her gaze, her hands on her hips. He was often struck by how cute she could be, especially without all the makeup. But it was her fiery spirit that had kept him coming back for more.

He set down both bags and took a step toward her. "You got me down here at considerable risk. I would think twice before you crossed me. I'm not even sure I can get us both out of this town alive and we sure as hell can't stay at the cabin any longer. We'll have to pack and leave as soon as we get back."

He was within inches of her.

"I'm not leaving without my car," she said, staring him down.

Snow fell in a white shroud around him as he disconnected and pulled away from the curb. As he drove out of town on Alternate Highway 14, headed for the mountains and Tomahawk Lodge, he wondered where his brother was. On this road into the mountains?

The Greybull police had already put out a BOLO on a dark-colored pickup and had a partial description of the man behind the wheel. The driver of the hit-and-run pickup would be anxious to get out of town. There would be damage to the pickup, and with the police looking for him… With luck, they would pick him up.

But Dillon knew someone else had Tessa. Halbrook had sounded surprised. Or maybe he was just a good liar, even when caught off guard. It didn't matter. This was about the rifle. Tom Grady had confirmed that.

What Dillon couldn't believe was that his brother was part of this. If he was, then Dillon really had never known his twin. The thought struck him to his core. Either way, he would find the damned rifle—and his brother.

He tried not to think about what would happen when he came face-to-face with Ethan after all this time. Ethan had let him believe he was dead, would have gone on letting him if it hadn't been for Tessa.

Tessa had seen him in downtown Greybull—not long after Tom Grady had been run down in the street. He swore again under his breath. Ethan had not only involved him, he was now endangering the woman carrying his child. What was wrong with his brother? It broke his heart to think about it.

ETHAN HAD SUSPECTED Ashley would have holed up at one of the motels in town. He'd driven by a few last night, including the one he'd seen her in with Tom, but he hadn't spotted her sports car. It had been snowing so hard, he'd given up and found himself a place to stay for the night.

Now he parked down the street from where he'd seen Luke stop. Luke had gotten out and gone into one of the motel rooms just minutes ago. Since he'd lost track of Luke and Ashley over a year ago, he had no idea how their relationship was going. Yesterday she was with Tom. Today it was Luke. That might very well have described Ashley's relationship with men.

The motel room door on the end of the units opened. Luke looked out, then, taking Ashley by the arm and a suitcase in his other hand, practically dragged her out to the pickup. She carried a small case and looked not just nervous—it would appear she wasn't all that excited to be going with Luke.

Luke shoved her into the passenger side, apparently avoiding taking her past the smashed-up front end of the truck. After shoving her none too gently into the pickup, he went around to climb behind the wheel. Had Luke told Ashley what he'd done to Tom? Ethan was betting not.

As Luke headed out of town the back way, Ethan started his truck and eased out. He took a route that paralleled the way Luke had gone. He caught only glimpses of Luke's older brown truck. It wasn't until Luke turned onto Alternate Highway 14 and headed toward Ranchester that Ethan remembered something Luke had once told him about an uncle who lived in that area.

The uncle had died, as Ethan recalled. But the uncle had owned a lodge in the Big Horn Mountains, where Luke had spent summers. Luke had told so many stories, half of them outright lies. But Ethan had a feeling Luke might have been telling the truth this time.

If so Ethan had a pretty good idea where Luke was headed. He now also knew just how far Luke would go. Had he really thought that Luke Blackwell would give up the rifle without a fight? He'd been deluding himself if he had. As far as Luke was concerned, the rifle was his. He was the one who'd gotten the combination for not only the safe but for the hidden gun safe that no one but he had known about.

The thought struck hard.

Ethan was going to have to kill someone.

He'd spent his life ripping off people, getting into all kinds of trouble, but he'd never come close to killing anyone.

What would happen now would be a culmination of those misspent years. He wouldn't have a choice—the stakes were too high. Halbrook wanted the rifle, and he had the money, the clout and men bad enough to make that happen.

Halbrook Truman played for keeps. Ethan knew that firsthand. But why would Luke take out Tom? He almost laughed as he realized the answer. Ashley.

Ethan swung by his motel and picked up the duffel bag he'd hidden there. He was coming out of his room when he caught movement out of the corner of his eye. He didn't even get a chance to duck.

TESSA FOUGHT THE panic. She'd been grabbed from behind as she'd come out of the café ladies' room. A hand had clamped over her mouth as she'd been lifted off her feet and carried quickly out the rear door into the storm. Moments later, she'd found herself in the back of a service van.

She'd fought the man at first until he'd whispered in her ear that if she kept it up, he would hurt her— and the baby.

She had lain on the floor of the van, the man's arm like a vise around her throat. All she'd been able to think about was Dillon. He would realize she was gone. What would he do? He would find her.

She listened, hoping to get some idea of where they were taking her. But all she could hear was the pounding of her own heart and the steady clack of the windshield wipers. It was snowing hard again.

Her abduction had happened so quickly that she hadn't had time to be terrified. But now, lying on the van floor, she felt panic prickle through her.

Where were they taking her? She knew this had to have something to do with Ethan. Dillon had done everything he could to keep her safe, and still, here she was in the back of this van going— Going where?

Her thoughts shifted as the van slowed, then turned and stopped. The man pulled her up into a sitting position. A moment later, the side door of the van grated open, letting in a flurry of snowflakes.

For an instant, she was blinded; then the man was hauling her out into the storm, leading her toward a small old house standing alone out in the Wyoming countryside.

The room they put her in was small and dark and contained nothing but a double bed. Off to the side was a tiny bathroom with a sink and toilet. All she could think as she looked around the room was that somehow, she had to get out of there.

She quickly checked her purse, surprised she still had it. The .45 was gone. Nor was there anything else in there she could use as a weapon, which was probably why they had allowed her to keep it.

There was one small window in the room, too small for her to get out of even if she hadn't been pregnant and as big as a house. She could hear voices outside the room. Two men had brought her here. They'd let her see their faces. She feared that meant she would never leave here alive.

Terror rocketed through her as her baby kicked and she felt her stomach cramp. *Not now, sweet baby. Oh, please, God, don't let the baby come now.*

CHAPTER TWENTY-TWO

"WE NEED TO talk about where you put the rifle," Luke said as he and Ashley neared the mountains.

She'd been watching her rearview mirror since they'd left town. She wouldn't sit still and it was making him nervous. He didn't know what had happened since he'd last seen her. Ashley had admitted to spending time with Tom, but had she seen Ethan, as well?

"Ash?" He glanced over at her. Why did she keep looking behind them? In this storm, she couldn't see ten feet past the rear bumper. "Ashley, stop doing that and talk to me." He hadn't meant to snap, but he had, and now tears welled in her eyes.

"Halbrook is going to kill us," she cried.

"Probably," he agreed, because he was in no mood for all this drama. "Get a grip. We'll pick up the rifle and leave for South America in the morning."

That stopped her sniveling. She wiped her eyes and looked at him. "Really? Do you really mean it, Luke?"

"I wouldn't have said it unless I meant it." A lie, but maybe she was right. Maybe they should skip the country. Hal was a maniac with an ego the size of Montana, but he wouldn't follow them clear to South America.

"They have these really big cattle ranches, I've heard, in Argentina," Ashley said. "You can get a job on one, I bet."

He wasn't going to wrangle cattle the rest of his life. Once he had the rifle, he'd sell it. If Hal wanted it back so badly, it must be worth a pretty penny. Anyway, he'd be glad to be rid of it.

Once he had the cash… Well, then what? he wondered as he glanced over at Ashley. She was going on about Argentina and some *National Geographic* special she'd seen on television. He felt an odd pang of regret as he met her gaze and smiled as if he was listening. Ashley wouldn't be going with him. She made him too crazy. He knew there would be other "Toms" and he knew the next time, it might end him up in prison. If he got away this time.

"So maybe we could go there some weekend after we get to Argentina," she said, finally winding down.

"That's great, Ash. But we aren't going anywhere without the money from the rifle. Tell me you hid it somewhere safe and that it is out of this weather."

She smiled like a kitten curled up in the sun. "You'll see," she said, and settled back into the seat. "Once we have it, we leave, right?"

"Right," he said, trying to hide his irritation and concentrate on his driving. The highway had turned into a series of hairpin switchbacks that wound up the mountain through the snowstorm, and the road, dangerous when dry, was covered in fresh snow.

Tessa turned at the sound of someone entering the room and went weak with relief. "Dillon." He stood in the doorway, filling it with his broad shoulders. She was overjoyed at the sight of him. She'd known he'd find her.

But more than anything, she was just happy to see that he was alive.

She rushed toward him, but stopped a few feet short of reaching him. The hair on the back of her neck spiked as a chill rippled over her skin. The man in the doorway looked exactly like Dillon. But in that instant, she knew better.

"Ethan," she said, and covering her belly with her hands, she took a step back.

"Sorry to disappoint you," he said as he was shoved from behind into the room, the door slamming and locking behind him.

"Where is Dillon?" she demanded.

"I don't know." He studied her openly for a moment. "I'm sorry about all this, Tessa."

She shook her head, anger boiling up from deep inside her. "You're *sorry?* You and your past are going to get us all killed." Tears of fury burned her eyes. She brushed at them with the back of her hand. "You didn't just involve me and my baby, but your own brother. Your *twin.* You let him believe you were dead for a year?"

She saw his reaction to her disgust on the face she'd once thought was the most handsome she'd ever seen.

"I've been trying to make this right. I saved most of what I made in construction and what I borrowed from you to pay Halbrook back, but without the rifle…"

She winced at the word *borrowed* but let it go. "You're talking about the old Henry rimfire."

Ethan looked surprised. "You know about that?"

"Where is the rifle?"

"Luke. He has it. I was trying to get to him when I ended up here. But don't worry. I'll make a deal with them and get you and Dillon out of this." His gaze softened as he took a step toward her. "You look great."

She let out a snort.

"Really, pregnancy makes you even more beautiful."

"Save your breath, Ethan."

He bowed his head for a moment. "I know you hate me. I don't blame you. But I had to get away from you to keep you safe."

"Do I look safe, Ethan?"

"You can't blame all this on me. What are you doing in Greybull?"

"Isn't it obvious? Looking for you. I have something I need you to sign." She picked up her purse, dug out the form. It probably wouldn't matter now, but she wanted him to sign it. Needed him to. The form was wrinkled, but she smoothed it out on the bed and handed him a pen. "Sign it."

He took the pen, his gaze locked with hers for a moment, before he picked up the form and read it. His blue eyes lifted to meet hers again.

"This is what you want even if I get us out of here?"

"You and I are done."

He gave her a slight nod. His smile was heart-rending but resigned. "I'm sorry I had to take your money. I offered it to Halbrook, but unfortunately, he seems to want more than his money back."

"*You think?* I doubt Halbrook is going to be happy until we're all dead because of you."

He took the form over to the small desk and signed it, then he returned the pen and paper to her. "There you go. You won't ever have to see me again after this."

Tessa stared at the man, wondering how she could have fallen for him. She'd always been driven, had been forced to be that way to survive. So falling for a man who was just the opposite probably made some kind of weird sense. At least, if it was true opposites really did attract.

But Ethan and all his good-ol'-boy charm hid a lack of integrity, honor and substance. It was as if Dillon had gotten all of those things and Ethan had been overlooked entirely.

"I wish there was some way I could make all this

up to you," Ethan said. "I really did want to change because of you and the baby."

There was the sound of the dead bolt on the door being thrown back. The door opened and a figure filled it. Tessa caught the glint of a gun in the man's hands.

"The boss wants to talk to you," the man said, motioning to Ethan.

He nodded as if this came as no surprise. But before he left, he moved to Tessa and planted a kiss on her cheek before she could avoid it. "I will always love you and I'll do what I can to keep you safe," he whispered. Then he turned to grin at the man in the doorway. "Let's not keep the boss waiting."

ETHAN DIDN'T FALTER until he was outside the room. He stumbled. One of the men tried to grab him. "Keep your hands off me," he snapped and jerked free. He wanted to put his fist through a wall or wail like a wounded animal. But he could do neither.

He'd seen the look on Tessa's face when she'd first seen him. She'd thought he was Dillon. Dillon come to save her. Once she'd realized her mistake…

He swore under his breath, telling himself that all he could do was try to convince Halbrook that he would get the rifle and bring it to him—if he let Tessa go.

"Hey, Hal, how's it goin'?" he said into the receiver.

Halbrook Truman let out a string of curses before he said, "I should have let them kill you."

"Yeah, but I might be the only person who can get your rifle back. You know I've been trying to."

"And apparently failing. Why didn't you mention you had a twin brother who was an undersheriff?"

"It just never came up in polite conversation."

"Now he's *involved*." Halbrook swore some more. "Tom Grady at least was helpful."

"Before you killed him," Ethan said, but the rancher either didn't hear him or ignored him.

"Tom told me where we can find Luke—and the rifle," Halbrook was saying. "But unfortunately, I'm afraid he might have also told your brother. With your brother involved, that complicates things."

"Let me worry about my brother. I will get you the rifle and make sure my brother doesn't bother you any further. But you have to do something for me."

Halbrook instantly went off again. "You aren't in any position to—"

"This is a deal breaker, Hal," Ethan interrupted. "And without me, you aren't going to get the Henry back. By now my brother could have already found Luke and be in possession of the rifle. He's a lawman first and foremost."

"What do you want?" the older man snapped.

"Let Tessa go. Hell, man, she's about to pop any moment. Have your men drive her to the hospital and leave her there. I will deal with my brother. I promise you, you will get your rifle back."

"You promise?" Halbrook let out a bark of a

laugh. "A promise from Ethan Lawson. Now, there's something I can take to the bank."

"I haven't lied to you yet," Ethan said. "But time is a-wasting. I can tell you exactly what my brother will do if he gets his hands on that rifle."

"Let me tell you how this is going down. Luke apparently has been hiding out at a place called the Tomahawk Lodge down there in Wyoming. Ashley is with him." Halbrook sounded as if he was gritting his teeth. "Tessa isn't going anywhere until I know you are in possession of the rifle. As you say, this is a deal breaker. If you refuse to do this, I'll take care of all of you my own way."

Ethan hadn't expected Halbrook to let Tessa go, but it had been worth a shot. "You just make sure nothing happens to her. If it does—"

"I'm tired of being threatened by you and your brother. You have only yourself to blame for this mess. Put Gus on."

"Which one is Gus? The big ugly one? Or the little ugly one?" Ethan asked, turning to look at the two men standing nearby.

"You really don't have a lick of sense, do you?" Halbrook said. "The big ugly one who is about to thump you."

Ethan laughed. "Seems he wants to talk to you." He handed over the phone and waited with his heart in his throat. He listened to Halbrook chew out the man. Apparently things weren't going the way Hal had hoped.

DILLON FOUND HIMSELF driving slower and slower. Snow whipped across the road, swirling around him, making it next to impossible to tell where the narrow highway started and ended.

The drive should have taken an hour. Instead, hours had passed and he still wasn't near the summit yet.

The snow was getting deeper. He saw where the plow had gone through earlier, leaving only a single lane. Not that it seemed to matter. He hadn't seen another vehicle since he'd left Greybull.

He kept thinking of Tessa. He couldn't help worrying. What if she had the baby? The highway had narrowed as it began to climb in a series of tight switchbacks. He could see why the road wasn't open in the winter. Snow was still piled high on each side of the road where the plow had come through earlier.

Was this really where he could find Luke, and ultimately Ethan? Dillon was having his doubts as the landscape looked more wintry as he drove. Tom must have known he was dying when he'd told him about the Tomahawk Lodge. Would a dying man lie to protect his friends? But they weren't his friends. He'd already ratted them out.

Still, he might have lied. Ethan had lied to all of them. Dillon still had trouble believing his brother was alive. Or maybe it was believing that his twin would put him through what he had a year ago. He'd thought he'd buried him. He'd thought he'd lost him for good.

Ethan was still lost to him, he realized. Tessa had seen him across the street and yet Ethan hadn't contacted them. He silently cursed his brother for hurting Tessa. Worse, for involving her in his mess.

"I never had a dog."

The words this morning at breakfast had taken him by surprise.

"A dog?" he'd asked, thinking he must have heard Tessa wrong.

She'd nodded. "All my friends had gotten puppies but my grandmother was allergic. At least that's what she said. She had cats. I always wanted a dog. My daughter will have one."

She had said it with such defiance that Dillon had laughed.

"I'll make sure she has a puppy," he'd promised.

Tessa had said nothing. In the silence that had followed, he'd realized she might not want him in her baby's life any more than she said she wanted Ethan.

As he remembered the conversation from earlier, he was reminded that sometimes he forgot that he was a constant reminder of Ethan's betrayal because, at least on the surface, he was just like his twin.

He couldn't think about that now, he told himself as the road began to flatten out, the snow falling harder. Since this highway had connected with Alternate Highway 14 a few miles back, he'd seen only one set of tire tracks ahead of him.

As the storm got worse, Dillon's doubts grew. What if Tom had set him up? Or sent him on a wild-

goose chase while Ethan, Luke and Ashley disappeared again?

All possible, he thought as he kept driving. He
had to believe that a dying man, one who had obviously been double-crossed, wouldn't lie.

Dillon was counting on that being true for Tessa
and her baby's sake.

TESSA DIDN'T KNOW how many hours had passed. The
room they'd put her in was dark and cold. She'd finally climbed under the covers on the bed to stay
warm. She'd also found that if she lay down, the
cramping stopped.

The baby had quieted down as well, which scared
her until she felt her daughter move again. She tried
hard not to be afraid. Seeing Ethan had upset her,
but not for the reasons she would have thought. He'd
signed away his rights to their daughter—what man
did such a thing?—and yet she was thankful. Ethan
knew himself, knew he couldn't be a father for this
baby.

So where was Dillon? She knew he was looking for her. He would turn this town upside down
until he found her. She had no idea how far out of
town the van had driven before they'd reached this
house. It wouldn't be easy to find. She shoved that
thought away.

When she'd first been brought to the room, she'd
gone right to the window and looked out. All she'd
seen was snow. The window was apparently the only

way out and it was definitely too small for her to escape in her condition. So she'd paced, until she realized she was probably making the cramping worse.

For a while, she'd thought Ethan would come back. He hadn't. Nor had she heard any movement beyond her room. Had they just left her here?

Tessa refused to let her mind wander down that path. She thought instead of the day she and Dillon had danced in the kitchen at the ranch, and felt her eyes fill with tears. Dillon had never made her feel large and awkward, even though she certainly felt that way being so pregnant.

Dillon, with all his patience and his kindness, was the man she'd wished Ethan had been. He would find her. But would he find her soon enough?

The baby began to move, reassuring her, but also worrying her, because a few moments later, she felt the cramps start up again.

ETHAN KNEW HALBROOK was right as he was dropped off at his pickup at the motel. He'd made this mess. It didn't matter that for the first time in his life he'd been trying to fix something he'd regretted doing.

Now everything was even more complicated, with his brother the lawman looking for the rifle. Dillon must have thought the same thing he had. Get the rifle, settle up with Halbrook and make all of this go away for Tessa and the baby.

The only problem now was if Dillon got to the rifle first, he wouldn't want to hand it over. His straight-shooter brother would go after Halbrook Truman with a vengeance.

But what bothered him more than he wanted to admit was the memory of the look on Tessa's face when she'd thought it was Dillon coming to save her. He'd seen the disappointment before even the anger. Not that he blamed her. Everything she'd said about him was true.

All he could do now was try to keep his brother and Tessa and the baby from getting killed. He knew he would die trying, because what he'd told Tessa was the truth. He would always love her and always regret the life he'd lived before he'd met her. If he could do it all over... But he couldn't, he thought as he drove through the raging snowstorm.

He reached the edge of town and the turnoff, but went only a short way before he saw the flashing lights ahead and swore. Across the road, a barricade had been placed. It read Highway Closed.

The damned storm, he thought. He'd heard on the radio that a foot of snow was expected in the valley, with two to three feet in the mountains.

Stopping a few feet short of the barricade, he stared out into the storm, trying to decide what to do now. Luke had been ahead of him. He would have managed to get through before the highway department closed the road more than a couple hours ago.

Dillon would have gotten through, too. According to Halbrook and what he'd gathered from his goons, Luke, Ashley and Dillon had gone to Tomahawk Lodge. That was hours ago. He could already be too late to help his brother—let alone get the rifle and save Tessa and the baby.

Then again, they could all be caught in the storm up in the Big Horn Mountains. Ethan told himself there was nothing he could do. He would be a fool to go around the barricade and try to reach the lodge.

His only other option was waiting until morning and hoping the road would be open. By then, it would definitely be too late, he thought, remembering how Tessa had held her stomach as he was leaving the room.

He had no choice. He drove around the barricade and headed for the mountains, praying he could get through at all—let alone get there in time.

CHAPTER TWENTY-THREE

ETHAN TOOK A corner in the snowy highway and felt the back end of this pickup start to come around. He let up on the gas and straightened it out again. He knew he was driving too fast, but once he'd gotten up on top, there had been only a few tracks ahead of him in the new snow.

He had no way of knowing if either of them was Dillon's or Luke's, but he'd driven as fast as possible and felt as if he might be catching up to them. The falling snow was hypnotic. He kept fighting the feeling, trying to keep his mind active, as if the dangerous driving wasn't enough to keep him alert.

He thought of when he and Dillon were boys growing up. It always surprised him that Dillon was the one with the bad memories. Sure, the old man had been tough on him, but Ethan thought he'd had it coming. Burt Lawson believed in the old expression Spare the Rod, Spoil the Child.

Ethan was okay with that, at least with his growing up. He wouldn't feel that way with the baby he and Tessa had made, though. He would protect that child, probably to the ruination of her, just as his brother had protected him. But kids needed discipline and stability. Another reason Dillon would make a good father.

He thought of Tessa. Of course she was furious with him. It was the least of what he had expected. He'd always liked her fire. But he sensed she was also over him, probably had been for months. He'd known she would be able to take care of herself—if she didn't find the photo and ultimately find Dillon.

He'd also known she would go looking for him. The form she'd dug out of her purse was no surprise. He'd been happy to sign it, knowing it was for the best. Tell that to his heart, though.

The only thing that gave him any consolation was that she wouldn't be alone. She had Dillon now. She hadn't had much family growing up. He'd known she would want all she could get for the baby. Now, if his brother didn't blow it by getting himself killed, everything would work out.

FROM WHAT DILLON could tell, it appeared only two vehicles were ahead of him. The SUV plowed through the drifts, snow blowing up, blinding him. The wipers worked furiously to clear the windshield, the visibility clearing one moment and nothing but white the next.

The climb up out of the Big Horn Basin had been a white-knuckle series of switchbacks, but now, finally on top, all he had was the blowing snow to contend with.

Fortunately, he didn't have to go far before he

reached an area with tall pines on each side of the road. The trees kept the wind from drifting snow across the highway, making the visibility better.

A few more miles up the road, just when he was worried that he'd missed it, Dillon caught a glimpse of the sign through the falling snow.

The sign was weathered, the once-painted letters faded and almost unreadable, but he could make out the name. Tomahawk Lodge.

He slowed as another sign appeared out of the storm. Horses for Rent, Tomahawk Lodge. This sign leaned as if always fighting a fierce wind. Like the other one, the lettering was faded, a symbol of another time now lost.

Ahead, he caught sight of something large and dark beside the road. A dark-colored pickup immerged from the storm. He slowed even more, barely crawling now, and spotted a structure back in the woods.

As he pulled up behind the pickup, his headlights filled the cab. It was empty. He turned off his lights and motor and sat for a moment, listening.

The snow fell in a shroud-like silence that was unnerving. He wouldn't be able to see anyone coming at him until it was too late. But then neither would they, he thought as he checked his gun, put on his hat and climbed out.

The boot tracks in the snow at the pickup were still fresh enough that they hadn't filled in with snow. Two sets of tracks. One larger than the other.

As he walked around the front of the truck, he saw the busted-out headlight, the dented bumper, and felt his pulse kick up a beat.

Whoever had been driving this pickup had killed Tom Grady.

He looked up the snow-filled road to the lodge. It hadn't been plowed when the highway had reopened after winter. Several trees had fallen across the road, making it impossible to drive down it even if winter's deep snowfall wasn't still lying in it.

The two separate boot tracks from the pickup had gone up the road through the new snow. He began to follow them, his gaze going from the tracks to what he could see of the lodge ahead.

A series of small older cabins sat back in the pines with one main lodge building, some small outbuildings and a large old barn. He moved toward the main lodge through the silent pines, snow drifting down around him. But as he neared, he saw that it was boarded up tight. No footprints in the snow to it.

Instead, the tracks headed toward the cabins in the woods. He caught a glimpse of a light through the pines and snow. Someone was in one of the cabins. Following the tracks, he headed toward it.

Back in the pines, the visibility improved enough that he could see other cabins appear as he walked. The snow glare made an eerie light. Not like daylight and not like darkness, either. The mountaintop was caught in a cold, white place somewhere between them.

Most of the weathered log cabins had once been boarded up. Some looked as if the shutters had been torn down by trespassers, their doors standing open, snow piled inside.

A golden slat of light glowed behind one of the shuttered windows of the cabin where the footprints had lead. Dillon moved quickly through the storm to the corner of the building. The cabin was small, reminiscent of those the KOA campgrounds rented. It had a tiny porch. No back door.

Listening, he heard no voices. He pulled his gun and inched along the edge of the cabin. The lantern light inside flickered as if in a breeze. He pressed his face to the crack and peered in. A curse escaped his lips. In the distance, he heard a vehicle on the highway. Luke Blackwell and Ashley Rene Clarkson didn't hear a thing. They were both dead.

THE CLOSER ETHAN got to the Tomahawk Lodge, the more he remembered what Luke had told him about it. Luke had spent summers up there working for his uncle. He was in charge of the horses, something he'd actually liked.

"I had this place in the barn where I used to hide out and smoke weed," Luke had said. "It was great. I had my first girl in that room," he'd added with a laugh. "A tourist girl. Sweet sixteen. I really hated it when my uncle closed the lodge. I used to sneak out at night when my uncle was asleep. There was this back way by the barn."

Ethan saw the first sign announcing the now defunct Tomahawk Lodge, and pulled over to the edge of the highway.

The back way brought me out right by the first sign to the lodge. I could always hitch a ride into town from there.

He grabbed his flashlight, jumped out and took off through the snow in the direction of the lodge. As luck would have it, he found the back road and caught sight of the barn through the storm. Part of the barn roof had caved in, but otherwise it was still standing.

Ethan hurried to it, pushed open the door, snapped on his flashlight and ventured in. It was cold and dark inside, with an empty vast feel that was chilling all by itself.

A padlock hung open from the door of the only small room in the barn Ethan could find. His heart dropped at the sight. If the rifle had been here, someone had already gotten it.

When Luke had told him about the room in the barn, he'd envisioned it as being much cooler than it was. The room smelled musty with just a hint of aged manure.

"How romantic," Ethan said as he shone the flashlight beam around the old tack room. Luke would have hidden the rifle here, Ethan knew that much about him, because he would never have trusted Ashley.

He was counting on Luke still having the rifle. It was the one thing that would keep Ashley with him.

She had to know how Tom felt about her. He was a much better bet than Luke—unless she was counting on Luke eventually selling the Henry and taking her to South America, like he'd been promising.

The rifle wasn't there. No big surprise, given the open padlock.

As he stepped out of the room, he saw something he'd missed. An alcove on the outside of the tack room. It was just wide enough for a rifle. Why Luke would have put the rifle there of all places, Ethan had no idea, but as he shone his light into the dark crevice, he saw the old Indian blanket that the rifle had been wrapped in.

It took a moment to work it out of the hole. This wasn't like Luke at all. Was it possible someone else had hidden it here? Once Ethan had it out, he laid the bundle down on the soft dirt floor of the barn and peeked inside the blanket. He smiled, relief flooding him as he looked at the old Henry, but only for a moment. He felt rather than heard someone come into the barn.

THE REPORT OF a gunshot filled the air, making Dillon jump. He pressed himself against the side of the cabin for a moment, trying to figure out where the shot had come from and, more to the point, if it had been directed at him.

The second shot sounded farther away. Through the falling snow, he saw tracks leading away from the cabin where Luke and Ashley had been killed. They led in the direction the shots had come from.

As he edged around the corner of the cabin, he saw that the tracks headed into the woods in the direction of the barn. He caught glimpses through the falling snow of the large old barn.

Dillon moved quickly along the edge of the pines. He felt his phone vibrate and started to check it when another shot filled the air. This shot had come from inside the barn.

Ignoring the phone, he ran to the barn, leaning into the side of it as he listened. There were two sets of tracks in the snow, both fresh. Holding his weapon at the ready, he slipped into the cavernous cold of the massive structure and almost fell over a body.

A man lay dead just feet inside the barn. As his eyes adjusted to the darkness, he saw that it wasn't Ethan. It wasn't anyone he recognized. Relief washed over him. He'd come so far to find Ethan—

A flashlight beam suddenly snapped on, illuminating a corner of the barn. He watched as his brother shone the light on the ground, then knelt down to pick up something from a blanket spread there.

Even if he hadn't seen the way Ethan held the rifle, almost with reverence, he would have known it was Halbrook's antique Henry .44 rimfire.

NETTIE HAD BEEN on pins and needles all day. She'd had no choice but to open the store. She didn't want to bring any more attention to herself than she had to.

All day she'd expected Deputy Bentley Jamison to drive up and arrest her. Every time the bell jangled over the front door, she'd jumped. She knew she'd gained a dozen grey hairs today.

To make matters worse, she hadn't been able to reach Frank. She'd called his landline at the house and his cell. Having watched enough crime scene investigation kind of shows on television, she knew better than to leave a message that could get either of them into trouble. Nor had she called more than a couple times. That, too, might make them look suspicious.

She knew she was being paranoid, but there was a killer out there. Maybe two, if the man who killed Billy wasn't the same one who'd killed Pam. Nettie had thought a lot about who might have killed Pam. The father of her baby? The one thing she didn't believe any longer was that Pam had had someone kill her just to frame Frank. Not since she had turned out not to be sick and dying but instead pregnant with another child.

Nettie was glad when she could lock up the store. It had been raining all day, so store traffic had been light—if not almost nonexistent. She had spent too much of the day going over last night in her mind. She needed a nice glass of wine and to go home and sit in front of the fireplace with her feet up and relax.

She would be glad when Frank returned. She really needed to talk to him, she thought as she hurried through the rain to her house on the mountainside above the store.

Once inside, she quickly built a fire in the fireplace and, kicking off her shoes, went to the kitchen for the wine. She had to turn on lights even though it was still early. The storm had made the day dark and dreary, as if it hadn't been already.

The wind rattled the shutters and made the house creak. Nettie had never minded living here alone since Bob had left. She'd felt more alone when her ex-husband had been here.

But tonight she felt anxious. When she'd opened the store this morning, she'd expected Judge Bull Westfall to show up and read her the riot act. But she had seen neither hide nor hair of him. He had to know why she'd been to see his sister. Not that she'd gotten any information from her—well, at least not what she'd gone there looking for anyway.

But she could see how Pam might have been able to swindle Charlotte out of her money. The woman was addled as could be, and who knew how long she'd been that way?

A gust of wind rattled the windows. A pine branch scraped against the side of the house an instant before lightning lit the dark sky. Nettie jumped as thunder boomed so close it made the hair stand up on the back of her neck.

Frank, she saw, had finally texted to say Tiffany was in trouble. He was at the state mental hospital and would call her later.

Another jagged flash of lightning. This time the thunder sounded as if it was right over her head. Rain began to fall harder, pelting drops that beat at the windows.

If only Frank would call. She needed to hear his voice. As if willing it, the phone rang. She picked up. "Hello?" Another bolt of lightning lit the sky outside her window. Thunder boomed. "Frank?" She heard the soft click of someone hanging up.

LOST IN ADMIRING the weapon, Ethan didn't hear his brother approach until Dillon was only feet away.

Ethan spun, bringing up the rifle to point it at him. "I wondered when I would see you."

"I wondered the same thing," Dillon said, feeling his anger bubble up. His brother looked good, certainly not as bad as a man who had put his family through hell should.

"Put down the rifle, Ethan. Even if it was loaded, you know you aren't going to use it."

His brother chuckled. "If you were sure of that, you would have already taken it away from me."

"That you let me think you were dead for the past year… That aside, how could you do what you did to Tessa and that baby girl she's carrying? How could you, Ethan?"

"So it's a girl, huh?"

"Give me the rifle. I don't have much time."

His brother looked past him in the direction of the barn door and the dead man.

He noticed the blood on Ethan's clothing. Something deep inside him curled up and died. "What were you going to do with the rifle?"

"What do you mean?"

"Were you going to use it to rescue Tessa? Or were you going to skip out on her again?"

"How can you ask that?"

"Because you're the last one alive who was involved with the theft."

"Luke and Ashley?"

"Both dead. But you wouldn't know anything about that."

"No, I wouldn't."

Dillon shook his head. "It doesn't make any sense. Why would Halbrook Truman, even with his ego, take a chance on killing so many people?"

Ethan looked past him again.

"What is really going on?" Dillon demanded, remembering Halbrook's surprise when he'd told him Tom Grady was dead.

"I might have gotten involved with the wrong people."

Dillon let out a bitter laugh. "The body I buried is Buck Morgan, right?"

"Buck was just in the wrong place at the wrong time," Ethan said.

"And Luke and Ashley?"

Ethan glanced away for a moment. "I would imagine Luke thought that man over by the door of the barn was sent by Halbrook. He probably drew down on him. Luke was that way."

"That man doesn't work for Halbrook?"

Ethan shook his head.

"So you got them all killed. You never answered me. What were you planning to do with the rifle?"

"Originally? I was going to sell it, take the money and try to pay off some drug lords I inadvertently got involved with."

He shot Ethan a look. *"Drugs?"*

"I wasn't selling them. I just came across a duffel bag full of money, that's all."

Dillon glanced at the duffel bag Ethan had put between his boots. "Is that the money?"

He shook his head. "I gave them back their money, but I guess there is some principal involved. The fact that I took it knowing it was theirs…" He shrugged. "They tend to hold a grudge, it seems."

"So what's in the duffel bag?"

Ethan glanced down at the bag at his feet. "Close to twenty-five thousand dollars. Don't give me that look. It's mine— Well, most of it I saved. I borrowed some from Tessa. I came up here to get the rifle back. I didn't think Luke would just hand it over. I had planned to try to buy it from him—if appealing to his better nature didn't work."

Clearly his brother hadn't thought out a lot of things. "If I hadn't found you in the barn, would you really have taken the rifle to rescue Tessa?" He saw the hesitation in his brother's eyes and swore.

"I would have," Ethan argued. "I might not be good enough for her, but I do care."

"You have a funny way of showing it, but Tessa loves you."

Ethan laughed. "She loved the part of me that is like you." He shook his head.

"So it was the drug cartel that tried to kill you down in Arizona, not Halbrook?"

His brother nodded. "I thought it was Halbrook at first."

"But Halbrook's men are who have Tessa, right?" His brother nodded. "Give me the rifle, Ethan."

"I can't do that, bro. You don't really think that all you have to do is hand over the rifle and Halbrook's men are just going to say thank-you, now take your woman?"

"*Your* woman, Ethan."

He shook his head. "She's too good for me and we both know it."

"She's carrying *your* baby."

Ethan looked as if he was going to deny it.

"If you dare say that baby isn't yours I swear I will shoot you."

His brother laughed, a familiar and yet heartbreaking sound in the cold empty space. "I was just going to say Tessa and the baby would both be better off without me. I'm not cut out for marriage, let alone fatherhood."

"I don't believe that. I think you love her or you wouldn't have been trying to get the rifle back."

"Maybe I was just trying to save my own neck. Either way, I can't give you the rifle. This is something I have to do. The men who have Tessa won't hurt her. They just want the rifle. These other guys…" He shrugged.

Dillon swore. "Tessa could be having your baby right—" He caught movement behind his brother. "Ethan!" A wounded man stumbled into the barn. He was holding his side with one hand, a gun in the other.

As Dillon started to fire around his brother, Ethan stepped between them. "I thought I killed you," Ethan said and raised the rifle.

Dillon yelled, "No!" sure the rifle his brother held wouldn't be loaded. He jumped to the side to try to get off a shot.

There was the click of the empty rifle as Ethan pulled the trigger, and the boom of the other man's gun, followed in a breath by Dillon's shot.

The man staggered, started to fire again then dropped.

Dillon ran to his brother, who had fallen to his knees. He was bleeding from the gunshot wound to his chest.

"Hang on. I'll take you to the hospital—"

"No, go get Tessa. Don't worry about me."

"If you think I'm leaving you here, then you don't

know me." Dillon helped his brother to his feet and picked up the rifle from the ground.

Ethan chuckled. "You just can't help being the good guy, can you, Dillon?"

CHAPTER TWENTY-FOUR

WHEN FRANK CALLED Lynette, she sounded strange. "Is everything all right?"

"Did you call me about thirty minutes ago?"

"No, why?"

"It was probably nothing."

She didn't sound as if it had been nothing. "I'm sorry I couldn't call sooner. It sounds like it's storming there."

"Raining cats and dogs."

"Lynette, what's wrong?"

A few minutes later, after she'd told him about going to Billy's office to get the file, Frank bellowed, "You did *what?* Have you lost your mind?"

"I didn't have to break into Billy's office, as it turned out," she said quickly. "The door was open. Billy was in there sleeping off a drunk."

Frank swore. "Lynette, you're scaring me. I got a call this morning from Deputy Jamison. He told me Billy committed suicide around 1:00 a.m., so what are you trying to tell me?"

"Billy didn't kill himself," Lynette cried. "I was there. I heard the whole thing."

"What are you talking about, Lynette? What do you mean you were *there?*"

"How was I to know that someone was going to come to the office and kill him?"

"Just tell me what happened." He listened as she told him.

"I took her file but there is nothing in it that tells us any more than we already knew. I wasn't going to look, but when I couldn't reach you…"

Frank groaned. "Why do I suspect there's more to your story that you're not telling me? Lynette, listen to me. Whatever you took, don't do anything with it until I get there. Do you hear me?"

"Yes. Where are you?"

"As you know from my text, Tiffany tried to escape last night. She… Well, she's in much worse trouble. I drove up here thinking I could help, but they haven't let me see her."

"You should stay there and see her, then."

"I'm much more worried about you. At least Tiffany is locked up in a room where she can't hurt herself. You, on the other hand—"

"I won't do anything until I see you. Frank? I'm sorry. I was just trying to help. I love you."

"I know, Lynette." He sighed. "I love you, too. I'm almost home. I'll be in Beartooth within the hour."

DILLON LOOKED OVER at his brother in the passenger seat. He'd bandaged Ethan up as best he could. Now all he could do was get to the hospital as quickly as possible. He could see life seeping out of him.

He prayed Tessa was safe and that Ethan was right about the men not hurting her. As long as she didn't go into labor...

"This is like when we were boys," Ethan said.

Dillon wasn't in the mood to reminisce right now. "Why didn't you tell anyone you had a twin brother? You didn't even tell Tessa."

"Maybe I didn't want to bring my troubles down on you."

He knew that wasn't it, because ultimately Ethan had sent Tessa to him. "I never understood why you hated being a twin."

"But then you met Tessa," Ethan said.

Dillon shot him a surprised look.

His brother let out a laugh that turned into a pained gurgle.

"You shouldn't try to talk," Dillon said, wishing he hadn't brought it up.

But Ethan had never taken any advice from him and didn't now. "Trust me, she knows the difference between us. When I saw her where they're keeping her? At first she thought I was you. She started to run to me.... It only took her a second, though, before she realized her mistake." He laughed. "Then she let me know what she thought of me."

"She was all right when you saw her?" He hated that his voice gave away just how worried he was about her and more.

"Yeah." He could feel Ethan's gaze on him. "She's amazing, isn't she?"

Dillon didn't answer. He concentrated on the road, praying Tessa would be safe and that they would be able to rescue her without anyone else getting killed.

NETTIE HUNG UP from talking to Frank. Outside, the wind whipped the pine boughs and slung rain against the windows. The storm seemed to have centered itself over the Crazies, which meant the thunder and lightning were too close for comfort.

She threw more wood on the fire and poured herself another glass of wine, promising herself that was all she would drink. She knew she would need her senses about her when Frank arrived. He'd been upset with her, but who could blame him?

Another flash of lightning lit the room, followed by thunder that rattled the windows. The lights flickered. "Don't you dare go out," she said to the overhead fixture. She was getting up to make sure she had candles ready just in case when she practically jumped out of her skin at the loud knock at her door.

Nettie couldn't imagine what anyone would be doing out on a night light this. She thought of Deputy Sheriff Bentley Jamison and braced herself as she went to the door.

She was instantly relieved to see that it wasn't the deputy, but equally surprised to find Judge Bull Westfall's wife standing on her doorstop. "Cora?"

The tiny gray-haired woman had the usual vague expression on her face. "May I come in, Nettie, dear?" she asked in her small voice from under her umbrella.

Nettie looked past her, expecting to see Bull, but the woman's husband apparently hadn't come with her.

"Of course, I'm sorry. Please come in."

Cora stopped on the porch to shake out her umbrella before leaving it under the porch roof. She glanced into the house as she wiped her feet on the mat and entered.

"Are you alone?" she asked. "I thought Frank might be here."

"He went to see his daughter."

Cora nodded, giving Nettie the impression that she somehow already knew that. Her suspicious mind wondered if that had been Cora who'd called earlier. The number on the phone had been blocked.

As she closed the door behind them, Nettie wondered what was so important that Cora would venture out on a night like this. "I could put on some coffee—"

Cora waved the invitation away. "I wanted to talk to you about Pam Chandler. It won't take long."

Nettie had been curious before. Now she couldn't stand the suspense. If anyone knew about Pam, it might be Cora. She'd known the woman since Pam had come to town years ago. The woman lowered herself to the edge of the couch, clutching her purse in front of her as if she might get up and leave at any moment.

Nettie quickly took a seat, impatient to hear what had brought Cora out on a night like this.

"I heard you visited Charlotte."

She nodded. "I saw Bull there."

"He told me." She pursed her lips. "He is so protective of her, the poor dear."

While the words sounded compassionate, something in her tone said just the opposite. "Since I'm unaware that you have ever visited my sister-in-law before, did you get what you went there for?" Cora asked, and there was no doubt about the sharp edge to her tone now.

Feeling a little uncomfortable, Nettie decided rather than beat around the bush, she'd come right out with it. "I heard that Pam Chandler had swindled Charlotte out of all her money."

"If you heard it, then I can assume it's all over town."

Apparently the kid gloves were off. "Is that what you came to tell me?"

Cora shook her head. "I'm sure you know that Pam was very close to me and my family."

Nettie didn't like the way this conversation was going and decided it was time to cut it short. "You really didn't come all this way in a storm to tell me what a wonderful woman Pam was, did you? Because if that is the case, you've wasted your time." She was on her feet. "The woman tried to kill me, but that is nothing to what she's done to Frank and their daughter."

"Sit down, Nettie. I didn't come to sing Pam's praises. As well as I thought I knew Pam, Bull got to know her even better."

Nettie lowered herself back into the chair. "Are you saying what I think—"

"Please, did you really not know that she went after my husband?"

Nettie couldn't imagine Pam and Bull... "You mean, *romantically?*"

Cora laughed bitterly. "Is that what you call it when a gold digger tries to seduce your wealthy, older husband?"

"Surely Bull didn't—"

"He's a man, isn't he?" She sounded angry and impatient. "Close your mouth, Nettie. Yes, Pam had an affair with my husband."

"Then it was *Bull's* child she was carrying?" Nettie burst out.

"So you know about that, too. My, I have underestimated you, Nettie. You are a much more clever woman than I thought."

Nettie was confused why Cora Westfall was sharing such personal information with her. "Well, Pam didn't succeed in taking him away from you."

Cora gave her an impatient look. "Only because she's dead."

That sank in. "I should get us something to drink." Nettie started to rise when Cora's hand dipped into her purse.

"Please sit back down," the woman said as she pulled a small pistol from her purse and pointed it at Nettie's heart. "We aren't quite done here yet."

THE BABY WAS coming. Tessa breathed through the contraction. She'd pounded on the door, trying to get someone's attention. But when no one responded, she'd taken to the bed. She'd done everything she could to slow down her labor. She held no hope that Ethan would be back.

Dillon would find her, though. That thought kept her from getting more panicked than she already was. She'd prepared for the birth of the baby, getting towels ready. She found a nail clipper in her purse to cut the cord. Other than that, she didn't know what else she could do but pray.

As the contraction eased, she calmed herself by thinking again of when she and Dillon had danced in the kitchen at the ranch. She felt her eyes well with tears at the memory. He'd made her feel pretty that day, not large and awkward as pregnant as she was.

She thought of the kiss and had to wipe her tears. He would save her because that was what he did. But when he looked at her and her baby, he would always see Ethan between them.

Another contraction. The next pain doubled her over. She hugged her stomach, paralyzed with the pain and the realization that she and her baby were on their own.

NETTIE STARED AT the gun in Cora's hand, telling herself this wasn't happening.

"I just assumed Charlotte told you everything," Cora was saying.

"It must have been one of Charlotte's bad days," Nettie said as the pieces of the puzzle dropped into place. "*You* killed Pam and framed Frank for her murder?"

"He made it too easy, since if he had gotten to her first, I'm sure he would have killed her himself."

Nettie didn't argue the point. "But how did you get his gun?"

"Pam underestimated me. A lot of people do." Cora smiled. "She really thought Bull would leave me for her and her bastard child. When I agreed to meet her somewhere…private, I took my own weapon. I'd heard that Frank was claiming Pam not only beat him up but took his service pistol. I guess Frank was right because when I searched her purse, there it was. See what I mean about Frank making it too easy for me?"

"How does Billy fit into all of this?" Surely it

hadn't been tiny Cora she'd heard that night on the stairs going to Billy's office.

"You really can't believe I would kill my own grandson?"

Nettie wasn't sure what she believed. She'd never expected to see Cora holding a gun on her after admitting to killing Pam Chandler.

"But Billy is the one who was helping Pam."

Cora gave her another impatient look. "Did you really think Bull was the only man caught up in her web?"

Nettie stared at the gun. "I don't understand what you're doing here."

"Don't you?" Cora said. "You just can't keep your nose out of things. When I saw you at the grocery store the other day talking to the hired man who'd overheard Bull and I arguing about Pam, I knew I was going to have to do something about you. Then when Bull told me you'd been to see Charlotte…"

"But Charlotte didn't tell me anything, and neither did your hired man."

Cora smiled. "As if that would have been the end of you butting into things that don't concern you."

"I was only trying to help Frank Curry. Cora, you can't let Frank go to prison for something *you* did."

"I'm a murderess, Nettie. Everything else pales beside that. It's time to go down to the store."

Nettie looked at her to make sure she was being serious. "The *store?*"

"Yes, Nettie, you're about to be robbed and I really

would hate to soil such a beautiful carpet here at the house, but I will if you don't cooperate."

"It makes no sense to kill me," she said, stalling for time. Frank had said he would be here within the hour. But how long ago was that?

"I suggest you put on a coat—just as you would if you'd forgotten something at the store and decided to go back down in the storm. Or if you saw something suspicious down there."

"Cora, you won't get away with this. Frank will track you down if it is the last thing he—"

"Frank will be in prison, unless he gets the death penalty, and then he will be dead."

The words fell on Nettie like quarter-size hail. Cora *could* get away with this.

"You go first and, Nettie, don't do anything stupid. I don't want you to suffer because I was forced to wound you more than once."

It was the cold, calculated way Cora was going at this that turned Nettie's blood to ice and made her cooperate. She didn't doubt for a moment that Cora would shoot her as many times as it took.

"Remember Elizabeth?"

"Ethan, don't." Dillon stared at the road ahead. They were almost off the mountain. Dillon remembered seeing hospital signs. If he could just get Ethan to help, then find Tessa.... Hadn't the men said they would call?

"I lied, Dillon. She didn't know it was me that night. I know I told you she knew that she wanted the wild brother...."

"I'm not listening to this."

Ethan shook his head. "I have to tell you. That night—Elizabeth figured it out and demanded I take her home. She was so angry...."

Dillon felt his breath still, his heart a sledgehammer in his chest. "Don't."

"I said, 'Why him? Why not me?'"

He closed his eyes for a moment, hearing his brother's pain. Hadn't he suspected Ethan was in love with Elizabeth? "Ethan—"

"She told me there was something wrong with me. Something broken inside me."

"No, she was wrong. There was nothing—"

"And that it was why the old man loved you and hated me. That was why..." His brother's voice broke. "I'm why Mama died. She couldn't bear to think she'd raised a son like me." Ethan was crying now, his chest shuddering with his sobs.

"No, no," Dillon pleaded. He could see the lights of Greybull through the falling snow. Just a little farther. He thought he could never hate Elizabeth. He'd put her on a pedestal for years, holding her up against every woman he met. "She shouldn't have said that. She was wrong, Ethan. Ethan, are you listening to me? There was nothing wrong with you. You aren't broken. You were the gentle one, the loving one."

His brother shook his head. "I killed Elizabeth."

"Ethan—" His twin grabbed his arm, his fingers digging into his flesh.

"I have to tell you *now*." The urgency in his voice made Dillon swallow back his words. He didn't want to hear this. Not now. Maybe after Ethan was better. But as he looked into his brother's face, he knew Ethan wouldn't be getting better. This was going to be all they had.

"We were fighting. Elizabeth told me to stop the truck. I was driving too fast. She pleaded with me to slow down, but I was so angry."

"It was an accident."

Ethan shook his head. "She took off her seat belt and opened her door, threatening to jump out if I didn't slow down."

Dillon held his breath but he knew what was coming.

"I reached for her, but she didn't want *me* to touch her. She jerked away from me. I hit a bump and... and she was gone. I swerved and lost control of the truck."

"It was an accident." As he slowed at the edge of town, he reached over and brushed his brother's hair back. It had never been strange looking into a face so like his own. He loved Ethan's face and couldn't bear the thought that he might never look into it again.

His brother was trembling hard now. Dillon had pulled his jacket off and tucked it around him earlier. He saw that it was soaked with blood. "Did you hear me? It was an accident. You were never the bad one."

His brother's blue eyes shifted to him. He saw in that moment so much love that it would have buckled his knees if he hadn't been driving.

"Sorry. Here." The words came out a whisper from Ethan's trembling lips as he pressed something into his brother's hand. "Call the number. Tessa and the baby…"

"You don't have to worry about them. Once you're back on your feet—"

"Take care of them for me."

"You know I will. That's why you sent her to me."

His brother smiled. "She's a good woman."

"Yes."

Ethan held his gaze. "I knew I could depend on you. Here." He pressed a small pocket knife into Dillon's hand. "For luck. It once saved my life." Then he closed his eyes.

Dillon felt him go. *"Ethan! Ethan!"*

CHAPTER TWENTY-FIVE

THEY MOVED THROUGH the pouring rain, Cora holding her umbrella with one hand and the gun in the other. Nettie hadn't been allowed to grab her own umbrella.

"Really, Nettie, do I look that stupid to you? If I let you have anything you could use as a weapon, you'd be foolish enough to try to stop me. A little rain won't hurt you."

At the back door of the store, Nettie opened it and Cora shoved her inside. She turned on a light, her mind racing. There were all kinds of things she could use as a weapon now that they were in the store. Cora must have thought the same thing.

"Head right for the cash register," she said. "And please don't touch anything along the way. I have spent many hours shooting tin cans off the fence at the ranch. I won't miss."

At the cash register, Cora instructed her to get a can of peas from the shelf and break open the cash register.

"I'm supposed to be a rather stupid thief?" she asked Cora. "The cash register isn't locked. And why would I think there would be any money in it?"

"Because this is a small town. You don't make

enough to take the receipts into the bank in Big Timber every day, nor do you have a safe."

"I don't?"

Cora smiled. "You don't. You're a Montanan. You're very trusting and you've never been robbed. Until now."

Nettie hated that the woman was right. She retrieved a can of peas from the nearby counter. For a moment she considered throwing them and making a run for it, but when she met Cora's gaze, she saw that the woman was expecting just that.

She moved to the cash register and, clutching the can of peas in her hand, began to beat on the register until it finally broke open. Because she'd been busy, she hadn't emptied it, just as Cora has suspected. There was close to a hundred dollars in the till. Maybe Cora was right and a real thief wouldn't have bothered to try to open the cash register before beating it to death with a can of peas.

"Now take the money. You can put it in a shopping bag."

Nettie did as she was told.

"I'll take the bag. Thank you. Now get a roll of duct tape."

"Cora, this is silly. No one is going to believe this."

"Of course they will. This time of year there are all kinds of degenerates passing through the state, not to mention all those oil workers headed up north. Times are bad enough that I'm sure at least a few of them have had to knock over a little old store in the country for gas money. Now I want you to sit down on the floor and tape your ankles. Do them good and tight."

She had no choice. But she moved slowly, trying to give Frank a chance to reach Beartooth before Cora finished what she'd come to town to do.

With that done, Cora moved to her and, keeping the gun within her reach—not Nettie's—she taped Nettie's wrists.

"I just don't understand what you hope to accomplish here," Nettie said.

"I'm saving my family. That's what a woman does. She doesn't let anyone destroy her family."

"That explains why you killed Pam, but—"

"You were there the other night, the night Billy died in that horrible accident."

Nettie blinked. "How did you—"

"Bull smelled your perfume. He remembered it from when he caught you at Charlotte's house."

"*Bull* threw his grandson out the window?"

"It was an accident," Cora snapped. "Billy was drunk and Bull..." She shook her head. "Billy thought he could blackmail us. I don't know how he knew that I'd killed her, but he did. He was going to turn me in if Bull didn't give him money."

Bull's precious grandson, Nettie thought. No wonder he was so furious.

"If he had just listened to reason... It was a horrible accident," Cora repeated.

"Then what is the point of this?" Nettie demanded, motioning to the faux robbery scene.

"Billy's death has been ruled a suicide. You're the only one who can put Bull there that night. Without you…"

"I won't say a word."

Cora laughed. "Nettie Benton not saying a word?" She ripped off a piece of tape and plastered it across Nettie's mouth. "*Now* you won't say a word."

She rose to her feet, picked up her gun and the sack with the money in it. "Just a few things more and I'll be on my way. Sad," she said, looking around the store. "This place is such a landmark." She moved to the barbecue lighter fluid and matches.

"No!" Nettie tried to scream through the tape as Cora began to douse the hardwood floors and merchandise with the flammable liquid. Then she struck a match. There was a poof and a flash of light. An instantly later everything began to flame and burn.

"One last thing to take care of. Goodbye, Nettie."

Over the crackling of the flames, she could hear the woman in her office, ransacking it. Nettie scooted on her behind as far from the growing flames as she could. She fought the tape, but realized it was futile. The fire in the old building was spreading too quickly. She began to slide herself toward the hallway that led to the back door, praying Frank would arrive in time.

Nettie heard Cora still rummaging around in the

office. The flames licked closer, the smoke billowing up into a black cloud across the ceiling.

Sliding on her behind, Nettie inched her way down the hallway. If she could just reach the back door without Cora seeing her... The smoke was getting so thick, and with the tape on her mouth she couldn't cough, couldn't breathe.

She had to keep moving. As she scooted toward the door, she could still hear Cora in the office where the smoke wasn't so bad. Just a little farther. If she could reach the back door—

"Where do you think you're going?"

IT WAS LATE by the time Frank reached Beartooth. He'd been anxious to get to Nettie, but a semi rollover on Interstate 90 had held him up.

He was worried about her, and for good reason. She'd gone to Billy Westfall's office with every intention of breaking in and stealing Pam's file. He shook his head. He hadn't really thought she would go to such extremes.

That made him laugh. This was *Lynette*. She didn't do anything halfway. That thought made him smile. He couldn't wait to see her. They would sort this out and hopefully she wouldn't end up behind bars. Hopefully neither of them would.

He frowned as he came over a rise and saw smoke billowing up from what appeared to be the general store. He called it in, tromping down on the gas as he raced toward the store, all the time telling himself that Lynette was safe up at the house, when his instincts told him differently.

When he'd talked to her, she'd promised to stay at the house and wait for him. But this was Lynette. If she'd seen the flames, she would have headed for the store, sure as the devil.

Normally a near ghost town, Beartooth was like a tomb tonight, no doubt because of the pouring rain. Only a few pickups were parked down the street in front of the Range Rider bar. He swung in front of the café across the street from the store, killed the engine and the lights and jumped out.

A small river of water ran down the main street as he ran across. The front of the store was ablaze. He ran for the back door, praying Lynette wasn't inside.

At the door, he grabbed hold of the knob and pulled. The door swung open.

Frank would never forget that instant when he'd opened the back door of the store and seen Lynette bound on the floor and the flames rushing toward her. There'd been a rush of air. He'd heard a door slam. But all he'd been able to take in was Lynette gagged and bound on that floor.

He knew he must have frozen for a moment as smoke and heat rushed at him, he had been so shocked, but somehow he'd reached her before the flames had. Somehow he'd gotten her out of there.

If he'd reached her any later, she would have burned to death.

Frank ran out the back door with her in his arms,

into the pouring rain, and laid her down in the dried pine needles beneath a tree, out of the hardest of the rain.

For a moment, he'd been afraid she was dead. "Lynette! Lynette!" He'd been screaming her name like an insane man before he'd grabbed the tape over her mouth and ripped it off. She began to cough, heaving as he pulled out his pocket knife and cut her restraints.

"You're all right," he said, "you're all right," not sure if he was reassuring her or himself.

Nettie finally caught her breath and looked back at the store. He could feel the blistering heat even from here.

"Cora."

At first he didn't catch what she said. "What?"

"Cora Westfall. She's—" Lynette began coughing again, doubled over with it. "She's in the…office."

He looked toward the store, remembering a door slamming, remembering belatedly the stuck door. "Cora?" He started to get to his feet, but Lynette grabbed his pant leg. He knew she was right. There was no saving anyone inside that store. The entire structure was ablaze.

"I don't understand what Cora—"

"She tried to kill me."

He felt his eyes widen as he stared at her. *"Cora Westfall?"*

Lynette nodded. "She had a gun." She coughed. "Pam was pregnant with Bull's baby. She killed Pam.

Billy knew. Bull went to his office…" She began to cough again, but Frank was pretty sure he knew what was she was going to say. Bull and Billy had fought and Billy had gone out that window.

"Cora swears it was an accident, but Billy was blackmailing her and Bull."

In the distance, he heard the sound of sirens. Too late for the store. Too late for Cora. Bull must have helped Cora after he found out she'd shot Pam. Cora couldn't have gotten that body to the old mine on her own.

Fire trucks began to arrive, but there was no fighting the fire. Frank swept Lynette up in his arms and walked down the hillside toward the road and the flashing lights of the sheriff's department patrol SUV.

DILLON PLACED THE call to the number Ethan had given him. He tried not to look at his brother lying dead in the seat next to him. "I have your damned package. But you aren't getting it until I speak with Tessa."

"You aren't in any position—"

"I speak to her and right now or I am taking this rifle to the sheriff's department," Dillon interrupted. "What's it going to be?"

Silence, then, "Just a minute."

He waited, his heart in his throat. He could hear footfalls, then the opening of a lock and a door creaking open. "He wants to talk to you," the man said.

"Hello?" Tessa sounded as if she was in pain.

"Are you all right?" Dillon asked, fear edging his voice. "The baby?"

"I'm in labor. Please hurry. I'm not sure—"

"You talked to her," the man said after snatching the phone away from her. "I suggest you get here right away." He sounded panicky as he gave the directions to the house. Fortunately, the house was on the edge of town off the highway and sounded easy to find, because he had already hung up.

Dillon thought about calling the man back and demanding he take Tessa to the hospital, but he didn't have time to argue. After what Ethan had told him, he didn't think he would have any trouble once he reached the house. He would gladly give over the rifle, he thought as he found the road and turned down it. He would deal with Halbrook later.

The small house loomed ahead as he raced down the road toward it, praying Tessa and the baby were going to be all right.

When he saw the van with Montana plates from the Big Hole area, he first called 911 and requested an ambulance. Then he called the sheriff and gave him the plate number of the van, asking him to detain men and take possession of a stolen rifle.

He pulled up beside the house, jumped out with the rifle and ran toward the door. As he entered, he could hear Tessa in the back of the house, hear her cries. He swore as he shoved the rifle at the biggest of the men and stormed past. The door to the room where they had been keeping her was open. She lay on the bed, writhing in pain.

"We have to get her to a hospital," he cried to the men over his shoulder even as he heard them both hightailing it to their van. The engine turned over and the men took off, wanting nothing more to do with this.

Wouldn't they be surprised when they were pulled over before they crossed the state line?

Her water had broken and one look at her and he knew she was having the baby right here, right now. He'd hoped to get her out of there, one way or another, and take her to the hospital. But there wasn't time.

He took Tessa's hand. "It's going to be all right." As he squeezed her hand, he looked around, taking in what he could use in the room. The place was reasonably clean and there was a bathroom.

She smiled up at him, and then a contraction pinned her to the bed. He'd never birthed a baby. He'd given a couple sheriff's department escorts into Big Timber with his lights flashing and siren blaring, but that had been the extent of it. So this was going to be a first, he thought as he rolled up his sleeves and stepped to the sink to wash.

He saw that she'd gotten some towels and other items together. His hands had been shaking earlier; now they were still. He could do this. This was his niece. While he wanted Tessa in a clean, warm hospital with trained personnel who knew what they were doing, he would make do.

Tessa lay back on the pillow on the bed as the contraction finally ended. Her hair around her face was damp with perspiration. He stepped into the bathroom and got her a wet washcloth. While in there, he accessed the number of towels and anything else he could use.

In the medicine cabinet, he found a few first-aid items and took those back into the room. "Here," he said as he laid the wet washcloth on her forehead. She looked up at him, her big blue eyes wide with a new kind of fear.

"It's going to be all right," he assured her again. Or maybe he was assuring himself.

"Have you delivered a baby before?" she asked as another contraction started.

"I wanted my niece to be my first," he said, all hope of levity falling short as another contraction took her.

"I can feel the baby," she said between gasps. "It's coming!"

"Okay, I need to get you ready after this contraction."

He went into the bathroom and let the hot water run. There were a half dozen towels, all clean. He would need something to cut the umbilical cord. Nothing in the medicine cabinet. He'd seen a nail clipper by the bed. Tessa's? Had she planned to cut the cord with that?

He felt the knife in his pocket that Ethan had pressed into his hand. *For luck,* he'd said. *It once saved my life.*

Dillon opened the knife and dropped it into the steaming water as he heard Tessa cry out. He rushed in to find her partially sitting up. He could hear sirens in the distance. Too late to move Tessa. He caught sight of the top of the baby's head. His niece had a thick head of dark hair like her mother.

"I can see her," he told Tessa. "Get ready to push."

The baby's head emerged an instant before her little body came out in his hands. Dillon cradled it there for a moment before he hurried to cut the cord and wrap the child in a towel. A small cry escaped the baby's lips as he quickly turned her over and let the tiny infant take her first breath of air.

"Is she…?" Tessa cried as the EMTs came rushing in.

"She's perfect," Dillon said. "Beautiful. Just like her mother."

Tessa began to cry as he laid the baby on her chest and she got her first look at her daughter.

CHAPTER TWENTY-SIX

FRANK HELD NETTIE's hand as they gave their statements to Deputy Bentley Jamison. He'd taken them to a corner booth at the Branding Iron Café across the street. Once the café owner had been called about the fire, she'd come in from the ranch and opened the café up, serving hot coffee to the officers and firefighters.

Smoke billowed up from the charred remains into the dark, rainy night. Nettie could see law enforcement officers and firefighters moving around the black skeleton of what had been the Beartooth General Store for more than a hundred years.

"Has Bull been picked up yet?" Frank asked.

Jamison shook his head. "I sent someone out to inform him and bring him in for questioning but I suspect he'd heard about the fire, already heard…" He hesitated to say it. "Heard about his wife. The ranch hands said he'd saddled up and ridden up into the Beartooths. As soon as it is light, I'll send some men up to look for him."

Frank nodded, but Nettie doubted they would find him alive. The man had lost everything that mattered to him. She'd overhead a deputy tell Jamison that the ranch hands had said that all Bull had taken with him was his pistol. He hadn't even taken his dog along.

"Once the dust settles, you'll be reinstated," Jamison said. "It will be nice to have you back, Sheriff." He stood and shook Frank's hand.

As Jamison left, Nettie turned to watch the men working across the street in their dark hooded rain jackets, flashlights flickering like fireflies. When she saw the coroner's van back up to what had been the front of the store, she looked away.

"Are you all right?" Frank asked, squeezing her hand.

She felt numb. Frank had insisted she have an EMT check her out before he would let the deputy ask her questions. Her throat felt raw, her wrists and ankles ached from the duct tape, but mostly she felt numb inside. She knew that tomorrow it would hit her. All of it. The almost dying, the loss of the one constant in her life, the store. Cora. She told herself she hadn't heard the woman screaming over the crackling of the flames, but she knew she would once she closed her eyes and tried to sleep.

Nettie looked up as the new waitress, Callie Westfield, refilled her coffee cup. The young woman lived upstairs over the café and had gone to work the moment Kate had called her down to help.

"Thank you," Nettie said, watching her even after she moved away.

"Is something wrong?" Frank asked.

"That woman. I told you I hired Billy. I needed

to get a good look at his office so I told him I was suspicious of the new waitress."

Frank groaned, no doubt remembering the old Nettie Benton, who'd been suspicious of Kate Lafond to the point of obsession.

"I know," she said. "I picked her because I thought he wouldn't find anything of interest on her. Apparently he found something suspicious. He was going to tell me what, but he never got the chance."

Frank watched the young waitress as she put on another pot of coffee. The café was busy, what with fire inspectors and the MDCI across the street going through the ruins of the store.

"I'm sure it was nothing," Frank said.

Nettie nodded and turned back to him. She had more to think about than other people's secrets. "I thought I was a goner."

"I know," Frank said, and reached across the table to cover her hand with his again. "I've never been so afraid."

"Me, either."

"But you're safe now," he said.

She nodded and looked across the street. "What am I going to do, Frank?"

"Whatever you want, Lynette. Whatever you want. Just don't do it without me."

Tessa couldn't take her eyes off her baby girl. She was so beautiful. Every face she made, every movement, felt like a miracle.

She heard Dillon come into her hospital room. He stopped just inside the door. She motioned him over to the bassinet by the bed. "Come see," she said. "You brought her into the world. If you hadn't gotten there when you did—"

"You would have done just fine," he said with his usual humility.

She didn't know about that. She was strong and determined, no doubt about that. But yesterday she'd been terrified that something would go wrong and that her baby would pay the price.

"She's so precious," he said with a kind of awe that made her heart beat a little faster.

"She's going to need a name."

He nodded as he reached down to touch the baby's cheek with one callused finger. So gentle. Tessa remembered him with the filly the first day she'd laid eyes on him. The thought made her heart ache. Was that when she'd started falling in love with this man?

"What did you say your mother's name was?" she asked.

"Jessie."

"Jessie," Tessa repeated. "Jessie Dillon Winters for the man who brought her into this world."

He glanced over at her with eyes bright with unshed tears. She saw him swallow as if fighting emotion. Their gazes locked for a moment.

She thought he might try to argue with her, but managed to say, "Thank you."

Tessa smiled. "You see it, don't you?"

"What?" he asked as if he needed to hear her say it.

"That when I look at you, I see Dillon Lawson and no one else."

He gave her a shy smile, this cowboy lawman, as if he wanted to believe that was true. He'd been through hell for her, but they'd both come out of it stronger, she thought.

She took his hand and squeezed it as she saw him look into the bassinet again. "I'm so sorry about Ethan." She'd known Ethan was dead the moment Dillon had come into the room where she was being held. Sadness and yet a resolve had been on his face. He'd already buried his brother once. Now he would have to do it again. She doubted it would be any easier a second time. Except this time, a little of Ethan would live on.

The doctor came in then, and Dillon excused himself.

"You should be able to take your wife home tomorrow," the doctor said before Dillon got out of the room.

Tessa saw him open his mouth to correct the man, but then he closed it, his gaze grazing over hers. "Good," he said to the doctor.

JESSIE DILLON. DILLON tried to swallow around the lump in his throat. Jessie Dillon *Winters,* he reminded himself.

His heart ached for so many reasons. Ethan was

gone. This time for good. He'd already grieved his brother's death for a year.

He thought of his brother's last words. At least this time, he had gotten to see him before he lost him again. And there was little Jessie. His heart swelled with the memory of holding that precious baby in his hands when she'd taken her first breath.

As he walked down the hospital hallway, he saw the sheriff waiting for him.

"I had to cut the two men we picked up loose this morning. Their boss made bail," the sheriff said. "But I have your rifle. If you come down to my car, I'll have you sign a release for it."

"Thank you." He wanted to be the one to take it back to Halbrook Truman. If Ethan was right, the man hadn't been responsible for Buck Morgan's death. Luke had killed Tom Grady. Some drug cartel gunman had killed Luke and Ashley...and Ethan.

But Halbrook had hired two men to take Tessa, and he wouldn't get away with it. He'd already bailed them out of jail. He would no doubt hire the men the best lawyers money could buy. The men would never admit that Halbrook had hired them to take Tessa.

Dillon followed the sheriff out to his patrol car parked outside the hospital. As the lawman pulled out the rifle, he said, "It's a beauty. Dates back to the Civil War, right?"

Dillon nodded. "You ran the ballistics on it?"

"Told them it was urgent."

He shook the man's hand. "I appreciate your help

with this. I want to be the one to take the rifle back to its real owner."

"I'm sure you do. I'm anxious to hear how it all turns out."

"You will," Dillon promised as the sheriff handed him the ballistics report. Dillon read it over, smiled and put it in his jacket pocket.

Halbrook Truman would have to wait a little longer to get his rifle back. Right now Dillon's first priority was Tessa and the baby.

"I'm sorry about your brother," the sheriff said.

"Me, too."

"How's your wife?" the lawman asked.

Dillon was sure the sheriff knew that he and Tessa weren't married. The man was being polite, just assuming that was his baby in there. "She and the baby are doing fine."

"I heard you delivered it. Good thing you got back to town when you did."

"Yes, it was," Dillon said. "Thanks again for your help."

"I'll let you know when your brother's body will be released." The sheriff gave a tip of his Stetson and left.

SPRING BROKE IN a brilliant display of sun and blue sky. A few cumulus clouds bobbed along on a warm breeze over the snowcapped Crazy Mountains.

Dillon loved days like this. But he loved more having Tessa and the baby at the ranch. He'd talked her into staying—at least until she was strong enough to return to her job in California.

This morning he found her out on the porch, her feet curled under her as she sipped a glass of iced coffee. He'd checked the baby and found Jessie sleeping like the little angel she was in the crib he'd bought. "For visits to Montana," he'd said when Tessa had raised a brow at the new crib.

"How is she?" Tessa asked now.

"Sleeping like a baby. I swear I could watch her sleep for hours." Just the sight of her made his heart soar. It was a strange feeling, this connection he felt to Jessie through his twin, through the shared blood. Tessa smiled and slid over on the swing to make room for him.

He joined her and looked out at the Crazy Mountains. They were so familiar, after spending years looking at this very view, but somehow he felt as if he was seeing them for the first time. The rugged peaks took his breath away. The new snow on them was the color of the clouds floating in Montana's big sky. The green of spring ran across the valley to the pale purple of the rocky cliffs, all of it dramatic in the morning light.

"It's beautiful here," Tessa said. "So peaceful."

"Some would say boring. The closest mall is miles away."

She laughed and looked over at him. "Is that something you think I would be interested in?"

"Aren't you?"

"I guess not, since the thought of it being miles away doesn't bother me in the least."

"You're a woman after my own heart," he said with a chuckle, but stilled as her eyes locked with his.

"Is that true?" Before he could answer, she continued. "I called my job this morning. They're anxious to have me back."

That didn't surprise him and he said as much. "You have friends down there, too."

She nodded. "I told my boss I'd let him know soon."

He felt as if he'd been punched in the heart. For a moment he couldn't speak. He swallowed. "Probably a good idea."

"I didn't get to make a snowman. I've always wanted to."

He couldn't bear look at her. "You could come back next winter. Maybe you and Jessie could come for Christmas." He could see a huge tree in the living room covered with lights and ornaments and presents piled high under it. It would be a first, since he didn't bother with decorating, living by himself. "That is, if you don't have other plans," he added, unable to let himself even hope for a Christmas like that with Tessa and Jessie.

"Yes, if I don't have other plans," she said, and looked away. "When are you going to take the rifle to Halbrook?"

As badly as he wanted to confront Halbrook, he didn't like leaving Tessa and the baby.

"I know you're anxious to have it over with. Jessie and I will be fine," she said as if she knew him better than he knew himself.

He studied the toes of his boots, not sure what to say. Afraid to say what he really wanted to. If he kept sitting there he was going to blurt out how he felt. "I should get going."

She glanced over, worry etching her face. "You'll be careful?"

He nodded and gave her a smile. "Don't worry."

"When will you be back?"

"This evening. I could call to let you know when."

"That would be good," she said, making him wonder if he would return home to find her gone.

He'd been expecting it for weeks now.

FRANK LOOKED UP at his telephone line. A dozen crows looked back at him. Several cawed. He laughed, swearing he recognized the birds, as well as their caws. They'd come back. His family had returned.

The crows were acting as if they'd missed him as badly as he had them. He knew it sounded crazy. He didn't care. He felt that as bad as things had been, they were getting better.

Frank had invited Lynette out for dinner tonight at The Grand in Big Timber. He had never been this nervous in his life. He had a whole lot more than dinner on his mind.

"Do you think she'll like it?" he'd asked Kate. He'd been carrying the ring around for several weeks in his pocket, waiting for the right moment. The right moment hadn't presented itself.

"It's beautiful," Kate had said that morning when he'd stopped by the café for coffee. Lynette had been in town, taking care of some last-minute insurance papers on the store. "When are you popping the question?"

"Tonight." He'd said it with such finality that she'd laughed.

"It's been a long time coming, huh?"

He'd nodded and wondered if everyone in the county knew how long he'd been in love with Lynette Johnson Benton. "I was waiting, you know, after what happened, the fire and everything."

"Probably wise, but no reason to wait any longer, I would imagine."

He still couldn't believe that he'd almost lost her. Not once, when Pam had tried to run her down in the street, but twice, when Pam's killer had tried to silence Lynette forever.

"I'm still shocked that it was Cora Westfall," Kate had said, voicing what most everyone in the community had been saying. "She seemed like such a sweet little lady."

"Well, she had to be tough, married to Bull."

"What a family tragedy. Not surprised that Billy would try to blackmail his own grandparents, though," Kate had said with a shake of her head. She'd smiled then at Frank. "Glad it has a happy ending. I never believed you killed your ex, and now you're going to start a new adventure. Good luck proposing to Lynette tonight."

"There's no way she'd say no, right?"

Kate laughed. "No way on this earth."

CHAPTER TWENTY-SEVEN

DILLON DROVE OVER to the Big Hole area, anxious to see Halbrook Truman. He'd called first to make sure the rancher hadn't skipped the country. He'd told him he was bringing him something, just not what. For so long, the man had thought himself above the law. He hadn't had the good sense to run. Probably because he believed he would get away with everything. In his way of thinking, he was the one who'd been wronged and whatever he did to get his property back was within his rights.

As Dillon drove into the Double T-Bar-Diamond Ranch, he passed a truckload of men leaving. It wasn't until he pulled up in front of the house that he noticed the absolute quiet. There were no vehicles parked near the house or barns, no sign of anyone.

Had Halbrook purposely sent everyone away?

Dillon checked the weapon at his hip as he climbed out of his patrol SUV. The quiet followed him up the steps and across the wide veranda to the huge wooden door.

He knocked and wasn't surprised when Halbrook himself answered the door. At Dillon's pretended surprise, the rancher said, "It's the staff's day off."

He just bet it was.

Halbrook's gaze went to the package under Dillon's arm. "What's that?"

"You'll have to tell me, since you never told me what my brother and his friends took from you."

He eyed the package. "I suppose you'll want to come in," the rancher said, and turned to lead the way into the living room.

The rancher went straight to the bar. "Can I offer—"

"I'm fine." He noticed the way the older man's hands shook as he poured what was obviously not his first drink.

"Sorry about your brother. I didn't have anything to do with all that. I heard his pregnant girlfriend was taken." Halbrook shook his head. "Glad to hear she and the baby are fine. I wouldn't be surprised if all of that was Ethan's doing."

Dillon wanted to smash his fist into the man's smug face. Instead he said, "Yeah, that's what the two men claim. About what was recovered at the scene... I was led to believe my brother took a rifle from you. So I hope this belongs to you so we can put this whole thing behind us. If not, I'll have to take it back and try to find out who they stole it from and if any crimes were committed with it."

"I would have thought you would do that anyway," Halbrook said as he dropped another ice cube into his glass.

"The crime lab's backed up. We try to sort these

things out first before we go to the expense and trouble," Dillon said.

Turning from the bar, the rancher motioned to the coffee table. "Let's have a look."

Dillon put the package on the table. He could tell Halbrook was anxious although trying hard not to show it. Dillon pulled out Ethan's lucky knife.

He had purposely taped cardboard around the rifle, wanting to see the rancher's reaction when it took a while to free the rifle from the covering. The man definitely was nervous as Dillon struggled for a moment with the tape.

"You know, one of my rifles has been missing, now that I think about it. There's no reason to open it up," Halbrook said. "If that's what your brother said he took from me, you can just leave it with me."

"Sorry, but I need to make sure it's yours."

The rancher had to work to tamp down his irritation. "Fine." He watched Dillon struggle a moment longer before he said, "Here, let me." With obvious growing impatience he pulled out a pocket knife and cut the tape. The cardboard fell away.

"You certainly wrapped it well enough," the rancher said as he began to deal with the bubble wrap Dillon had wound around the rifle.

He watched as Halbrook tore into the wrap. When it, too, fell away, the rifle came into view.

The rancher let out a surprised, disappointed sound. "That's not it." In those few words, he managed to verify what Dillon already knew. The Civil

War rifle was what Ethan and the rest had taken. He'd expected Halbrook to deny it.

For so long he just hadn't known why the rancher was so determined to get it back. Not just determined. *Desperate.*

"No?" Dillon asked as if surprised. He'd wrapped up an old rifle he had at the house and was enjoying tormenting the rancher.

"I don't know why Ethan would have told you it was."

"Good thing we opened it," Dillon said. "I suppose we'd better check the other one."

"The *other* one?"

"There was one other rifle found at the scene."

Halbrook looked as if he was about to bust. "By all means, let's see the other one."

Dillon went out to his patrol SUV and brought in the second package. The rancher tore right into it, no longer able to hide his impatience.

As the antique Henry came into view, Dillon watched him. The expression on the man's face was priceless. The rancher almost fell to his knees with relief.

"This rifle means a lot to you," he said to the rancher. Halbrook had kidnapped Tessa over this weapon. The thought burned in Dillon's belly.

"You went to an awful lot of trouble and expense trying to get it back. I'm glad I was able to return it to you. But there is one more thing, though. I probably had better ask if there is any way you can verify that it is yours."

"Sure. Whatever." The rancher gingerly picked up the rifle, walked over and leaned it against the fireplace before going to a sideboard. He opened a drawer and returned with a framed photograph.

"You can see it's the same rifle and that it's mine," the man said as he handed the photo over.

The snapshot was of a much younger Halbrook Truman. He was squatting on the ground, grinning hugely next to the same dead elk as the mount over the fireplace. The gun was in the photo, clear enough the lab should be able to make a positive identification even without the wire that Dillon was wearing.

"If you don't mind just signing this release form," Dillon said.

The rancher didn't even bother to read it, just signing and went back over to the gun to admire it, his back to Dillon. The undersheriff sent the text that would not only signal the local authorities to move in, but would make his phone ring. A moment later it rang.

He pretended to check to see who was calling and said, "I need to take this."

"It sounds as if you need to get back to work," Halbrook said. "Don't let me keep you."

Dillon stepped away, but not so far that he couldn't keep an eye on the man or make sure that the rancher heard him.

"What have you got?" he asked and pretended

to listen, darting glances at Halbrook as he did. He watched the rancher become more and more agitated before he disconnected.

"If we're through here…" Halbrook said, and started to turn toward the front door. He stopped after only one step, no doubt seeing the sheriff's department patrol cars pulling up out front.

"I suppose this won't come as a surprise to you," Dillon said, "but two murders were committed with your rifle. Your wife's death and one of your wranglers'. The cases were ruled accidental because the murder weapon was never found. Until now."

"You'll never prove it," Halbrook spat. "I'll deny that I ever saw that rifle. Now that I look at it, I realize it isn't mine."

"You just signed a form saying it was your property."

"I'll say you framed me to get back at me because you think I had something to do with that mess down in Wyoming, which I did not."

Dillon's cell rang again.

This time it was Frank. "I thought you'd want to know. Since hearing that the rancher is going to be arrested, the two men who took Tessa have decided to talk."

Dillon had everything he needed. As he disconnected, he smiled and pulled his revolver. "Halbrook Truman? You are under arrest for the murder of your wife and your hired hand and the kidnapping of Tessa Winters. I'll take that rifle now."

The rancher swung the barrel of the rifle toward Dillon and pulled the trigger. A loud click filled the air an instant before the undersheriff grabbed the barrel and shoved hard. The rancher stumbled back and fell hard onto the floor.

"Let me add resisting arrest and assaulting an officer of the law, with witnesses," Dillon said as the local sheriff's department officers streamed into the room, guns drawn.

"Those charges won't hold up. This was entrapment. My lawyer—"

"Is going to have a hard time getting you off," Dillon said. "Sheriff Frank Curry just took statements from the two men you hired to kidnap Tessa Winters. That along with what I picked up on the wire I'm wearing…"

The local sheriff cuffed Halbrook and proceeded to read him his rights. Along with the ballistics report from the rifle, Dillon didn't think a lawyer would be able to save the man. But at least now he knew why Halbrook was so anxious to get the rifle back. It was the only thing that tied him to the murders.

"If you had just let them get away with stealing from you," Dillon said. "Some collector would have bought the gun and it might never have surfaced again."

THIS WAS IT.

Tessa felt her body quiver as she heard Dillon's boots on the wooden porch. He'd called as promised to say he was on his way and tell her about Halbrook Truman's arrest.

Now, though, he hesitated at the door, and for a heart-stopping moment she thought he might suspect what she was up to and turn and run. But he wasn't Ethan. She heard his hand on the doorknob and closed her eyes at the memory of that large, warm hand at the small of her back as he'd pulled her to him for that kiss.

She gathered her courage as she heard the door swing open. She'd known earlier that she couldn't let another day go by without making a decision. Her boss in California was anxious to have her back. Her friends had been calling. They all couldn't wait to see Jessie. She should have returned home weeks ago.

Except that little apartment in California didn't feel like home anymore. Dillon had insisted she settle in at the ranch and get her strength back. She had, but it hadn't taken long for her to heal. What kept her at the ranch was watching Dillon with the baby. It broke her heart to even think about taking Jessie away from him.

She'd kept hoping he would see how she felt about him. He had to know, and yet… His stubborn pride would let her leave, she was sure. It would keep him from finding happiness, as if he thought he didn't deserve it.

If he would just look at her, really look at her, he would see that she was in love with him and had been for some time. What if she couldn't reach him, though? Worse, what if she didn't try?

"Tessa?" Dillon sounded alarmed, as if he had just noticed how dim it was in the living room. She heard him clear his throat and mumble, *"Candles?"*

She stepped out of the hallway and stopped. He had been looking toward the fireplace where she had a small fire going and a bottle of wine chilling. As he turned, his gaze locked on her.

She wanted to run to him, to throw herself into his arms and show him how much she loved him. But she stood where she was, waiting, afraid he would turn her away. Afraid he would never accept the truth.

She felt self-conscious. It had been six weeks since she'd given birth, but she hadn't lost all of her baby weight. She ran her hands down the sides of the dress, her palms moist, her heart a thunder in her chest. She almost laughed at how ridiculous she felt. It was as if this were her first time.

If her prayers were answered, it would be her first time with the man she'd fallen in love with.

Dillon pulled off his hat. "You look…beautiful."

She smiled and felt her heart start beating again. His blue eyes shone in the firelight.

He still held his hat in his big hands. "Tessa," he said, his voice a hoarse whisper as he seemed to take in what she was wearing. "I don't think this is a good idea."

She laughed softly. "I think it's a great idea."

"You're leaving soon."

"Am I?"

He met her gaze. "Aren't you?"

They stood like that, eyes locked. She felt as if there was no air in the room.

"Have you thought about me staying?" she asked, fear making her voice tremble.

"Of course I have," he said, his own voice breaking.

"Why haven't you asked me to stay?"

He rubbed a hand over his face. "How can I? You have a job, friends, a life in California. You can see what I have to offer you." He motioned to the old farmhouse.

"I love this house. We first danced in this kitchen."

He smiled at that, his blue eyes sad. "You deserve more."

"More than a man who loves me and my daughter?"

"I didn't say—"

"That you loved me and Jessie?" She laughed. "You didn't have to, although I wouldn't mind hearing you say the words."

He met her gaze again. "Of course I love you and Jessie. You're—"

"Family," she said with a nod as she took a step toward him.

"If you take another step, I can't promise I can keep my hands off you."

She took another step. "Do you want me, Dillon?"

He groaned. "You have no idea how much."

Tessa smiled. "As much as I want you."

"It's too soon after the baby."

Tessa shook her head. "I saw the doctor yesterday." She took another step.

"Woman, you'd better be sure about this," he warned her. "Because once you're in my arms…"

She was so close she could smell his masculine scent. "Do you know when I first fell in love with you? It was that day at the corral when I saw the way you were with the horse." She reached up and removed his hat, tossing it in the general direction of the hooks along the wall. "When I lost my heart to you was that day in the kitchen when you danced with me."

He groaned and grabbed her around her waist. He dragged her to him. "You should know I'm not the kind of man who takes this lightly."

She laughed softly. "I know."

DILLON BRUSHED BACK her hair, staring into her eyes for a long moment.

Love. How could he have not seen it before? He'd thought he'd caught glimpses, but he'd been afraid that he was deluding himself. He'd wanted Tessa so badly, but he hadn't dared believe he was the man she wanted. Until that moment.

He dragged her to him. "I love you, Tessa," he said as he swept her up into his arms.

She smiled. "I know."

He laughed softly as he carried her into the bedroom and gently lowered her to the bed.

Tessa pulled him down. She stroked his face, then took one of his large hands and looked again at his scars. Slowly, she lowered her lips to one scar, then another as her lips made all the old pains go away.

He groaned and cupped her face in his hands and kissed her again. She was so beautiful. He slipped the thin strap of the summer dress from her shoulder and let his fingers caress the soft skin there. His hand cupped one large breast, making her arch against it, the nipple hard in his palm.

Heat rushed through him. Desire coursed through his veins like hot lava as Tessa unsnapped his Western shirt and pressed her warm palms to his bare skin. Ripples of desire spread through him. He pulled the sundress over her head, not surprised to find her naked.

For a moment, he just looked at her lush body. Her trembling fingers worked the buttons of his jeans. He slipped out of them and moved onto the bed next to her. Drawing her into his arms, he lost himself in her blue eyes and then her warm, lush body. Like teenagers, they explored, relishing in each stroke, each soft caress, until their passions ran white-hot.

Later, both spent, they lay spooned together. "Do you want to know when I fell in love with *you?*" Dillon whispered against her hair.

"It was that night in Greybull. You're a sucker for a woman with a .45."

He laughed. "No, it was when I came home that night and caught you dancing in my kitchen."

She snuggled against him.

"I knew then that I wanted you more than anything in the world."

NETTIE STARED AT herself in the mirror. Not bad for a woman who had almost burned to death, she thought. Her hair had been singed, but a beautician in Big Timber had fixed it. She liked the shorter do and the new red color.

It surprised her that the nightmares about Cora being locked in that office had waned. For several weeks, she'd dreamed that she could hear Cora screaming for someone to let her out. All Nettie recalled of the night of the fire was the roar of the blaze.

The knock at the door made her jump. In time, she wouldn't be afraid, she thought as she went to answer it. First there had been Pam trying to kill her, then Cora and for a while, she'd been terrified that Bull would be coming for her. He would blame her for Cora's death—just as he had in her nightmares.

But Frank had called earlier to say that Bull's body had been found back in the mountains. Just as she'd suspected, he'd taken his life. It made her sad to think about the Westfall family. Pam had set all of that into motion, destroying Billy, Cora and finally Bull before she was finished.

Nettie opened the door to find Frank standing on

her porch, looking more handsome than ever. He was dressed up, she noticed, wearing his new boots and Stetson.

"This must be an occasion," she said.

"Why would you say that?"

"New boots *and* a new Stetson?"

He looked embarrassed. "Only the best for you."

She noticed that he seemed nervous as he led her to his pickup. She was reminded of other summer nights like this, riding in his old pickup out across the valley. The air smelled of fresh-cut hay. She breathed it in as he headed toward Big Timber.

"How are you?" he asked after a moment.

"I'm always wonderful when I'm with you."

He smiled as a song came on the radio. "Remember this one?"

Tears filled her eyes. It had been *their* song.

Suddenly Frank threw on the brakes and pulled to the side of the road. He turned up the radio and climbed out.

"What in the world are you doing, Frank Curry?" But he was already coming around her to her side. He opened the door and held out his hand and suddenly they were both young again and dancing in the middle of the empty road on a summer night to their song.

He pulled her close as they danced under the starlight. "I love you, Lynette," he whispered. As the song ended, he drew back. "I had planned to do this at dinner, but I can't think of a better time or place."

He dropped to one knee in the middle of the road. "Lynette Johnson Benton, will you be my wife?"

Lynette's eyes blurred with tears. She'd turned him down once—there wasn't a chance she would ever make that mistake again.

"I would love nothing better than to marry you," she said, her voice breaking with emotion.

He rose to put the ring on her finger. The diamond caught the starlight as they walked hand in hand back to the pickup under that same summer sky where they'd fallen in love so long ago.

EPILOGUE

THE DAY TESSA married Dillon, the sky was robin's egg blue. Only a few clouds hung over the Crazies. Originally the ceremony was going to be small, just the three of them—Tessa, Dillon, baby Jessie—and the preacher.

But word got out and cars began arriving early. It turned into a party out behind the ranch house under a stand of cottonwoods. The entire county wanted to celebrate. Country bands played, with neighbors setting up makeshift dance floors and stringing lights.

The ceremony was short and sweet, just as they'd planned. The crowd erupted in applause as the preacher declared them husband and wife. Dillon kissed his beautiful bride and his precious daughter.

"It's wonderful," Tessa said, fighting tears later as the festivities continued behind the house. "I've never seen anything more beautiful. They all love you and are happy for you."

"For us," Dillon said as they put the baby to bed, and leaving her with the babysitter, went back out where neighbors and friends had thrown a huge barbecue in their honor.

"As I recall, you like to dance, Mrs. Lawson," he said, taking her hand.

She smiled as he pulled her into his arms. They danced, lights glittering all around them. As he pulled her close, Tessa realized she'd found the home and family she'd always yearned for.

"I might want a large family," she'd told him a few days before the wedding. "I don't know how you feel—"

"I had given up hope that I would have a family. I figured I'd be an old bachelor, mean and ornery, living alone out here because I never met a woman I wanted to have a family with...until I met you."

"Then you wouldn't mind having more children?"

He'd laughed. "Mind? I want as many children as you want to have. This is Montana. We have lots of wide-open spaces for our kids to run. I'll teach them to ride. I'll—"

She'd kissed him then, caught up in his excitement. "I love you, Dillon Lawson."

Now as they danced, she looked up into his handsome face. The music played, the celebration a send-off neither of them would ever forget. This ranch had never been more of a home for either of them, she thought as Dillon bent down to kiss her.

NETTIE BENTON SAT in the Branding Iron Café, staring at the charred remains of the store the next morning. *Her* store. It had been her life for so many years, she felt as if there had been a death in the family.

"Every time I look out the front window, I'm startled. It just doesn't feel right not having the store over there," Kate said as she refilled her coffee cup and moved away.

It certainly didn't feel right to Nettie. The store had been her anchor. It had kept her sane through the years, given her something to do, provided her with income. Everyone had been encouraging her to rebuild, but she wasn't sure she had it in her. She could never put it back as it had been any more than she could be the same. Did she even want to be that woman?

She had no idea what she was going to do now. For so many years she'd lived with regrets over not marrying Frank and foolishly marrying Bob. That was all behind her. She looked down at the ring on her finger. Engaged. To Frank. Her heart beat a little faster.

"Are you going to have a big wedding?" Kate asked after complimenting the ring. It made Nettie feel good to see how happy everyone was about the upcoming nuptials.

"I think we might elope to Vegas," Nettie said. "Or have a small wedding out at the ranch." She and Frank had been at Undersheriff Dillon Lawson's wedding and she knew the same thing could happen to them if word got out. Dillon had been in the café earlier to show off the baby. He'd looked so proud and happy.

"I'd love to cater it if you decide to do the latter," Kate said.

Nettie thanked her. As Kate hurried to help a customer, Nettie listened to the talk around the café.

"It's such a shame. A big piece of Beartooth's history is gone," one of the rancher's said at a nearby table about the loss of the store, before the men changed the subject to the weather and the price of feed.

"Who inherits the Westfall Ranch?" someone asked at another table. His question was met by shrugs around the table.

"I suppose Charlotte. There aren't any other relatives, are there?" said another.

One of the ranchers laughed. "Every cowboy in the county is going to be wanting to marry Charlotte."

"I heard she's not in her right mind."

"What woman is?" a couple cowboys said in unison, and they all hooted.

"What *will* happen to the ranch?" Nettie asked as Frank joined her. She knew he'd heard the cowboys talking about the Westfall Ranch.

"I have no idea. Kin often come out of the woodwork when something like this happens," Frank said. He'd been reinstated as sheriff. She'd never seen him looking happier. "Charlotte's money that Pam stole has been found, I heard. So Charlotte is now a very wealthy woman again."

"Who will look after her now that Bull is gone?" Nettie wondered.

Frank shook his head. "Let's hope another Pam Chandler doesn't come along and move in with her."

WHEN DILLON GOT the call that Ethan's body had been released, he asked that it be sent to the local mortuary in Greybull and that his cremated remains be shipped to Big Timber.

Tessa had agreed at once when he told her why he'd made that decision.

"Ethan was a free spirit, never staying in one place long," Dillon told her. "I've already buried his memory once here. There is a headstone, in case you or Jessie ever want to visit it. But I'm thinking Ethan would have liked his ashes scattered in the Yellowstone River. It flows from here to the Missouri and joins the Mississippi and finally ends up in the Gulf of Mexico. From there… Who knows. A little of him could end up anywhere in the world."

Tessa smiled. "I love that. It's exactly what he would have chosen."

"Do you want to come with me when I take his ashes to the river?" Dillon asked her.

"I already said my goodbyes to him, but Jessie and I will come with you if you'd like."

"I would like that."

Dillon drove them to a stretch of the river where the water pooled a crystal clear green. A breeze stirred the pines at the water's edge as a flock of geese honked in the pale blue sky overhead. The dark V threw a shadow over the water for a moment.

They stood at the water's edge, Dillon holding the canister with Ethan's ashes. "I feel like I should say something."

"He knows."

He slowly poured his twin's ashes into the moving water, then he put his arm around Tessa and Jessie. Together, they stood and watched the river take Ethan. In the stillness of the afternoon, Dillon let his brother go.

* * * * *

CINDY DEES

ON THE RUN AND UNDER FIRE...

CINDY DEES

CLOSE PURSUIT

Is redemption possible when the past won't let go?

Providing medical relief in a war-torn region helps Alex Peters forget his past and focus on the job—delivering babies. Less easy to overlook is his blonde comrade-in-arms, who knows nothing of the trouble he's running from. Katie McCloud makes the assignment bearable, although her perky innocence proves to be an arousing distraction. Then, as combat explodes around them, their only option is flight.

A kindergarten teacher seeking adventure, Katie hoped this humanitarian mission—and the mysterious, sexy doctor sharing it— would push her out of her comfort zone. With Alex, she starts taking tantalizing risks and becoming the survivor she knew she could be.

But back on U.S. soil, Alex and Katie face a new threat, and this time they're the target. Forced into close confines, neither can believe the other isn't the intended mark. With only each other to depend on— and suspect—Alex and Katie can't avoid the simmering attraction between them. But to stay alive, they'll have to trust more deeply than ever before....

Available wherever books are sold!

Be sure to connect with us at:

Harlequin.com/Newsletters

Facebook.com/HarlequinBooks

Twitter.com/HarlequinBooks

HARLEQUIN® HQN™

www.Harlequin.com

PHCD848

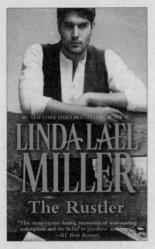

REQUEST YOUR FREE BOOKS!

2 FREE NOVELS
FROM THE ROMANCE COLLECTION
PLUS 2 FREE GIFTS!

YES! Please send me 2 FREE novels from the Romance Collection and my 2 FREE gifts (gifts are worth about $10). After receiving them, if I don't wish to receive any more books, I can return the shipping statement marked "cancel." If I don't cancel, I will receive 4 brand-new novels every month and be billed just $6.24 per book in the U.S. or $6.74 per book in Canada. That's a savings of at least 22% off the cover price. It's quite a bargain! Shipping and handling is just 50¢ per book in the U.S. and 75¢ per book in Canada.* I understand that accepting the 2 free books and gifts places me under no obligation to buy anything. I can always return a shipment and cancel at any time. Even if I never buy another book, the two free books and gifts are mine to keep forever.

194/394 MDN F4XY

Name _____ (PLEASE PRINT) _____

Address _____ Apt. # _____

City _____ State/Prov. _____ Zip/Postal Code _____

Signature (if under 18, a parent or guardian must sign) _____

Mail to the Harlequin® Reader Service:
IN U.S.A.: P.O. Box 1867, Buffalo, NY 14240-1867
IN CANADA: P.O. Box 609, Fort Erie, Ontario L2A 5X3

Want to try two free books from another line?
Call 1-800-873-8635 or visit www.ReaderService.com.

* Terms and prices subject to change without notice. Prices do not include applicable taxes. Sales tax applicable in N.Y. Canadian residents will be charged applicable taxes. Offer not valid in Quebec. This offer is limited to one order per household. Not valid for current subscribers to the Romance Collection or the Romance/Suspense Collection. All orders subject to credit approval. Credit or debit balances in a customer's account(s) may be offset by any other outstanding balance owed by or to the customer. Please allow 4 to 6 weeks for delivery. Offer available while quantities last.

Your Privacy—The Harlequin® Reader Service is committed to protecting your privacy. Our Privacy Policy is available online at www.ReaderService.com or upon request from the Harlequin Reader Service.

We make a portion of our mailing list available to reputable third parties that offer products we believe may interest you. If you prefer that we not exchange your name with third parties, or if you wish to clarify or modify your communication preferences, please visit us at www.ReaderService.com/consumerschoice or write to us at Harlequin Reader Service Preference Service, P.O. Box 9062, Buffalo, NY 14269. Include your complete name and address.

ROM13R

B.J. DANIELS

83793	CARDWELL RANCH TRESPASSER & BIG SKY STANDOFF	___ $6.99 U.S.	___ $7.99 CAN.
83787	JUSTICE AT CARDWELL RANCH	___ $5.99 U.S.	___ $6.99 CAN.
77780	FORSAKEN	___ $7.99 U.S.	___ $8.99 CAN.
77757	REDEMPTION	___ $7.99 U.S.	___ $9.99 CAN.
77673	UNFORGIVEN	___ $7.99 U.S.	___ $9.99 CAN.

(limited quantities available)

TOTAL AMOUNT	$ _____
POSTAGE & HANDLING	$ _____
($1.00 FOR 1 BOOK, 50¢ for each additional)	
APPLICABLE TAXES*	$ _____
TOTAL PAYABLE	$ _____

(check or money order—please do not send cash)

To order, complete this form and send it, along with a check or money order for the total above, payable to Harlequin HQN, to: **In the U.S.:** 3010 Walden Avenue, P.O. Box 9077, Buffalo, NY 14269-9077; **In Canada:** P.O. Box 636, Fort Erie, Ontario, L2A 5X3.

Name: _____

Address: _____ City: _____

State/Prov.: _____ Zip/Postal Code: _____

Account Number (if applicable): _____

075 CSAS

*New York residents remit applicable sales taxes.
*Canadian residents remit applicable GST and provincial taxes.

HARLEQUIN® HQN™
www.Harlequin.com

PHBJD0314BL